"Alexander, Do You Remember How It Was Between Us?"

A bolt of desire shuddered through him as she lowered her hands and moved them slowly over his broad, muscled back.

"You don't know what you're doing, Liz," he said hoarsely. "This is madness."

His lips hovered inches from hers. Her uneven breaths whispered against his mouth, her husky voice coming to him in the darkness, low and seductive, irresistible in its wanton invitation.

"I know. But then there was always madness between us, wasn't there?"

ANN MAJOR
has developed a style of engrossing stories that have won her many admirers. She lives in Texas with her husband and three children and not only writes, but manages a business and household as well.

Dear Reader:

Romance readers have been enthusiastic about Silhouette Special Editions for years. And that's not by accident: Special Editions were the first of their kind and continue to feature realistic stories with heightened romantic tension.

The longer stories, sophisticated style, greater sensual detail and variety that made Special Editions popular are the same elements that will make you want to read book after book.

We hope that you enjoy this Special Edition today, and will enjoy many more.

The Editors at Silhouette Books

ANN MAJOR
Dazzle

Silhouette Special Edition

Published by Silhouette Books New York

America's Publisher of Contemporary Romance

SILHOUETTE BOOKS
300 E. 42nd St., New York, N.Y. 10017

Copyright © 1985 by Ann Major
Cover artwork copyright © 1985 by Franco Accornero

Distributed by Pocket Books

ISBN: 0-373-09229-6

First Silhouette Books printing April, 1985

10 9 8 7 6 5 4 3 2 1

Map by Ray Lundgren

Books by Ann Major

Silhouette Romance

Wild Lady #90
A Touch of Fire #150

Silhouette Special Edition

Brand of Diamonds #83
Dazzle #229

Silhouette Desire

Dream Come True #16
Meant to Be #35
Love Me Again #99
The Wrong Man #151
Golden Man #198

Silhouette Intimate Moments

Seize the Moment #54

To the special families I married when I married my husband—The Cleaves, the Brakebills, and the Acords. The lives of these people have been indelibly interwoven with mine, both their joys and their pain.

To Helen and Wilbur for being wonderful grandparents.

To Kitsie and Kent for running their "Acord Hotel."

To Connie and Dave for their love.

To Gini and in loving memory of her Mark.

And to Rusty, Dinah, Lisa, Missy, and Cathy for giving so much to me.

Chapter One

*T*he slim, golden girl walked lightly across the exquisite perfection of gleaming teak joinerwork on the
yacht's deck. In one hand she carried a large brown
envelope that had just arrived by special courier, and in
the other hand a drink she was being careful not to
slosh. When she saw Alexander she stopped abruptly,
her mind in turmoil as to what to do.

Gazing down at the dozing man, she thought he
looked dangerous even in sleep. He could be so unpredictable, so wild, so terribly reckless. Since his wife ran
away seven years ago, he did exactly as he wanted as if
he had no care of the consequences.

Tina's courage fled. The address on the package was
familiar. Whenever Alexander received something
from this Mr. Henson he would glance at it and then
tear it to shreds with a pretense of indifference, but he
would be brooding and difficult for days.

She remembered his abominable mood of the night
before and made the cowardly decision not to wake

him. She knelt and slid the envelope stealthily beneath the *Financial Times*. Then she set an iced soft drink garnished with a sliver of lime beside the stack of mail and newspapers.

A moment later Alexander awoke. When he opened his eyes, Tina was gone, though her fragrance lingered upon the things she had touched. He saw the drink and stretched a dark arm toward it. He was surprised she'd ventured on deck. He wondered idly if it was a peace offering because of their quarrel the night before.

He did not see the fat brown package beneath the *Times*, hidden as cozily as a time bomb.

Sipping the tart, fizzling drink, he reached for a section of the *Times* and began to read with the fascination of a man who'd long been married to the business world. He frowned as he noted Dazzle's stock had fallen a point while Radiance's had risen.

On first glance, he did not appear the entrepreneur at all. Prince Mikhail Alexander Vorzenski had the look of a pirate about him. He was tough and lean, a tall man who was so powerfully built and so awesomely male, he made even the tallest woman feel small and enchantingly feminine. His eyes were piercing gold; his broad, white smile deliciously and disturbingly cynical. He had the stormy good looks most women find so attractive, and his teasingly bold manner told them he knew it. He could be arrogant and insolent when pushed, and cynical when confronted with maudlin sentimentality in others or himself. Despite his charisma and his easy smiles, he was a difficult man to know well. Women had the feeling that he deliberately closed off that most vital and exciting part of himself, but this aura of mystery only made him all the more fascinating, especially when they caught stirring glimpses of his passionate, hidden soul.

He was so charming, when he chose to be, that women forgave him all these faults and many others.

Into his arrogance they read self-confidence, and into his insolence, a sensitive temperament. In his cynicism they saw intelligence. When he was dominating, they defended him by saying that this only made them feel cherished and protected, but none of these women understood him.

Only one woman had glimpsed beneath his surface hardness. Only she had discovered the lovelessness of his childhood, which had made him the proud and lonely man he was. Born of parents who had no time for him—his father a titled playboy, his mother a workaholic—Alexander had thrown himself into sports in his youth, playing to win because he wanted to gain the brief approval of his parents. Only Liz knew that business was a game to Alexander and that winning had become supremely important to him because his mother applauded only the winners.

For the briefest time Liz had shown Alexander a world where love could be had without the need of conquests. He'd glimpsed the fulfillment a happy family life might have brought him. After her, he was harder and lonelier, his victories in the business world more ruthless than before.

Alexander was, as usual, thinking of the business problems that faced the international perfume company he ran. Though he lived his personal life with reckless indifference, he was dedicated to his company. He was ostensibly vacationing, but in truth he'd left Paris so that he could isolate himself and concentrate on several very disturbing realities he'd just become aware of.

The sun gleamed in a cobalt sky and warmed the sheer rock cliffs. It was summer, and Alexander's skin was bronzed from skiing in the Swiss Alps, where snow lingered even in July, and from having just sailed from his elaborate villa in Sardinia's secluded Porto Rotondo.

Alexander stretched his long, lean frame on the narrow strip of navy towel he'd thrown down upon the foredeck of his immense Swan, the latest and loveliest of all his yachts. In the marine world, the name Swan has a connotation similar to that of Rolls-Royce in automobiles, Rolex in watches, or Godiva in chocolates. It is a reputation based not upon fabulous price alone, but on quality.

Prince Alexander, who'd sailed all his life, was very pleased with his new yacht, with the way it had sliced through the Mediterranean the previous afternoon like a freight train in twenty-seven-plus knots of wind, its lee rail dipping under a single reef.

He was a man who sought the very best of everything. It was a fact of his character that he demanded nothing less from himself or the men who worked for him.

His strength served him well. If it were not for the sheer ruthlessness and drive of his powerful personality, he would have long ago lost the presidency of Dazzle Ltd., the vast family-owned international company he controlled, for there were those who wanted to take it from him. Indeed, his hold on power had never seemed so perilous. There were officers in the company who said he was too hard, that he took too many risks. They wanted to go back to the slow pace of the old days. They said that these were good times, that on the downside, Alexander would bring the company to ruin. Worse, they said, he was a pirate, a man who disregarded all rules but his own. Others still blamed him for what his wife, Liz, had done seven years ago.

Alexander's power was intact only because Dazzle had prospered under his leadership. The majority of the board was afraid to get rid of him; his successes had been too brilliant and too timely. His enemies were watchful, resentful. Dazzle, a leading manufacturer of perfume in England and Europe, had been sailing through rough seas for the past few years, and it had taken an iron hand at the helm.

A sudden reversal of fortune had made many who had cheered his successes forget them in the wake of a series of disasters that had struck the company. The worst and most recent had occurred only ten days before. The explosion in one of Dazzle's top-security chemical labs in the Alps had rocked the very foundations of Dazzle. Alexander was blamed by several board members for the incident because he had personally overseen the installation of all the security measures at the plant.

Alexander rolled onto his stomach. He felt strangely restless. He wished he hadn't agreed to this party Tina had demanded. He wanted to be sailing, not tied up at a mooring. He lay back, watching the pink pages of the *Financial Times* ruffle when he tossed it aside. The article in the *Times* about Dazzle and the explosion had not improved his mood. The journalist implied that arson was at the bottom of the tragedy, and publicity of that nature was the last thing Dazzle needed.

A week ago Alexander had flown to the site himself and examined the black debris; he'd talked to the injured men and to the Swiss police. What he'd learned had shaken him.

Alexander tried to relax. The quiet, familiar sounds of the Mediterranean came to him: the gentle lapping of wavelets against the snowy fiberglass hull, the distant purr of the incessant summer traffic of Monte Carlo, the roar of a nearby ski boat slicing through the dimpling, gleaming waves, and the gentle laughter of one of his more enchanting female guests, who graced the grand salon below. Suddenly these peaceful sounds were shattered as a passionate tirade of Greek music blasted from the salon.

Mon Dieu! Did they have to play that? He combed bronzed fingers through his thick, black rumpled hair, brushing aside the lock of hair that had fallen across his brow. Alexander frowned wearily at himself for his reaction to the music. What was wrong with him? He felt so unamused by all the things that had once so amused him. He should be glad his guests were having a good time. It was rude of him to ignore them, but he'd invited them for Tina. He hadn't come to the Mediterranean to entertain the same sort of people the perfume business forced him to associate with in London and Paris.

His mistake was that he'd invited Tina. She was like a child who demanded constant entertainment—incessant flirting, gambling or partying. He shouldn't have brought her! It was just that he hadn't wanted to be alone with himself, with all the memories he normally kept himself too busy to face, and with the great unresolved mystery that still haunted him.

He hadn't realized until yesterday how completely unsuited to his personality Tina was. Tina abhorred the peace and silence he sought, and last night she had dragged him to the main casino of Monaco to play the roulette wheels. He'd strolled restlessly among the gamblers, pausing in the Salon Rose where he'd looked up, observing with cynical amusement the unclad nymphs floating about the ceiling smoking cigarillos. Unfortunately he'd grown bored with the ceiling long before Tina had grown bored with roulette. When he'd retrieved the sulky and losing Tina, she'd dragged him to the equally opulent and crowded Hôtel de Paris. She'd stopped beneath the bronze statue of Louis XIV's horse and whimsically stroked its extended golden fetlock for luck as was the custom among gamblers in Monaco. Afterward she'd insisted upon at least stopping at the frenetic Café de Paris. There Tina had gambled away the last of her, or rather the last of his, loose change in the slot machines between her too-frequent Bloody Marys. Later, things had been even more difficult than usual between them.

Ice tinkled against crystal glasses as a never-ceasing abundance of expensive liquor was consumed by the prince's guests on his yacht. Tina and her friends drank heavily for ones so young. He had no common bond with any of these people.

Why then did he hang around with shallow pleasure-seekers who bored and dissatisfied him? Why did he choose for his companion a woman of Tina's inclinations when his own passions were neither shallow nor visceral? Alexander shrugged these questions aside; the last thing he wanted to dwell on was their answer.

The papers beside him began to flap. A brisk westerly gust would have sent newsprint flying had Alexander not seized them. He felt the lumpy brown mailer beneath them. Curious, he secured the *Times* beneath two magazines and examined the bulky envelope. In bold black letters Henson's unmistakable scrawl flowed across stiff, brown paper: "Raymond Henson and Sons, Private Investigation Ltd."

Alexander's pulse thudded with startling violence. A terrible premonition gripped him as he ripped open the package.

"Liz! Damn! What a hell of a time for her to surface!" he muttered savagely, knowing even before he spilled the contents of the envelope onto the deck what they would contain.

Seven years ago Alexander had hired Raymond Henson to find his wife when she'd run away. Alexander had wanted to find her to prove that he was innocent of the destruction she'd deliberately wrought upon Dazzle and upon him, but when he'd failed, he'd managed to salvage his position in the company. He'd reshaped a world for himself that no longer included her, and he'd continued his search for her for one reason only. When she'd left him, she'd been pregnant, and he was determined to find his child.

Alexander was accustomed to Henson's monthly reports. The slim white envelopes that invariably contained a single carefully typed page that informed him there was still no trace of Liz's whereabouts had arrived with unfaltering regularity—until now.

Three glossy photographs, a sheaf of typewritten pages neatly clipped together, and an exquisite, handsomely packaged twelve-inch doll lay before him. He studied the photographs first; two were of Liz.

He lifted one of them and stared at it, his handsome face hardened by his grim determination not to be affected by her. Even on paper she dazzled like a brilliant jewel, tempting him from his harsh stance. Her slender, pale face was vibrant with emotion, her black eyes ablaze as she tilted her chin at that defiant angle he remembered so well. She was talking to someone that Henson had not photographed. Alexander could almost hear her voice, that incredibly silken and yet so very American sound that could fall sexily hushed against his ear.

He remembered the brief time he had had with her, the only time in his life he had not felt alone. A flare of intense excitement shot through him. There was another feeling too—an overpowering relief to discover she was alive.

How was it possible that a mere photograph could make him feel electric with tension? Hatred, he'd been told, was as powerful as love.

She still wore her red hair the way he liked it, rippling like a mane of fire over her shoulders. He remembered suddenly the silken touch of it, the scent of those perfumed tresses falling across his pillow when he'd slept with her in his arms.

On closer inspection he noted she was thinner, as though her life had not been easy. Her bright hair accentuated the extreme pallor of her cheeks. Yet there was an air of gallant bravado about her that would have triggered his admiration had he not instantly stifled it.

She was dressed in one of her wild and extravagant costumes that no one but Liz could have carried off. Apricot silk swirled around her body. The dress looked like an Indian maiden's, its hem edged with the most exquisite and lavish of embroideries.

The male in him noted that the fabric clung to the uptilted shape of her breasts and to the slim curves of her hips. In her bright hair she wore a headband twined with strands of gold and trailing with white feathers. It was outlandish. Ridiculous. It was Liz.

The second picture was a close-up of her face. For the first time Alexander noted a new sadness, a vulnerability in her expression that he had never seen before.

He set the pictures quickly aside, not wanting any further contact with a woman who'd brought him so much pain.

The third photograph was of a boy uncannily like the boy he'd been himself at the age of six. A surge of fatherly pride swept Alexander. It was an emotion more intense than any in his life. He gazed at his son with rapt eagerness.

For seven years he had waited for this. At last, a picture of his child! He remembered how he'd hungered for his own father's regard when he'd been a child, and never received anything but indifference. His father had been too busy womanizing and racing cars and spending the allowance his rich French wife indulged him with in gratitude for the title their marriage had brought her.

His older half brother, Paul, had resented both his mother's second marriage as well as his young half brothers, and, therefore, had ignored them when they were growing up. Servants had raised Alexander and his younger brother, Sasha; kindly teachers and coaches had played father in wearying succession to the little boys starved for love. When Alexander had become a tennis star in college, his mother had taken a mild interest in him. "I think you've got the instincts of a winner," she'd said proudly after he'd become an amateur champion. "Welcome to my world. You have a job at Dazzle when you graduate." He had accepted her offer, glad for the chance to prove himself and win her approval.

Alexander wondered about his son. Who did his own child turn to? Did he long for the father he had never known? Or had Liz taught the child to hate him? Was he being brought up by servants and neglected?

In the photograph the black-haired child, his golden eyes alight with daredevil exhilaration, stood on the edge of a precipice formed by a rock above a pool. It was obvious he had every intention of jumping. A look of terror contorted the Indian features of the girl behind him, who was trying to dissuade him. Then Alexander saw Liz in the water, her bright hair flowing loosely, her arms encouragingly outstretched toward the child.

Alexander drew a quick, sharp breath. Idiotically he wondered if the boy could swim, if the pool was deep, if it was sanitary. He felt new fury toward his estranged wife that she could be so reckless with his son. But then Liz had always been reckless. If she hadn't been, she never would have dared to marry him and attempt to destroy him.

Alexander stared at the picture of his son. He did not hear the Greek music, nor did he feel the sea breezes, cooler now because of the sinking sun.

He wondered if Liz had deliberately allowed herself to be found by Henson. Did she realize how dangerous it would be for him to associate with her right now, even if his interest were solely because of his son? Was she trying to complete the task she had almost succeeded in accomplishing seven years ago—his destruction and that of Dazzle? If so, she'd unerringly placed the most tempting of all baits on her hook when she'd let Henson get close enough to photograph the child. Despite the danger to himself, Alexander was inexorably drawn to the child. He scarcely understood his feelings; he didn't realize that all his life he'd yearned for someone to love, that what he'd once sought from his father and his older brother, he would now seek from his son. Alexander knew only that he had no choice but to go after him.

At last Alexander read the report. Henson had located Liz because he'd received an anonymous tip that Jock Rocheaux was traveling from Paris to Mexico City nearly once a month, and the reason for his trips was to visit Liz Vorzenski.

An anonymous tip. So Liz had wanted to be found. Alexander bristled at the thought of Jock having anything to do with his son. Damn Liz! How could she be blind to the kind of man Jock was? Superficial charm concealed his reptilian cold-bloodedness.

Jock was Alexander's own first cousin, and they'd been boyhood friends. Together Jock and Alexander had been the most promising junior executives at Dazzle. The first break in their relationship had occurred because of an unfortunate incident involving a young woman they had both been dating.

The severe rupture happened on a hairpin curve at a speed of over two hundred kilometers an hour. Jock decided winning a certain Grand Prix tour on the French Riviera was worth any price. Unfortunately the price had been Sasha. Jock had floored the accelerator of his race car and sent Alexander's younger brother, who was driving the car beside him, hurtling through a barricade and over a cliff in a ball of crystal flame.

Alexander publicly blamed Jock for Sasha's death and used all his stature in the company to have Jock thrust out of it. In the end Jock resigned in a rage and went to Radiance, Dazzle's rival. . . .

Alexander continued to read. Henson reported he had nearly returned from Mexico City without discovering anything until he'd happened upon a collection of exquisite dolls in a department store. The doll he enclosed to Alexander was a model of the shepherdess in Zurbaráns painting in London's National Gallery. The scarlet dress was a replica of the gown Liz had designed from the same painting for herself to wear on her wedding day. Henson had discovered the sloping L, Liz's signature as a designer, hidden upon the heel of the doll's foot. Henson had learned that a hacienda in the mountains outside of Mexico City was the factory where the dolls were made. Jock had visited the village near the high-walled, Spanish colonial hacienda several times. When Henson staked the place, he'd photographed Liz and the child.

Alexander set the report aside. The sky was lit with fiery brilliance. Greek music swirled in the soft evening air. Soft waves caressed the white fiberglass. He came back to his world with the jolt of a man who'd traveled a long way.

Everything was the same, but everything was different. Liz had come back into his life. Once, in a moment of dark anger, he had promised her the most terrible revenge.

Now all that mattered was his son. He would go after the child even though to do so held monumental dangers for him. He would take his son away from a mother who would no doubt be no more than the most destructive and shallow influence upon him. What kind of woman fled to an uncivilized Mexican village and tried to bring up a child far from the heritage that was rightfully his? To raise a child without the cultural and educational advantages he was entitled to was neglect.

What kind of woman deliberately denied a child his own father?

The stereo stopped abruptly, and the passionate Greek music was replaced by the clear sound of Barbra Streisand's voice. Tina's mellow laughter soared above the haunting notes. The deeper tones of a man's joined hers, and Alexander heard their enjoyment of one another without a trace of jealousy.

Alexander lifted a black brow. It was not Tina and her latest admirer that caught his interest, but the lyrics of the familiar song. From his Russian father, he had inherited his passionate response to music, a response he frequently sought to conceal, for it embarrassed him.

Tina must have changed the record. She was the only American on board, and she was as avid about Streisand as Liz had been. Sometimes Tina forgot that he did not want Streisand played.

The voice sang of lost love and all its deep anguish, and suddenly Alexander remembered the song; it had been a favorite of Liz's. The melody and its sensuous lament affected him, bringing back a tantalizing fragment of the glorious time he'd shared with her.

A wave of passionate longing washed over Alexander. It was a feeling that only one woman had roused in him. He knew with an acute, aching pain all that he'd lost, just as he knew how empty his life was without her. Tina was no more to him than his latest friend, and like all the others before her, she was a mistake.

No woman could replace the one woman he'd lost— not that he wanted to replace her. That was the last thing he wanted! He wanted to be free of her! Burning deep in his soul was the torture of a memory that was still too vivid—his unforgettable, his blazingly bold, his terribly defiant Liz. How he had loved her in those twelve brief weeks he had had with her.

He'd thrown her out in one blind moment of rage. He'd accused her without once giving her a chance to defend herself. But the evidence of her treachery had seemed so blatantly irrefutable.

If only she hadn't burst into his office to give him her news at the exact moment he'd just been confronted with the incriminating evidence of her betrayal. If he had had even an hour to cool down before he'd seen her, he might have handled everything differently. He'd been hurt, furious, sick with feelings of betrayal. He'd lashed out with all the violence of his nature, and he'd never behaved more brutally toward anyone.

He would never forget the way she'd flung herself from him. She'd run out into the rain. From his window he'd watched her slender form disappear in the gray, slanting storm, and he'd wished passionately that he'd never met her. He never wanted to see her again. She'd deliberately sought to destroy him, and she'd very nearly succeeded. She'd jeopardized his career, divided the board of Dazzle and brought the company itself to the brink of ruin. Because of her, his own family allied themselves with his enemies against him, even his brother, Paul.

Strangely, when Alexander's anger had abated, the only thing he could remember with crystal clarity from that terrible scene was the shattered hurt of her beautiful face when she feebly protested her innocence before he'd overridden her protests with accusations so vile that the lovely look of vulnerability had died in her luminous black eyes, and she'd merely stared back at him with a smoldering defiance he hadn't then realized was significant. Then she'd run away. What he hadn't known at the time was that she was pregnant; Henson had found that out.

At first he'd wanted to find Liz. He had to! He spent a fortune trying to find her. He wanted to try to understand why she had betrayed him. Now all the urgency was gone, and all he wanted was to have her out of his life, and out of his son's life as well, he amended.

Once she had laughed up at him, "Money won't buy everything, my darling. But it can buy freedoms most people can't begin to imagine." She had smiled enigmatically. "You can escape so completely when you're as rich as we are."

He'd thought she was speaking of *his* fortune. He hadn't known then who she really was and that she was incredibly rich herself, and that she knew all about money, that she who was such a bold, free soul was an expert at escaping, that she'd lost herself in countries, in cultures, in out-of-the-way niches in the world for months on end during the rebellious years of her youth when she'd defied her family. There had been so many secrets she had kept from him.

Once he had wanted to know everything about her. That time was past, despite any tricks his sentimental nature might play on him. All he wanted now was his child.

He could never want Liz again! He hated her for what she'd done, because above all things he despised disloyalty. He'd loved her, and she'd deliberately tried to destroy him.

His hatred had warred with his love for seven years, and in the end the harsher emotion had stifled the gentler. He'd never met another woman who mattered to him. How many women had there been? Beauties, heiresses, international celebrities, and so many of them Americans, had shared his company all because *she* was American.

The press said he had a taste for free-spirited American beauties. Tina, like so many of the rest, was American. But not one of them had made him forget. He didn't want to see Liz again, but he knew he had to confront her. She was no more than an intense memory he couldn't quite put behind him, a breathtaking illusion that had never really existed.

The music enveloped him, and his fierce mood was suddenly too overpoweringly painful to be endured. Alexander hated thinking of Liz. In seven years his hate and love had become as hopelessly twisted as a snarled vine. He felt violent and impotent at the same time, each emotion feeding and magnifying the other.

The haunting words seemed to go on. Was that song never going to end? Tina! Damn her! If it weren't for her, he'd be sailing instead of bitterly awash in memories!

Suddenly he had an immediate target for his explosive anger. He sprang to his feet. He ran lightly across the gleaming deck, his hard body lithe and fluidly graceful. He took the varnished teak stairs two at a time.

He burst into the throng of revelers near the bar and ripped the record from the turntable. There was instant silence. For a breathless moment not even an ice cube dared to clink in the glasses gripped with paralyzed, bejeweled fingers.

The faint odors of the Greek foods the caterers had brought on board at Tina's whim assailed him, mingling in unappetizing chaos—sizzling suvlaki, trays of pastitso, heaps of dolmathes, and the inevitable tiropitaki.

Alexander's head was pounding. Instead of comforting him, the silence was thick and suffocating like wads of warm cotton stuffed smotheringly against his face. Tina swirled her gilt head to glare at him in annoyance.

Alexander stared at her, sharply seeing her as though for the first time. She looked very young with her straight, cornsilk hair and with her wide blue eyes. Her flawless, honey-toned body was covered (if one could call it covered) by a crocheted string bikini. She was far too young for the sophistication of her lifestyle, he thought. She belonged on some American college campus in Colorado or Wyoming and not on a perfume magnate's yacht cruising off the south of France.

The moment between them was long and still.

His other guests watched with mild interest. Intense emotion was a novelty to them, and it was exceptional in their cynical and worldly Mikki, as Alexander was called by his intimates.

"Mikki, what the hell?" Tina began sulkily before she broke off, suddenly not daring to go on as she met the full force of Alexander's angry gaze.

His tanned, handsome face was as fierce as that of a warlord. He wanted to smash everything in the room. The pupils in his golden eyes had dilated. They blazed like black fire.

"I told you never to play that record in my presence, Tina," Alexander said in an ominously soft tone. He cracked the brittle plastic and let the black shards fall to the carpet. "You know I don't like American music." The fact was he liked it too well; Liz had taught him all her preferences.

There was a terrible, suppressed violence about Alexander, in his low voice, in the dangerous stillness of him, and Tina did not dare to defy him.

Then he was gone, leaving them to stare after him in mild, bored confusion, until one of the younger women, who'd been drinking too much, tittered a bit nervously as she exhaled a deep breath. "I never saw Mikki like that before! He's so . . . so magnificently pagan," she stated with a touch of breathlessness. "When you tire of him, Tina, darling, why don't you give him my number in Zurich. Passionate men can be so amusing in bed."

Tina's acid response was lost as the wild Greek music resumed.

In his cabin, Alexander made two telephone calls. One to Paris and the other to London. He refused to listen when his brother Paul told him it was impossible for him to postpone his return to Paris, that important decisions that he alone could handle had to be made. Alexander overrode every protest and gave orders for his Lear 55 to be flown at once to his private airport on his estate in Grasse.

He would go to Mexico City and catch Liz by surprise. She would not best him again. This time he was determined he would be the winner—no matter what it cost him. Dazzle had long been Alexander's life, but even if the price were the presidency itself, he would pay it to remove his son from the care of that irresponsible and destructive woman.

He would hire a nanny, tutors. He would have to find out what the best schools in England were. Hell! It suddenly occurred to him that he didn't know a thing about little boys. Well, he could learn.

Alexander had no intention of allowing Liz to pursue the disastrous course of raising his son as a half-savage in a remote Indian village in Mexico. Nor would he allow Jock to hold any influence over the child.

What in the name of God was Liz thinking of?

Chapter Two

$\mathcal{T}$he edges of Mexico City's smog reached the pine forests on the green mountain slopes, bringing with it the diesel smell from the distant city. Beneath the forest on the gentler terrain farmers were cultivating their terraced cornfields, some with primitive wooden plows. The peasants of the village called this annual breaking of new land the *barbecho*. The poorer farmers who still used the ancient Aztec cutting and burning system of hoe culture, locally known as *tlacolol*, were weeding their fields, which hugged the steeper slopes where a plow could not be used.

It was the rainy season, and the air was crisply cool and damp. Liz wrapped her *rebozo* more tightly about her shoulders and sipped her first cup of coffee that morning. It was strong, the way she liked it, and it tasted rich and delicious.

An unopened letter from Jock lay on the table beside her treasured photographs of her beloved Cornwall. Quickly she slit the envelope and then set it down without reading it. The letter would contain the inevitable demands. "Marry me. Leave Mexico and come to France. Forgive your father. Forget Alexander." Sometimes Jock enclosed a gossip magazine photo of Alexander with some young beauty to emphasize that the husband she had so passionately loved had long since forgotten her.

Because of Jock, Liz knew how wildly Alexander lived. She'd kept every photograph Jock had sent, studying those handsomely chiseled yet so coldly remote features, her heart filled with the pain of a woman whose hopeless love refused to die. It was little comfort that Alexander looked no happier than she despite his glamorous companions.

For the thousandth time she thought about marrying Jock. She did not doubt Jock's love, though her own fondness for him scarcely reciprocated the passion he professed for her. But if she married Jock, she would have to resolve the complex mess she had made of her life. She would have to face the issue of divorce.

The coffee cup clattered as she set it in its saucer. Divorce Alexander? Divorce the man she'd loved since the first moment she'd seen him? Even now she lay awake in the night, her dreams filled with sensual memories of him.

She was a fighter, and yet she hadn't fought for Alexander. She'd run away, because to fight for him had meant she had to fight him. Loving him as she had, she hadn't possessed the strength for that battle. Now, she knew that if ever she had the chance again, she would do anything to regain his love. However, she'd never have a second chance. Alexander did not love easily, and having let his guard down with her once and been hurt, he was not likely to do so again. He was vulnerable, but he shielded himself with an armor of ruthless hardness.

The haunting vision of Alexander's burnished maleness, his jet dark hair, his golden eyes, rose in her mind's eye. She saw him again as she'd seen him that first night. They'd met at a beach party in Deauville after a sailing regatta he'd won. Of course he'd won; that's what mattered most to him—winning.

Their meeting had almost seemed preordained. It was ironic that it was Mimi, her father's mistress, who had suggested a holiday on the coast of France.

Mimi had said, "A few days together . . . away from your father . . . will give us the opportunity to get to know one another."

Liz had wondered if Mimi sensed that she felt uneasy in her presence. Mimi had always been friendly, and yet from the first Liz had felt a reticence toward her. Even her father had noted it. He had said, "It is not easy for a man like me to live alone, Liz. I know Mimi is . . . different, but that is often the case with famous actresses. There is this ego problem."

Perhaps he was right, or perhaps it was only the normal jealousy a daughter might feel toward her father's mistress who was years younger than he. Nevertheless, Liz had not wanted to go to Deauville, but she had not known how to refuse.

They'd come late to the grand old château, which was aglitter and alive with laughter and music and dancing. Mimi, who was famous in France, was immediately in the midst of a throng of autograph seekers, and Liz was left to herself.

Liz noticed Alexander at once, even before he'd noticed her.

Women were swarming around him. His black head was thrown back and he was laughing. Yet even from across the ballroom she sensed a loneliness about him that only someone who had suffered as she had could understand. She knew too well what it was like to be with friends and yet to be alone, to be lost in a world of money and opulence and success. She fancied that none of the people he was with really understood him, that in some curious way he deliberately kept himself apart from them. Suddenly she'd felt the heat of his gaze upon herself. He smiled boldly because he'd caught her looking at him.

She flushed with an odd, embarrassed sensation. His male eyes ran over her dramatic gown, and his smile broadened. She was overdressed for a sailing party, but then she usually overdressed. He liked to win. That was his way of seeking attention, and she liked to dress outrageously for the same reason. Only the way he looked at her made her feel self-conscious, as though she'd blundered.

Her bodice of burgundy velvet studded with bugle beads and sequins tightly encased her full breasts and tiny waist. Puffed and slashed Renaissance sleeves gave the impression of a Tudor princess. Naturally all the other women were wearing slacks.

Liz tossed her head defiantly and moved quickly away. She was deeply conscious of his eyes following her, and an oddly breathless sensation made her slow her pace. But she was curious about him, and she had whispered excitedly in Mimi's ear a few minutes later, "Who is that man dancing beneath the potted palms? The conceited one with the black hair who looks so like a pirate?"

"A pirate!" Mimi's features froze. Her throaty voice didn't sound like her own. "You have been buried in Cornwall. That's Mikki Vorzenski. He's no pirate, *chérie*, but a real prince. He's the new president of his family's fragrance company, Dazzle. Quite a yachtsman too. A winner at every game he plays, or so it seems. In the game of love, they say he is a despoiler of women. Roger told me that his own family has exiled him to London. You must stay away from him."

"Mikki Vorzenski!" Liz murmured. "Oh, no." A

terrifying hollowness in her stomach made Liz feel sick. Of all men, he was the one she was bound to avoid.

Her attraction horrified her because her father had warned her and had made her promise to avoid him. "Mikki Vorzenski and I are old, old enemies, my child. He is a ruthless thief in the perfume world. He would like nothing better than to hurt me through you." Her father had made it clear that he wanted her to marry Jock.

It was inevitable that Liz would have met Mikki Vorzenski in France. What Liz could not have anticipated was her own instantaneous attraction to him.

She remembered Mimi's words. "A despoiler of women."

Mimi had disappeared.

One of the young women beside the prince was leaning forward so that her breasts spilled invitingly against her thin T-shirt. "Mikki," she cried laughingly, "dance with me."

"Another time, Monique."

It appeared likely that a number of the young beauties would have jumped at the chance for a little despoiling.

And how was she different from them? She understood them only because the same urge lay within her. Liz stumbled toward the door. She could not stay and chance any encounter with him.

Liz hurried blindly across the ancient cobblestones of the darkened garden. Heavy footsteps thudded behind her. Suddenly she was jostled hard against the lean body of a man who'd been running as swiftly as she. For a stunned instant she forgot her fear.

She was at once profoundly aware only of the man. She felt his warmth, his masculine strength when he touched her. She caught her breath at the dangerously provocative sensations his hard, groping hands evoked.

"Oh, excuse me," he said quickly, the warm, rich sound tickling her earlobe. "I'm terribly sorry." But of course, he was not sorry at all.

His touch lightened; his arms slid around her tiny waist to steady her. The strange desire for him to mold her against himself nearly overcame her.

She looked up into the passionate fire of his golden eyes, and she froze. Her black eyes went darker with recognition. She knew he'd followed her deliberately.

"Are you all right?" he asked in that deepest, that most melodious of voices.

She was afraid, but she nodded hastily. Her fingers still gripped his arm for balance. She liked to touch him, to hold on to him. She caught the faint scent of his musky aftershave mingling with the fresh male scent that was uniquely his own, and she liked that as well.

When she flung herself away from him with sudden, fierce determination, she noted that he was breathing hard, as though her nearness was as oddly disturbing to him as his was to her.

Liz was struck with the awesome electric quality of his male charisma. The way he looked at her set her on fire. The way he touched her made her feel thrillingly alive. And he was a stranger. She remembered who he was. Oh, if only he *were* a stranger.

His molten eyes held hers, as though he could not look away, as though he too were unexpectedly affected by her, as if he couldn't stop himself from having feelings he didn't want to have.

That night of their first awareness—one for the other—would be forever frozen in Liz's memory. She had never been so immediately aware of another human being as she was of this striking man, her father's enemy, whom she'd chanced upon in a summer ballroom amid the crumbling grandeur of an ancient château.

Liz knew then, as a woman always knows, that he was just as deeply affected by her.

"You're Mikhail Vorzenski, aren't you?" she gasped in a trembling tone. She dreaded his answer.

"Yes, I am." He smiled warmly. "Who are you?"

She couldn't possibly tell him. Some friends of his called to him, and she seized the opportunity and escaped.

She escaped France and her father and Mimi as well. She hid for a week on a Grecian island.

Alexander pursued her to London. It took him a month to find her. It was late on a golden afternoon when Alexander strode into Liz's shop, Isobel's, with that air of bold confidence he always wore. Liz heard the little bell jingle faintly as the door closed against the jamb.

Leaving a customer in the fitting room, she ascended the stairs and observed him without his knowledge as he browsed restlessly, perusing a grouping of hazy jacquards inspired by the Gobelin tapestries, and a table of velvet blouses with circular yokes recalling the filigree bib collarettes from ancient Egypt.

Alexander lifted a negligee from a low table. It was little more than strips of jade chiffon hanging from a plumed neckline. His low, male chuckle filled the shop as he let the nightgown float back to its place on the table. It did odd fluttery things in her stomach to watch so masculine a man finger such delicate lingerie.

Liz spoke at last in a strangled voice. "Have you found something that interests you, sir?"

He spun around as though electrified by her presence. She was just as profoundly affected by his, though she was determined to deny it.

"Definitely," was his dangerously smooth reply, which he punctuated with a smile that was even more dangerous. His golden eyes were direct and bold as they met hers before they lowered and swept her body with possessive insolence.

Liz stumbled backward with a gasp. He ignored her sputters of indignation and continued his raking scrutiny.

He stared at the mad pulsebeat at her throat and the faint tremor in her hands before she clasped them together. His mere presence was an assault upon every sense in her being. How dared he come here? She retreated into the deep shadows at the back of the shop in an effort to feel safe from him. Then she realized that there was no safety anywhere.

"Do you always undress a woman when you look at her?"

"Only a woman I want," he said, shrugging his wide shoulders lazily. There was laughter in his pleasantly deep voice. "Why did you run away from me in France?"

"You should not have come here," she said, and her words were low and desperate. She was afraid her eyes betrayed the treacherous excitement he aroused within her.

"Why shouldn't I?" he asked, moving nearer. "I always go after what I want."

She shrank against the wall. Her breasts tautened as if in response to his nearness. "Because I told you I wanted nothing to do with you."

He smiled into her glare. "I don't believe you." She moistened her lips, and he watched the curl of her pink tongue as though he found it tantalizing.

She rallied. "I have a customer downstairs. How can you stand there and tell me what's in my own mind?"

"Why not, when you won't?"

"You really are too much," she managed, trying to back away, an impossibility because of the wall behind her. His lean, dark body loomed threateningly nearer.

She forced her gaze from the expanse of his broad shoulders, from his large but surprisingly lithe body. "Look, I'm sorry that you find it so objectionable that I don't want to have anything to do with you."

"That didn't sound much like an apology," he chided silkily.

"It wasn't." She turned toward the back of the shop.

"Not so fast." Deliberately he stepped toward the door, blocking her escape. His grave eyes held hers. "I find it objectionable because you don't really know me." He spoke quietly, all the mockery stilled for the moment in his handsome face.

"I know of you, Mr. Vorzenski, and that's more than enough," she retorted. Her tone held dismissal, but there was a betraying quaver in her voice.

"You don't strike me as the kind of woman who usually lets other people do her thinking for her," his deep baritone taunted.

Her back stiffened, and she thought he knew he'd found a weak place in her armor. She dared a glance at him, her expression softening subtly.

"You're making a mistake," he continued, "to rely on hearsay when it would be so much more interesting to learn about me from firsthand experience." Again there was that dangerously seductive silkiness in his low voice that left her shaking.

"The last thing I want, Mikhail Vorzenski, is to learn about you through firsthand experience," she muttered, her thick dark lashes downcast.

"Is it?" Golden eyes flashed with amusement. "I wonder?"

Her cheeks were aflame. "I told you, I know all about you."

"Not all, surely? But that is why you intrigue me. You know about me, so I must learn about you."

"I don't want to intrigue you."

"But you do. The moment I saw you, I wanted to

know you. When you ran away, I was determined to find you. It was not easy."

"Such selfish determination is deplorable," she flung out hastily.

"Really?" Again he looked amused. "You prefer indifference or weakness in a man then? A boy, perhaps? Or a sissy?" His eyes that knew too much slid over her, those golden male eyes that viewed her with such disturbing intensity.

Everywhere his gaze touched her, her skin flushed as if singed by a tongue of flame. Despite herself, the faint beginnings of a smile played at the corners of her mouth. "I did not say that."

"You implied it."

"How am I going to get rid of you?"

"Perhaps you are not."

"What do you want?"

"Only the reward that I deserve for my trouble." Again he smiled.

"I should have known."

"Oh, I don't want money."

She hadn't imagined that he did.

"What do you want?" Her voice was a tantalizing whisper.

"You."

The single word was direct and bold—like the man.

Before she could give into her sudden wild impulse to escape him, it was too late. He seized her hand and drew her to him.

The shock of his touch compelled them both.

His heady masculine scent enveloped her. A powerful, unconquerable force bound them one to the other in a spell of electric enchantment. She was breathless, and so was he. The tension drained out of her as her fingers curled around his in mute acceptance.

Nor did she draw her hand away as he turned her slender fingers over in his palm and brought them to his lips caressingly. His mouth was pleasingly warm and vibrant against her flesh, and she shivered from the heat of his slow kiss.

She looked into his eyes, and all her timidity was gone. Her black gaze was bold and hot and wanton.

"Hold me," she said suddenly, "tightly. Oh, tightly!"

With a half-smothered groan, he crushed her slim body against the awesomely lean power of his. Her delicate body accommodated his even more perfectly than she could have ever imagined. In that first rapturous moment, the world stood still.

They'd both come so far, traveling through two lifetimes of loneliness to find each other.

She held herself motionless in his arms, her pulse hammering wildly and her breath faint and shallow. She did not speak. Her face was pale and still. Her only movement was the quick downward flutter of her long dark lashes over her eyes.

His hands slid over the soft flesh of her arms. His warm breath stirred in her perfumed hair. A thousand needs pounded in her body.

He lowered his mouth to possess hers, but she reached up and brushed his lips with her fingers.

"Not now," she said breathlessly, "not now." But her eyes caressed the sensual curve of his male mouth with a desire as heated as his own.

"Have dinner with me tonight," he said hoarsely.

"This is all so preposterous." Her husky whisper of protest was the most passionate assent any woman had ever given him.

The whole length of her body was heated by the contact with his.

"Seven, then?" he asked. "Wear that red dress you wore in Deauville."

She nodded. Her black eyes were still fastened upon his dark face, most of all upon his lips.

"The shop closes at six-thirty. I'll be ready then."

There was a blistering eagerness in her that warred with the lingering traces of her fear of him.

"Why are you so afraid of me?" he asked suddenly. "Why did you run away?"

"Because we cannot be."

"But we are," he said forcefully.

"Yes," she murmured. "And that is more frightening than anything." In agonized passion she nuzzled her face against the warmth of his throat, and his hands moved caressingly through her hair, pressing her head even more tightly against him to reassure her.

They dined in the Grill Room of the Connaught, considered by many to be the most desirable and exclusive public dining room in London. How Alexander had obtained his favorite table in the bay window on such short notice, Liz did not ask. But she knew that the Grill Room was sold out, lunch and dinner, every day, and that the most sought-after tables were the two in the bay windows. There were, in all, only eleven tables in the room. The black-haired, black-tied Giancarlo Bovo escorted them discreetly to their places.

The superbly prepared game and woodcock might as well have been cardboard, because they scarcely made an impression on the striking couple at the window table. They had eyes only for each other.

Liz was aglitter in the elaborate wine red gown with the slashed Renaissance sleeves. Her red hair was plaited in coils, which were wound high upon her head in an elaborate coronet of gleaming braids. There was a wildness in his eyes every time he glanced at her that made her blood flow as hotly as lava.

"If I'd known we were eating in the Grill Room, I would have worn something less extravagant," Liz said softly, tilting her face so that the golden light illuminated her flawless beauty.

"I'm glad you didn't," Alexander replied with one of his easy, warm smiles.

"This hotel prides itself on the understatement," she murmured.

"You couldn't look more perfect."

She studied the strong line of his jaw, the brilliance of his golden eyes. He was studying her as well, and she colored with pleasure beneath his intense, hot gaze.

Long silences such as this one fell between them from time to time, moments of hushed, expectant excitement that were powerful, unspoken eroticisms.

"What am I going to call you?" she asked a little breathlessly after one of these prolonged silences.

"Everyone calls me Mikki," he said.

That name jarred; that was the name her father had taught her to hate and fear.

"I don't want to call you what everyone calls you."

"My mother calls me Mikhail."

She frowned, and he saw that she didn't like that either. "What about Alexander?"

"No one calls me Alexander."

"Alexander." She said his name softly, sexily, possessively, and then she smiled. "It's a shame to have a name that no one uses. I will call you Alexander."

"What will I call you?"

"Why, Liz, of course."

"No choice?" he asked. "No last name even?"

"For a long time I have preferred not to use my father's name." Her expression was momentarily shadowed, her fleeting smile enigmatic. *Tell him,* a tiny voice sounded in the back of her mind. "No choice," she said in a strange, tight voice.

"I'm beginning to wonder if there isn't a basic unfairness in our relationship." His golden eyes flashed with amusement.

She laughed. "I certainly hope so, if it's in my favor."

"I'm not used to being dominated by a woman," he teased. His fingers wrapped the velvet warmth of hers across the table.

Her eyes met his. "No, I don't suppose you are," she whispered. "It will be a new experience."

"One must always seek . . . new experiences," he murmured, bringing her fingertips to his lips, having forgotten for the moment the restrained, formal atmosphere of the Connaught. "They say it is the secret of retaining one's youth."

"Is that what I am to you, a new experience?"

"That, and much more." There was an acquisitive gleam in his eyes when he spoke, and a certain teasing look as well.

She knew what he meant, and her fingers tightened upon his with an eagerness that more than matched his.

Afterward they'd gone dancing at the Savoy with the Thames sparkling behind them. Alexander was an excellent dancer, and Liz drifted happily in his arms as a piano tinkled softly.

Later they talked, holding hands, their voices soft and hushed, their faces rapt and golden in the dim candlelight. The ice melted in their untouched drinks, and their kindly waiter left them to themselves. Time passed quickly, as if on wings.

Alexander made himself deliberately charming, and Liz forgot the danger of him. The loneliness of the past year, her grief, her mother's foolish self-destruction, her own mad flight across a far-flung world—all these things were swept aside in the breathless thrill of her excitement.

Liz talked to Alexander easily, making light of the succession of tragedies that had befallen her. She told him everything, everything except her damning secret. She spoke of her childhood in Cornwall, the simple pleasures she'd found on those golden beaches with the man she'd loved as a father. She did not say that only recently she'd learned that man had been her step-father. She brought to life Killigen Hall and all its wonders. She told him, as well, of her despair that her mother had planned to sell her childhood home.

In his turn Alexander talked of his own life—a cosmopolitan world so different from hers she could scarcely imagine it. It was a world of high finance, of the struggle for power, of world-class yacht races, of resorts and beautiful women. Unlike her, he did not mention his childhood or his parents. He spoke of Sardinia, his occasional happinesses there before his brother Sasha's death. His was a fast-paced, exciting world, but it was a world of loneliness and emptiness as well.

They talked as if they'd always known each other. Why had her father warned her of this wonderful man? Alexander made her feel as she'd never felt before—beautiful, desirable and infinitely precious. He looked at her with glowing eyes that were as warm and radiant as firelight. She did not know that her face mirrored the rapture and thrill in his.

The hour was late when he took her hand in his and turned it over. He brought her palm to his lips and caressed it with a warm kiss that sent shivers throughout her body. His eyes met hers with a look that made her emotions rocket sky high.

"Liz, you know what I want, don't you? More than anything?"

The excitement that rushed inside her was hot. She dropped her eyelids. She was at a loss.

"Look at me," he said. When she did, he murmured, "I'm in the mood to follow the most dangerous inclination."

"Dangerous." Odd that *he* should choose that word. She trembled.

"I-I don't understand."

"I think you do."

There was no mistaking the sound of passion in his deep voice.

"You could have any woman."

"But I don't want just any woman."

"This is all so new to me," she heard herself say.

"The way I feel tonight is new to me," he admitted.

"You've had many women, while I—"

"They were not you. Until I saw you in Deauville, I never understood the instinct of other men to pursue one woman and forsake all others. I do now." His voice changed subtly, an edge of regret and cynicism having crept into it. "Of course, I can't promise I'm the changed man a woman like you deserves. I've lived a different sort of life for too long. I can only say I don't want to hurt you, that you are special to me, Liz. I don't know if that's enough."

He made her feel like a queen. The flickering candle had burned low in its pool of wax. Her fingers squeezed his. He'd been humble and honest, while she . . . She dismissed her guilt, and gave in to the tumultuous wonder of her feelings for him.

"It's enough," she said. "More than enough, for now."

"Will you come back with me to the Connaught?"

She did not speak, but she did not have to. They both knew the answer. It had been inevitable from the moment they'd first met.

Chapter Three

*W*hen Alexander and Liz arrived back at his hotel, and she knew they were going up to his room, her mood altered subtly. He was so sophisticated, and doubtless he preferred women who were experienced. She had never been with a man before. She knew only that she wanted to be with him. To delay, she insisted on walking up the handsome, six-story oak staircase to his suite rather than using the elevator.

"I love the Connaught," she said, tilting her head at a defiant angle when he protested the climb. "It's like a great English country house. It doesn't have all those empty, endless, Kafkaesque tunnels punctuated by anonymous doors other hotels have. I love the oil paintings and cupboards with china figurines. Have you seen the mounted stag's head?"

"I can't say that I have," came his dry reply.

"Then we must walk up."

He looked past her and eyed the stairs suspiciously as

though he wished he were living in a hotel with dull halls rather than fascinating ones, but he did not deny her her wish.

She dawdled, delighting in the discoveries of a chinoiserie cabinet, a tall case clock and an old map encased in a thick, plain frame. She laughed when he confessed he'd passed these treasures every day on his way to and from Dazzle without noting them.

When they came to his door, she grew silent. He was silent as well, and she wished he would think of something careless to say that would put her at ease. He led her inside, and when he locked the door, she blushed beneath his warm gaze. Her boldness was gone. She seemed overcome with shyness at being alone with him in the quiet intimacy of his hotel room. Her gaze made a frightened sweep of the vast bedroom, lingering with misgivings upon the bed.

She wished that his bed had not been carefully turned down by the maid, that the embroidered linen mat had not been placed beside the bed so that the guests' bare feet would not have to touch the carpet when they retired at night and rose the next morning. The room was obviously ready for the retirement of its occupants.

He came to her and circled her with his arms to reassure her, but she lightly skipped out of his reach.

He left her alone while he shrugged out of his jacket. He went to the bar and splashed brandy into a crystal glass.

"Would you care to join me?" he offered.

She did not answer him because she didn't hear him. She was standing beside his desk, where his research papers on Dazzle's latest fragrance were spread out. She could not stop herself from staring at them. So, her father had been right. Dazzle was preparing for a new launch.

It reinforced exactly who Alexander was, and why

they could have nothing to do with each other. Perhaps it was not too late to stop this madness between them.

Alexander was loosening the knot of his tie when she glanced up. The lamplight gleamed in his shining black hair. He turned to her; his dark face was flushed with some emotion she did not understand. She felt as guilty as a traitor to have looked at his papers. In the mirror her skin was as white as flour against her jewel red gown.

He strode to her, and she jumped away, too guilty and upset to speak to him. A tremulous silence hung between them. He caught her frightened glance and held it.

She forced herself to calm down. Of course, he could have no idea that she could understand his papers, that she was as inexorably linked to the world of gums, flowers, essences, concretes and absolutes as he. He would think her too ignorant of the business to understand perfume formulas. He did not know who she was, so he could not possibly realize his danger.

Shakily she dragged her eyes from his. "I must go," she choked.

"What?" Her behavior was incomprehensible to him.

"I don't know why I came out with you tonight, why I came up here," she whispered, trying to race past him. "I've made a terrible mistake."

He ignored her words. Reaching out, he caught her slim shoulders and pulled her against him. "What's wrong, Liz?" he demanded. "You must tell me."

"I can't explain."

Inscrutable golden eyes met her wavering glance. "We're no longer strangers on the street. I thought we were becoming friends." There was warmth in his gaze. "More than friends."

"You and I can never be friends."

"But why?"

She stared at him in mute anguish, giving him no answer. She was quivering like a frightened animal, and after her warmth all evening she understood why he was at a loss.

Despite her fear, the heat of his body against hers aroused her like a drug. Neither was he unaffected. She felt the rapid unevenness of her breathing. She was trembling everywhere her body touched his.

"Alexander, you must forget we ever met. Let me walk out that door, and don't come after me. You will never be sorry."

"You're wrong, Liz." He laughed softly. "I would be sorry every day that I lived. You can't leave me."

"I must!" She struggled to free herself.

Then he did the only thing he could to stop her. He pressed her even closer against his body so that she felt the heat of him and his need of her. Easily he captured her hands, which pushed against his chest, and twisted them gently behind her waist.

"Alexander . . ." She pleaded weakly that he stop even while her pliant softness shaped itself to his hard contours with womanly readiness, even while he seemed to sense something deep within her was yielding and that her excitement was causing her to lose control.

"Oh, Liz, can't you understand that there's no reason for you to be afraid? Not of me. If you'll only tell me what the trouble is, I'll help you."

His mouth brushed the softness of her hair, then across her forehead and eyebrows, trailing at last to her trembling lips. He kissed the velvet skin of her throat. Ever so softly he won her from her purpose, stroking her body, finding all the secret places where his touch aroused her. Desire quickened under his expert titillation.

She felt wanton and yet shy toward him. His hands

slid into her hair, and she felt his fingers freeing the pins, uncoiling the braids, until the silken mass flowed freely.

"I did not want to go to the party in Deauville, but when I saw you, I knew you were my destiny," he murmured, his lips trailing along the smoothness of her brow. "When you ran away, I was desperate to find you. Don't leave me tonight, not when I want you with me forever. I need you, Liz. I've never said that to a woman before."

His gaze was filled with stark longing, and she reached up and touched his face lovingly.

"I won't leave you, Alexander."

Gently he wrapped his arms around her and led her toward the bed. He removed her rich gown, and when next he held her she felt the smooth hardness of his bare skin against her breasts. Her nakedness seemed strange and scary, and yet thrilling.

"I-I've never been with a man before. I hope you don't mind," she whispered shyly.

"Mind?" Alexander's laugh was soft and tinged with desire. "Liz, that just makes you lovelier, my sweet virgin."

He lowered his black head and possessed her lips with slow, passionate mastery. His tongue played across the edges of her warm wet mouth. His hands moved against the satin warmth of her flesh; hands that knew too well where and how to touch a woman. His mouth smothered the passionate moan that erupted from her lips.

She clung to him. He seemed pleased when she let her tongue mate with his, when she pressed her trembling body even more tightly against him. He gazed into slanting eyes that had gone dark with a passion. Her hand came up to his roughened cheek and she caressed him with infinite tenderness.

"I love you, Alexander. I don't know how that's

possible, but I do." Her black eyes seemed filled with love, and sadness too. "I don't want to hurt you! Not ever. That's why I'm afraid."

He took the hand that brushed his cheek and kissed it gently.

"Hurt me? How could you ever hurt me, my darling?" Her obvious concern for him accentuated his tenderness.

Alexander bent and kissed her. He lifted her into the bed and quickly stripped off his own clothes to lie beside her. She had watched him in fascination, blushing at the bronzed power of his body, at the magnificence of his muscled shoulders, the flatness of his hard belly, at the swollen shaft of his manhood.

He gathered her shivering body into his arms. He was gentle and loving, restraining his own passion, arousing hers. He learned the feminine secrets of her, kissing her everywhere with hot exploring lips until she was scarlet with embarrassment even while little whimpers rose from her throat.

The time that followed was filled with the rapture and wonder of discovering one another.

Alexander crushed her to him and abandoned himself to the full glory of his desire. She returned his kisses feverishly, running her hands over his powerful body, reveling in the hard pleasure of his muscular frame, savoring the ripple of muscle and sinew beneath the light tracings of her fingers.

She gave herself to him, opening her body for his, emitting a soft sob of ecstasy when he came to her and showed her the wild thrilling joys love could bring to a woman.

Afterward she lay weeping silently in his arms, too deeply moved to say anything. Now she knew what she had wanted that first moment in Deauville when she'd watched him across that glittering ballroom and caught that hungry look in his golden eyes, and when she'd felt the strength of his arms on her body in the courtyard. She'd wanted him like this—wild and powerful and yet possessive and gentle.

Her languorous black eyes opened slowly to meet his. "I love you," she whispered.

Alexander's eyes shone with tenderness, and his fingers lazily caressed her cheek. "Marry me," he said.

"I—"

"I love you, Liz. I can't bear to live without you. Until this moment I've been alone."

This from a despoiler of women. She smiled shyly and reached up and kissed him because suddenly she knew that she couldn't live without him either. She had no one except him. She could not go back to that barren loneliness now that she'd known the glory of being close to him. Liz gave him a tremulous yes, and the temptation to confess her secret trembled on the tip of her tongue. Her courage failed her, and she lay in tortured silence, her omission a fatal step in the destruction of their love.

"Do you realize you've promised to marry me, and I don't even know your last name?" he probed gently.

"My last name," she choked, "is Killigen." It was the truth, and yet it was a lie. She found that she could no longer meet his gaze.

After he'd conquered her reluctance, there had been no stopping their soaring passion. She had known from the moment his name was whispered to her in Deauville that their love could never be, and yet she married him without telling him who she really was.

Now, seven years later, she was in Mexico alone with her two children, and he had his wild bachelor life in Europe. How blindly stupid she had been. Liz clasped her fingers together beneath her thick shawl to conceal their trembling.

Just thinking of Alexander could still bring a faint

tremor to her body. She wasn't ready to confront him in person. Crumpling Jock's letter, she threw it, unread, in the trash. She would have to keep putting Jock off, at least for now.

From the balcony, Liz could see the peasants walking up the winding road from their village to open the doll factory. They dressed as they had for centuries, the women with their dark-colored skirts and high-necked blouses, half-aprons, and rebozos, the men in their white cotton jackets and trousers, straw sombreros, leather huaraches, and sarapes.

Once these primitive surroundings had seemed alien to the thoroughly modern Liz, but now they were home. Here, with the help of a village midwife, Liz had borne her fraternal twins. The children were miniature replicas of their parents. Alex was bronzed and dark and muscular, as Alexander must have been as a child. Samantha, with her carrot red hair and beanpole slimness, was bold and mischievous. This was the only home they had ever known, and despite her own sense of isolation and bouts of homesickness for Killigen Hall in Cornwall, Liz had sought to make it a happy one.

Jock said the children would have more advantages in France, but she was not sure that was true. Mexico was not without a rich cultural heritage.

This morning the twins were sleeping even later than usual because Liz had driven into Mexico City to pick Samantha up from a visit with friends the previous night. The children frequently slept until nine because Liz liked them to stay up in the evenings when she could spend time with them. She lunched with them during the siesta hour as well. During the mornings a tutor came and worked with the children. In the afternoons they had the run of the hacienda under Esmeralda's doting supervision.

Liz sank back against the creaky leather of her handmade Mexican chair and savored this rare moment of relaxation. She was thinking of the excitement of her recent trip to New York, her first trip abroad since she'd come to Mexico. With a thrill of pleasure she remembered the buyers' enthusiasm for her dolls. "Exquisite," they had said. "Museum quality." "Delightful." Their praise was the fulfillment of a secret personal dream she'd conceived in this mountain village. She was going to have to work harder than ever to be able to fill their orders for her dolls.

The morning stillness was pierced by a sudden, earsplitting shriek of despair that startled Liz out of her reverie. The sound came from the doll factory, and a wave of alarm rippled through Liz. Besides her twins, her factory was the most important thing in her life.

Liz jumped up. Her shawl slid to the floor, but she did not notice it. The thick, roughly woven Mexican cotton dress with its lavish, jewel-bright embroidery work was long sleeved and warm.

A second scream erupted from the factory, and this was followed by a tumultuous chorus of cries.

What in the world could have happened?

Chapter Four

*H*er bright hair flying, Liz raced down the sun-splashed corridor. She crossed the courtyard, which was shaded by ancient poplars and draped with scarlet bougainvillea. Even before she reached that part of the hacienda she had converted into her doll factory, she saw the telltale signs of trouble.

Water trickled in a steady stream from beneath the doorway and pooled on the pink tile floor of the courtyard. She heard the muted cries of hopelessness. Not bothering to remove her huaraches, Liz sloshed through the water. When she opened the door, her heart caught in her throat.

Eyes from a hundred brown faces turned toward the tall, slender woman who looked far too young to be shouldering her massive responsibilities. To them she had always been like a goddess since she first stepped onto their mountain and moved into the dilapidated, high-walled hacienda that had been partially destroyed during the Revolution because it had once belonged to the most hated of all the *caciques*.

Liz surveyed the destruction. The entire factory was floating in three feet of water. Doll dresses, tiny wigs, spools of golden braid, beads, miniature shoes and hats, the machines—everything was soaked.

Juan, Liz's foreman, shushed the others to silence so that he could speak. "Señora, the water tower on the roof broke and flooded the factory." His low, Spanish voice held both anxiety and defeat. He was a man whom life had defeated too many times. "We have lost everything."

Liz felt as lost and defeated as they did. She had hundreds of new orders that had to be filled within the month, and they were already running behind. During the rainy season the villagers needed time to seed and cultivate their fields. She was too lenient with her workers, excusing them from duties to tend their land when she should have insisted that they come. She even excused Juan when he didn't work because of his drinking, but the peasants' lives seemed so relentlessly hard to her.

She thought of New York, where she'd found the vast new outlet for her dolls. She'd come back with hopes of expansion, and now this. If she disappointed her distributor, a hard man who would not tolerate failure, he would lose faith in her.

She waded through the water and picked up a sodden doll garment and a tiny soaked silk flower. She fingered the limp petals of the ruined flower reverently. She was overwhelmed by despair. Years of her own work and frustration stood behind her dolls. She remembered the loneliness and isolation she'd endured in this strange country that was so far away from England and everyone she'd loved.

Nor would she be the only one affected if this

calamity were allowed to destroy everything she'd worked for. The desperate Mexican villagers depended upon her factory for their livelihood. She was responsible for them. The silk flower was a symbol of their ruin as well as hers.

She felt the stinging fire of tears behind her eyelids, but she fought them back. She set the little flower on a table and smoothed the petals tenderly. She did not know what she could do to salvage her factory, but when she looked up, Liz's dark eyes flashed with the fierce determination that was her heritage, the heritage of the father she sought to deny.

"I will not give up. *We* will not give up," she said so softly they scarcely heard her.

Her Spanish was awkward. She had learned to speak the tongue the way she always did everything—by simply plunging in and doing it. But the people who worked for her loved the soft sound of her voice despite her confusing conjugations and hopelessly jumbled pronouns. They heard strength and hope.

Long ago, when Liz had first come to the deserted hacienda, the people had regarded her with suspicion. When she saved a child dying of malaria by driving the infant and his mother into Mexico City for medical help and remaining with them through the crisis, the hearts of the villagers softened. They gave her their sympathy when they learned she was pregnant and alone, their respect when she'd begun her factory, and finally their love because of her treatment of them. She had brought them work, hope and a new beginning. They could not know that by helping them, she had given herself the same things.

"We will have to work together," she continued haltingly because she had to pause to keep her voice from breaking, "as we always have. This will mean long hours. Six days a week. You must bring your cousins from other villages to help you in the fields. No vacations for a while if we are to clean this place up, dry everything before it mildews, and repair the machines. But if we can satisfy our New York distributors, it will mean a bigger factory very soon, better machines, more jobs, more money for you."

Now there were smiles instead of dark looks of despair. For an instant she was filled with doubt. There was a much easier way to save the factory. One telephone call to an opulent flat in Paris. One telephone call to her father and Mimi.

The mere thought strengthened her resolve. It would be easier to lose her factory, easier to starve, easier even to watch the villagers and their children starve than to call him. With an effort she forced Roger Chartres and Mimi from her mind.

Liz beckoned Juan and gave him specific orders. Then she telephoned Manuel Rodriguez, her partner, who was in Mexico City, and told him they had to have more machines at once. She carefully concealed her desperation. He would learn how bad things were when he returned.

"At once?" Manuel asked. "Liz, in Mexico you must learn the word *mañana.*"

"There are many things about the Spanish language that are beyond me, Manuel. The meaning of that word is one of them."

She hung up to the sound of his laughter.

She would succeed by herself. Already the demoralizing feelings of defeat were subsiding, and her fierce will to win despite all odds was taking over.

Liz worked long into the afternoon, racing between her office and the factory, making uncountable decisions as to what could be salvaged and what should be thrown out. It was a painful process.

An entire shipment of fifteen-inch dolls resembling miniature princesses from imperial Russia, all lavishly costumed to attend a dance in the tsar's Winter Palace, were soaked. The research that had gone into the creation of these dolls had been monumental, the labor in their gem-studded diadems, gossamer veils and rich ball gowns awesome. Now they were ruined.

Ruined as well were four dozen Japanese samurai dolls. These dolls were the finest and most authentic Liz had attempted to design and manufacture. They were dressed in rich brocade, and their equipment included the traditional two swords, a suit of armor fashioned of leather, metal plates, and silken tassels. Embossed miniature helmets hid heads of real hair. Clean-shaven chins reflected the samurais' fastidious customs. Liz had spent three months pouring over library books before she'd completed her design for the model of this doll.

She forgot about lunch and the siesta hour until Esmeralda tiptoed into her office. Then Liz's stomach growled ferociously as she realized it was long past the hour she usually had lunch on the balcony with the children.

They must be starving! She couldn't imagine why they had not bombarded her office an hour earlier, as they usually did when she became engrossed with her work. The spicy aroma of chile and tortillas drifted from the kitchen.

When Esmeralda said nothing, Liz glanced up and saw the misery contorting Esmeralda's face. With the instincts of a mother who realized her twins' numerous imperfections, some charming and some of them not so charming, Liz knew that a new catastrophe had struck.

"What have the little rascals done this time, Emmie?" she asked lightly, for she was an indulgent mother.

"Nothing, señora," Esmeralda wailed. "The little angels are gone!"

Panic rose like a hot wave in Liz's throat.

"Gone?" Liz's tired mind refused to accept a new crisis. "Surely it's one of their games."

"No, señora, they are gone. Even the burro Pablo. I left them in the meadow to ride Pablo, but he was being so stubborn he wouldn't move. When I came back they were gone."

"When was this? Have you looked everywhere for them? Someone must have seen them. Did you go down to the village?"

"I'm crazy with looking for them, señora. Mario told me he saw them with a gringo. *Un gigante.* A giant. He took them into the forest, Mario said. They were laughing as though they were friends. I am afraid of the forest. I cannot go after them."

Liz's fingers gripped her ledger. Esmeralda, like many of the other villagers, believed in all the gruesome local superstitions regarding the cliffs, mountains and forests. The villagers believed in a world filled with hostile forces whose goodwill and protection must be secured. The rain god would withold rain if he were neglected. *Los aires,* the spirits who lived in the water, might send illness to those who offend them. The superstitions regarding the mountain were so ridiculously frightening that Liz had never paid any attention to them before.

Liz looked past Esmeralda to the thick pine trees that climbed the steep slopes. Liz was not frightened by legends, but the forest and the mountain were dangerous with their unexpected precipices and cliffs.

A giant who laughed? Was there some reality to this? Liz remembered a foreigner she had seen in the village the week before. But none of the village men were giants. Only one man that she knew fit that description. Alexander was six feet four, his body so thickly muscled he would seem a giant to someone of Mario's smaller stature. She remembered her husband's broad grin, the pleasurable rumble of his laughter, and she was shaken.

"Oh, no! Don't let it be Alexander." Liz sank back, gasping. Was the man who'd come upon her last week, when she and Alex had gone swimming, someone Alexander had sent to find her?

She could fight the loneliness of exile. She could fight floods and the constant lack of money, but she could not bear to lose her precious darlings.

Had Alexander found her hiding place? Had he come and kidnapped the children? She had read stories of fathers doing that. What if he took them and went away as she had? She felt a twinge of guilt as she thought how he might twist her actions of seven years ago. But what she'd done had been different. Alexander hadn't wanted her, and he hadn't known she was pregnant. He hadn't wanted children from her. He'd sent her away, vowing the most terrible revenge if he ever found her. But what if he'd changed his mind? What if he wanted them now? What if he took them? With his vast resources, how could she fight him? Would she ever be able to find Alex and Samantha again?

Liz's stubborn, resilient will rallied. She mustn't allow herself to panic yet. The man last week did not have to be in Alexander's employ. The children were probably perfectly all right. She was overreacting because she was already in an anxious state from the flood.

Liz rose. She stood a head taller than Esmeralda. "Tell everyone we must search for the twins. I will go into the forest myself."

"But the giant, señora!"

"If he is so terrible, Esmeralda," Liz erupted, "do you think I will leave my defenseless children in his care in the forest?"

* * *

The brook gurgled as it flowed over amber pine needles and splashed over black lava ash. The shadows in the forest were darkening; the sun had sunk behind the lavender peaks. A sliver of moon hung in the sky. Liz had been walking for hours, and she was exhausted.

"Alex. Samantha. *Queridos.* Oh, my darlings. Where are you?"

Liz called the names repeatedly, and when there was no answer, her terror increased. Never had her bold, mischievous children seemed so vulnerable and in need of protection.

When she stepped on a twig that crackled, she screamed, so brittle were her nerves. She felt so tired and emotionally drained, she did not know how much longer she could go on. At last she sagged wearily against a tree and listened to the silence. For the first time she grew aware of the darkness. From somewhere deep in the forest came a sound that didn't belong. She strained to hear it again, but there was only the swift flapping of a winged creature in a branch overhead, the rustling of leaves and the hootings of an owl.

Her teeth began to chatter. Just when she thought she must return to get flashlights and warmer clothing, Liz heard the sounds of childish laughter mingling with the pleasant, deep resonance of a man's voice.

"Come on, Pablo. This way." Samantha was coaxing her pet, who was renowned for his stubbornness.

The chilled night air swirled around Liz, but her relief was so profound she scarcely felt it. She was about to call to Samantha when the velvet warmth of an all-too-familiar, amused male voice came to her.

"You're sure this is the way back, Samantha? Burros usually have a better sense of direction than people do—though I hate to credit this ragtag animal with any superiority."

"No, Daddy, I'm not sure," Samantha admitted. "Maybe Pablo is right."

"Daddy." The word that was so casually uttered by the daughter sliced through the mother's heart. Liz began to quiver, and was rational enough to know she was on the verge of hysteria.

It couldn't be. He couldn't be! Not here! Not Alexander! Not with the children! Had he come to take them away?

"Alexander?" Liz cried his name with hushed fear as she propelled herself into the darkness toward the voices.

"Liz. Is that you?" Her own name and his question with the husky French intonation reached out and enveloped her like a warm caress. Only *he* could make her name such a sensuous sound.

She saw him then, walking in the moonlight, and she stopped as though a witch had frozen her with a spell. Everything seemed to happen in slow motion, as though the purple darkness of the night had somehow enchanted the forest and everyone within it.

The children's laughter at Pablo's hoarse snort was fuzzy and sounded far away. Liz was aware only of Alexander beside them, holding Pablo's reins and the children's hands.

Liz felt his intense, devouring gaze. There was a look of astonishment scrawled on his handsome face. Their eyes touched before she looked quickly, too quickly, away. In that split-second glance she memorized every detail of his appearance.

He was as stunningly charismatic as ever. His hair was as black as the deepest shadows; his golden eyes were molten with hot, unfathomable emotion. It seemed he could not tear his gaze from her.

His face was leaner and more uncompromising

than it had been in youth. The hard experiences of life had carved his features, imbuing them with roughhewn strength. He was as compellingly handsome as she remembered, but the aura of rugged power he had always exuded had intensified. He was as awesomely virile as ever. Worldly cynicism curved his sensual mouth into a bold, insolent smile as he regarded her lazily. Yet there was about him a new and terrifying remoteness, a fierce determination to win no matter what the price.

Her heart began to pound like a frightened rabbit's. She went hot and cold.

All the emotions that she'd told herself were dead came alive like the searing, raw pain of an open wound, and she knew how terribly she had missed him, how terribly she still loved him. She wanted to rip away that chiseled mask he wore. Her independence these past years had been a valiant charade. She fought back the desire to beg for his understanding, to beg that this time he believe her.

Instead she stood stiffly before him. Pride silenced her and made her tilt her head upward defiantly, so that her gaze was almost level with his. She would not beg him again.

She struggled to fend off the overpowering emotions he so effortlessly engendered, feelings that left her weak and vulnerable and unable to fight him. But fight him she would. He represented danger. He could be hard and cold to his enemies. He might take the children from her.

"Mommy! Mommy!"

The spell of enchantment that bound Liz and Alexander was broken. The children sang in unison as they raced toward her. When they tumbled headlong into her arms, she knelt and cradled them against her breast, grateful for the security of their nearness. They were wriggling and breathless in their excitement.

"Pablo ran away, and Daddy came! We got lost in the woods chasing Pablo, but we weren't scared because Daddy was with us. Why didn't you tell us Daddy was coming, Mommy? Why didn't you?"

Liz hugged them closely, silently, frantically. When she gave them no answer, they shrugged free and peered at her with solemn, uncertain faces before they darted back to Alexander.

She felt bereft by their rejection, and she was in a state of bewilderment as she stared at her children clinging to their father. Never before had she had to share her children's loyalty. How had Alexander won their affection so quickly? It was an ominous sign.

"Daddy said you might not let him stay with us," Alex said. "We want him to." There was a mutinous note in his voice.

"Darling, how could he possibly stay?" Liz reasoned lamely. "Daddy lives far away. Besides, he's too busy." She glanced helplessly toward Alexander.

"He'll stay if you let him," Samantha cried passionately. "Mommy, please!"

Liz did not know what to do. Alexander's silence was no help. Why didn't he tell them it was impossible for him to stay?

It was terrifying that he could obtain an emotional hold over the children so quickly. Might he use longer periods of time to turn them against her?

As always, Alexander read her easily. His features hardened. She felt the thorough rake of his narrowed eyes sweeping chillingly downward over her body.

"It's getting dark, and the children are cold," Alexander said curtly as she stood up. "I think it might be best if we went back to the hacienda before we tried to talk."

It was a rational remark, but his tone of command sparked anger in Liz. "After seven years, you and I have nothing to talk about," she lashed out, speaking in French so the children wouldn't understand.

He responded in French that was as rapid and deadly as gunfire. "The hell we don't! I've come because of my children."

"Don't use them for an excuse. You couldn't possibly care about the children. You scarcely know them. You don't even know how to love in the first place."

A muscle spasmed in his jawline. "I do care about my children," he stated coldly.

Fear made her reckless. "Well, you have no rights at all where they're concerned. You threw me out when I was pregnant."

All of his careful control disintegrated, and as he moved nearer, she realized how stupid she was to provoke him.

"No rights, you say? I don't know how to love, you say, as if you do? You damned little . . ."

He was a tower of coiled fury looming over her, and for a minute she thought he might strike her. She cringed as he fought for control, and she noticed that the children were afraid and upset. Their faces were crumpled in misery.

Alexander glanced uneasily toward the children and saw their white faces. He swallowed his furious expletive even as he seized Liz by the shoulders and pulled her against his lean body.

His hard arms circled her tiny waist, and her hips were ground tightly against his. The heady scent of his maleness mingled with his cologne and enveloped her. Everything about him came back to her in a poignant rush.

She felt the heat of him, sensed his masculine toughness. Only her fury prevented the bold intimacy of his embrace from being a dangerously stimulating sensation.

Brown fingers tilted her chin so that he could inspect her face. She was afraid, and her mouth felt so parched she couldn't speak. When she trembled, it was his rock-hard body that supported hers. She felt branded by the muscular power of his body. She licked her lips, and he watched the motion of her tongue with hot, dark eyes.

His brows were drawn together in a deep frown as he studied her, his mouth twisted in sardonic anger. His expression was as intense and primitive as that of a predator who had stalked his prey and captured it.

There was danger in his hard look, and suddenly she was afraid. It was as if she were facing a stranger instead of the husband she'd slept with, the husband whose children she'd borne. His deep, golden eyes continued to rake her with frightening intensity, his penetrating gaze stripping away her defenses until her very soul lay dangerously exposed.

"No," she murmured breathlessly. "You should never have come. Let me go. You must. Be reasonable, Alexander."

He held her so close that the hushed warmth of her soft voice brushed the dark skin of his throat. Her hair sprayed like tousled silk upon his bare brown arms. She struggled wildly, but only became more hopelessly and intimately entangled with his steel-tough body. He did not release her. Instead he threw back his black head and laughed down at her harshly.

At last he stopped laughing. "I must? You really are too much, Liz. Why must I do anything you say?"

"Because . . ."

"I owe you nothing, my dear." She was very aware of his hands searing her bare flesh. "Let's get something straight," he said hoarsely. "I wouldn't have thrown you out if I had had the slightest idea you were pregnant. No matter how I felt about you, do you think I could deny my own flesh and blood? You deliberately left without telling me you were expecting a baby. When I found out, I spent seven damned years looking for you."

"I came to your office that morning to tell you," she replied quietly, "but you were already out of your mind with rage. There seemed no point then."

"Of course I was angry. You'd wrecked Dazzle and me in one staggering blow by stealing Paul's formula and giving it to Jock! Why, Liz? Why did you do that? What was worth all those lies and treachery, not to mention outright criminality?"

His brown face appeared contorted through her blinding tears. "I had nothing to do with that," she whispered. "I tried to explain. I couldn't have done that to you."

"No?" There was a jeering note in his hard voice. His fingers tightened cruelly on her shoulder blades, and he pressed her so tightly to himself that his body seemed to consume hers. "Then how did Radiance steal and launch the perfume Paul had been perfecting for more than three years? Explain why Jock named that particular essence Liz. And while you're at it, tell me those photographs used in that launch aren't of you, my darling wife. Tell me you weren't the model for Radiance in that stinking, crooked deal! Tell me you aren't Roger Chartres's daughter! Liz, why the hell did you try to destroy me?"

The anger in his voice was fierce and frightening. She realized with a sinking heart that seven years had changed nothing.

"Let me alone," she moaned. "You won't believe anything I say, so why should I defend myself?"

He held her as tightly as ever. "Answer me, Liz."

"I didn't . . ."

He gave her a hard shake. "I don't want your lies. This time I want the truth. Why?"

She was stung by his stubborn belief that she was so heartless, and she couldn't bear his bullying demands when he wouldn't even listen. Her fighting spirit returned, and she struggled, trying to break his grip. Kicking him again and again, she wrenched her hands free and pummeled his chest. She cried out in rage and misery, begging him to release her. Her fragile body writhed against the steely might of his arms until her heart pounded as though it might burst. At last she gave up. Against his strength, hers was as nothing.

"Tell me, Liz, was Jock your lover?"

"No!" The single word was explosive. She yanked a hand free, and would have slapped him had he not caught her wrist just in time. She was panting in fury. "How could you even think that?" she cried. "There's never been anyone except . . . except . . . you." Suddenly that angered her more than anything. "You rotten—" She bit back the rest of her sentence. What right did he have to answers from her now? How she wished she could return Jock's love. How she wished there had been many, many other men. It was all so hopeless. Her thoughts clouded as a terrible dizziness swept her.

"Let me go," she pleaded. "I feel so strange. I can't breathe. Please. Alexander, I think I'm going to faint."

The brutal disappointment of the flood, the hard work, her terrifying search for the children, and Alexander's fierce anger had all taken their toll.

His hold seemed to loosen, and yet she did not fall. She felt curiously weightless. His grave face blurred in a nauseating whirl.

She relaxed, but even his strong arms could not keep her from sliding into a void that brought swift, black oblivion.

Alexander lifted her into his arms. He stared into her still face. Her flaming hair fell across his shoulders.

"Why, Liz?" he drawled in a voice that was strangled by torture, repeating the question that had haunted him for seven years. "Why did you do it, when I loved you so?"

Chapter Five

Alexander strode with Liz in his arms. The children and Pablo trailed behind in a disorganized scramble. Liz felt excessively light and delicate against his body, and Alexander felt remorse at his treatment of her. She looked so innocent and sweet. His rage was gone and in its place was a baffling tenderness.

Samantha's curiosity bubbled to the surface with questions that intensified Alexander's guilt. "What's the matter with Mommy, Daddy? Why is she sleeping now? Why did she get so mad at you?"

"Your mother's tired, Samantha," Alexander replied gruffly, answering the first question and evading the second. Samantha's eyes, so like her mother's, remained doubtful.

The hacienda was brilliantly lit against the deeper blackness of the mountains, and as Alexander climbed the path leading to the front gates, Esmeralda, Juan and several other Indian peasants walked out of the house. Curious, worried black eyes accosted him with a thousand half-formed suspicions.

"My wife fainted in the forest," Alexander drawled in his heavily accented Spanish, emphasizing his relationship to her. "The shock of losing the children and seeing me again after our long separation was too much," he began. Deciding that their señora had come to no harm, they nodded in swift understanding and immediate acceptance of him while he marveled at how naturally the word "wife" slid from his tongue even in a foreign language and how right it felt to call Liz that.

Alexander could almost read the villagers' minds as they stared first at him and then at his son, Alex, who bore the irrefutable stamp of his paternity.

They were thinking, The señora's husband has come. Despite the seven-year separation he is the rightful man of the house and must be treated with respect.

In the village it was not the custom to question a man's behavior. The peasants' acceptance of him made Alexander accept his position in the household as well.

Liz's head stirred groggily against his shoulder. "I'm all right, Alexander. Put me down," she mumbled faintly.

Ignoring her request, Alexander commanded her servants with the ease of a man used to giving orders. "Take me to my wife's bedroom and bring hot tea and broth in case she's hungry."

Maria scurried to the kitchen while Esmeralda took the children. Juan led Alexander up winding tiled stairs to the señora's spacious bedroom, which had views of the valley and mountains.

Alexander kicked the door open, stalked inside and gently laid Liz upon her great, hand-carved Mexican bed. Juan lit an oil lamp before shutting the door, leaving the couple alone in semidarkness. The enormous chairs and ornately wrought candelabra cast flickering shadows upon the stuccoed walls, but Alexander could see the evidence of Liz's talent for making any room charming. Brightly colored Indian rugs covered the tile floor. Childish artwork decorated one wall, and he realized that their children must have inherited her artistic talent.

He saw the photographs of her beloved Cornwall on her worktable. Shelves were filled with the original models of the dolls Liz had designed. Snuggly baby dolls in yellow organza sat beside Mimi from *La Boheme* and two stern Amish dolls. Southern belles in ruffled hoop skirts stood next to the dolls from her International series. Goya portrait dolls smirked from their corner. Alexander scarcely noted them.

He brought the lamp to the bed, and Liz blinked from its brilliance. She flung her hand weakly over her eyes to shade them but the movement exhausted her. Her fingers fell away. In the golden light her cheeks were pale, her lush, half-parted lips temptingly rose colored. Her tousled red curls pooled in a riot of waves upon blankets.

He knew he should leave, but he felt intensely concerned. He hoped this was nothing more than exhaustion. It was not in him to hate someone who was so weak and defenseless.

"Alexander." Her voice was a soft whisper that stirred long-forgotten intimate memories.

He could feel the low thudding of his pulse. He had not contemplated what the effect might be upon himself were he to find himself alone with her in her bedroom, accepted by all in her household as her rightful husband.

"Come here," she begged. Her low tone was sexy. It was the way she had always spoken to him in bed.

He turned. His eyes moved over her, from the enchanting beauty of her face to the creamy flesh of her throat. She was irresistibly lovely. Her breasts rose and fell beneath the stiff Mexican cotton gown. For countless seconds he just stared at her. Then he leaned over her, his great body powerful above her slender form.

"Is there something you need, Liz?" he questioned gently.

"Alexander, is it really you?" she murmured, her anger gone because his was. Her voice held an aching tenderness that Alexander was incapable of ignoring. She lifted her hands to his cheek and caressed him wonderingly, inflaming him with her gentle touch. Her softly glowing eyes held his.

He had to get out of here at once. Still, he remained while her fingertips traced the curve of his hard jawline before outlining the edges of his earlobe with featherlight strokes. His skin was alive with sensation.

Alexander groaned inwardly and brought his own hand up to remove hers. Curiously, instead of removing it, his warm fingers wrapped hers. He brought her fingertips to his lips and kissed them one by one while he stared deeply into her eyes.

What was happening to him? This was the woman who had deliberately tried to destroy him. She had kept him from knowing his children for seven years. He had no business staying with her like this.

His blood throbbed as with a fever. He could fight her harsh words, but her gentleness was too potent a force for him to resist. He knew if he didn't go soon he would heartily despise himself in the morning.

Not that he had the slightest intention of remaining until morning. He would leave her quickly. He had only to make sure she was comfortable for the night. She was the mother of his children, and his unexpected appearance had given her a shock. If he hadn't taken the children into the forest, she would scarcely be in this state.

When he thought of the children she had given him, his bitter attitude toward Liz lessened. He had expected Alex, but Samantha had been a glorious surprise. Alexander wondered again how Henson had missed the lively little girl who reminded him of Liz. He already adored his daughter. He wanted desperately to play a vital role in the lives of his children.

"I'm so sleepy," Liz said dreamily. "So sleepy." Her black lashes lowered and lay still against her pale cheeks.

He viewed the stiff cotton gown twisted about her body and realized the bulky fabric was probably uncomfortable.

"Sit up, Liz," he whispered. "I know you're tired, but you can't sleep in that dress. Let me help you take it off."

She nodded weakly and sat up so that Alexander could lift the gown over her shoulders. He noted how soft and warm she was when he touched her.

Alexander tossed the dress over a chair and turned back to her. Her eyes were closed, and her dreamy expression gave her the look of an angel. Her form entranced him. Her waist was as tiny as a wasp's, her hips slimly curved. Beneath her lace teddy he saw the dark crests of her nipples. He remembered her wildness in his bed, her total lack of inhibitions, which had shocked even him at first. He remembered the way she had made love to him with her lips. He remembered the golden afternoon she'd seduced him in that secret Italian grotto on a tiny island off the coast of Sardinia.

He inhaled deeply, thrusting the memories to the recesses of his mind. He had to get out of there. He was rising to make a swift exit when her hands circled his neck. She fingered the inky tendrils that fell over his collar. A single fingertip twirled a ribbon of soft blackness around its pink nail. Every muscle in his body froze.

"Alexander, do you remember how it was between us?"

A bolt of desire shuddered through him as she lowered her hands and moved them across his shoulders, drawing him back down to her. He hated himself for his weakness.

"You don't know what you're doing, Liz," he said hoarsely. "This is madness."

His lips hovered inches from hers. Her uneven breaths whispered against his mouth, low and seductive, irresistible in their wanton invitation.

"There was always madness between us, wasn't there?" Her hands moved lower, touching him with the expertise of a woman who knows every vulnerable area of her man. "Alexander, you're the most magnificent man. Is it so wrong of me to want you? I've been alone so long and I'm still your wife."

"I didn't come here because I wanted you." He expelled the cruel words roughly, but his skin burned from her caresses.

"Really?" Her silken tone mocked him.

He couldn't think when she touched him like that, with her fingers circling lightly over his body. She slipped the strap of her silken teddy downward until the honeyed orb of her breast was revealed, her pouting nipple thrusting tantalizingly upward.

"Liz, don't do this!" he groaned, but he didn't prevent her trembling fingers from unbuttoning his shirt.

A strip of bronzed male flesh was exposed, and she leaned forward and slid her tongue across his warm skin, trailing a blazing, liquid path from his throat to his navel. She continued to kiss him there, her head buried against the dark hair of his stomach. He felt the flicking movements of her tongue, the warmth of her breath tickling his body, driving him insane with need.

"Alexander, stay with me."

"God, I want you, Liz. Damn you," he muttered forcefully, gathering her body in his hard, bruising arms. "I can fight everything but this."

"How do you think it's been for me?" she cried. "I still loved you when you drove me away. I tried to forget you, but when you're here, holding me, I can only remember how it always was between us. I want to know if it's still the same, if it's really over between us, if you really hate me as much as you say."

His dark face flushed with fury as well as desire. She was deliberately tempting him despite her knowledge of his dislike. Well, she'd pushed him too far. He despised her, and nothing she could do or say would ever change that.

"It's over, Liz."

"Is it? Then walk out that door, Alexander," she taunted softly. "That's all you have to do to prove it."

The violence of his emotions was unforgivable. Hesitating, he stared into her smoldering black eyes and was lost.

He felt the intimate pressure of her soft body beneath his. Desire surged in his blood in a powerful pulsing sensation. He had to have her, despite everything that had passed between them.

He seized her and pulled her roughly against his chest, hating her, loving her, wanting her, despising her. His arms were ruthless iron bands binding her against his tough male body. "You wanted this, Liz, remember that."

He crushed his mouth against hers, pressing his tongue deeply into her mouth. He was on fire with passion and anger, and his burning need consumed her as well. His hands forced hers to circle his neck. She trembled as though suddenly afraid of the overpowering emotions she'd aroused.

His fingers were tangled in her hair, and he jerked

her head back. The lamplight shone on her pale face and in the gleaming blackness of her eyes.

She'd taunted him with the memories of their past love. She wanted to know if he hated her. She'd dared to defy him by saying all he had to do to prove his hatred was to walk out the door. "Prove it," she'd said.

Well, he'd prove it, and there was a better way of showing her how he felt than walking out the door.

He ripped his clothes apart, not bothering to fully undress before he flung himself over her. His hands forced the ridiculous lace garment she wore downward, uncaringly shredding the flimsy material in his haste so that her body was fully exposed. He touched her everywhere but without even a trace of the infinite tenderness he'd once so lovingly shown her.

She lay very still, the expression on her lovely face uncertain, her body stiff beneath his hard hands, as if, too late, she sensed his callous intent. Then she began to struggle.

"Stop it! Stop, Alexander. I won't be treated so."

His harsh laughter mocked her desperation. "You were the one who wanted this, my love."

"But I did not want—"

Her words of protest were stifled by his hard mouth claiming hers. His caressing hands roamed over her with intimate familiarity until at last her body reluctantly responded. He lowered his mouth and kissed her white throat. His palm cupped her rounded breast, kneading its tip into a hardened bud. Her flesh felt hot beneath his lips and hands as though her passion washed her with waves of fire.

She fought him, but her strength was that of a child, his that of a giant. Mercilessly he overpowered her. He caught her flailing hands in one of his and held them high above her head. His mouth covered hers, and when she tried to twist her face on the pillow, he held her lips with his relentlessly.

His legs were long and muscled, his thighs like iron. Tears streamed down her cheeks, but her sobs were muffled from his kisses. When at last he released her lips, she muttered with a terrible sadness, "You've grown hard, Alexander. There's no softness left in you. You're a stranger."

"If I'm hard, Liz, you have only yourself to blame. If we're strangers, whose fault is that?"

She was silent then. His mouth found the rapid pulsebeat in the hollow of her throat. His hands moved over her bare arms, her waist, down her thighs, savoring every lush curve before his knees forced her legs apart.

Alexander's blood throbbed with the beat of a pagan drum. The sweet female scent of her stimulated every sense in his being until his desire consumed him.

He paused and kissed her with all the thorough, ruthless passion that was his nature, the heat of his punishing mouth insolent and demanding. She was shuddering, but her hands had raised to circle his neck again as if she were driven by a hunger as fierce as his. He felt her fingertips caress him.

He kissed her again and again until she was limp and unresisting, until her body melted against his. He soared on hot, flaming wings in a wild black night, and she came with him.

Her breathing was as labored as his. Their desire built into a wild crescendo of spiraling needs. For a timeless moment their hatred fell away, and they were lovers again, each glorying in the taste and the sensation of the other.

He took her then with the swift blind need of a man who'd been too long without the one woman he wanted. For a fleeting moment he glimpsed heights he'd thought he would never see again. His mouth moved over her in moist, intimate exploration, seeking all the intimate feminine places that would bring her the most pleasure. Then desire overcame him in a shattering burst of glory. In that final moment he crushed her beneath him as she whispered his name in complete surrender.

Afterward they lay in the hushed darkness without touching. His passion spent, Alexander's anger toward Liz returned. It was even more intense than before, augmented by the gnawing memory of a passion he had not wanted, augmented by the deep feeling of self-loathing for what he'd done. He should never have let this happen. There could be no closeness with her.

He had used her, not as the wife he loved, he reassured himself swiftly. She'd given him physical release, nothing more. Despite what had happened, nothing between them was changed. He felt no closeness with her, only a deep, unremitting coldness. Still, a new, unnamed unease lingered.

He slanted a hard glance in her direction. She lay as still as death upon the woolen sarapes. For an instant he wondered if she was unconscious. Then he saw the flicker of her lashes and the faint glimmer of her eyes behind them. No. She was awake, despite her exhaustion and his rough treatment. Liz was too bold to shrink from unpleasant realities. She was staring at the ceiling through her narrowly slitted eyelids. He wondered what she was thinking.

He remembered suddenly the long, languid lovemaking sessions of their past, so different from the violence of the present. He remembered the loving hours afterward, those balmy moments of satiated glory. He recalled the rapturous afterglow when they'd clung to each other after their wild excesses.

Now they lay without touching.

Despite the crisp mountain air sifting through the

partially opened windows, the room was stifling. Alexander rose abruptly, turning his back on the silent woman on the bed. He did not want to think of the past or of the present. He wanted no part of Liz. He had not meant for this to happen, and he swore that it never would again.

Chapter Six

L iz snuggled beneath the coarse cotton sheets and thick pile of woolen blankets and sarapes. Sunlight streamed into the room, its brightness indicating the lateness of the hour. Why hadn't she heard the children? Why hadn't Juan sent Esmeralda to summon her so she could handle any emergencies involving the factory?

Liz sat up, shading her eyes with curled fingers. The leaden weight of anguish lay upon her heart. With her fingertips she felt the crusted residue upon her cheeks from the countless tears she'd wept during the long night. She'd scarcely slept. Every time she'd wakened, thinking futilely of Alexander's passionate dislike for her, fresh waves of sadness had swept her.

How could she have been so foolish as to believe he felt anything other than hatred? He'd been like a stranger in her bed, using her brutally to satisfy needs he did not even want to have.

When he'd left her lying in the chill darkness, she'd

felt the most profound emptiness because she realized how deeply she still loved him, just as she realized how hopeless her feelings were.

Last night there had been no union of their souls, only the fierce mating of their bodies. His callous passion had shown her all that she had lost, but it had strengthened her longing to regain it, however futile that possibility seemed. If only she could have hated him for the way he'd used her in that time of wild darkness. Instead a part of her had reveled in it. She should feel ashamed for the way she'd seduced him against his will, but stronger than hatred or shame was the memory of his passion.

The furious rush of water splashing in the shower came to her, and she realized with a start that Alexander must be taking a shower. In her shower. Her heart fluttered in wild panic; he might walk in at any moment.

The shredded teddy lay on the floor where he'd thrown it. It would never do for him to find her like this. Her hair was disheveled and she knew she must look horribly wan. She leaped out of bed, picked up the torn garment and went to the dresser, where she hid it in a drawer. She worked swiftly, smoothing the worst tangles from her hair, wiping away the salt of her tears, dabbing blusher on her cheeks and putting on lipstick.

From her closet stuffed with outrageous clothes she grabbed the most dramatic garment of them all. The robe was a daring swirl of scarlet crepe de Chine with the sleeves cut out from the waistline. A wide sash made her waist as tiny as an hourglass. The robe, like many of her designs, was flamboyant rather than practical, but it was just what she needed to wear to make her appear bold and confident when she felt so uncertain.

Liz had designed the robe for her spring collection for Isobel's, her boutique in London. She'd never worn it before. She'd kept the original for herself when she'd sent Ya Lee, her London manager, the designs. Always when she was designing, Liz used her own secret fantasies as an aid to create clothes made to appeal to the woman who wanted to feel excitingly different.

Liz opened the drapes and looked out on the purple mountains and the broad valley. But this morning, the peaceful landscape did not bring harmony to her troubled mind. At the sound of the door, she spun around, her heart jumping chaotically.

In the sunlight her hair was spun flame. She was unaware of how extravagantly beautiful she was, because her attention was focused on the lean, dark man framed in the doorway.

He was unsmiling, his harsh stare as menacing as his lovemaking had been the night before. Well, at least he was not indifferent to her. Even his hatred was preferable to that.

It took all her willpower to maintain a surface calm when she felt so shaky inside. She did not know that the light from behind her outlined her body through the soft fabric of her gown. She was aware only of the swift intake of his breath, of a baffling intensity about him.

"Hello, Alexander," she said in a deliberately casual voice.

He said nothing, but there was a vital, sensual element in his hard, assessing gaze. His eyes lingered on her, following her as she moved from the long windows.

The force of his male virility seemed to capture her, and she felt a sudden breathlessness in the pit of her stomach. The way he looked at her made her feel positively undressed.

"Come in," she invited, not knowing what else to say.

He stepped inside, and she was never more aware of

how sexually appealing Alexander was to her as she watched his lazy, swaggering grace. Determined not to be intimidated, she tilted her chin defiantly.

Still, her senses registered his physically disturbing state. His blue shirt was half-buttoned, and a strip of his deeply tanned chest was tantalizingly visible. A sheen of dampness from his recent shower clung to his jet dark hair, and he smelled fresh and masculine. If only she could go to him. She wanted to touch him, but his remoteness quelled such impulses.

"It's a beautiful morning, isn't it?" she said composedly, as if there were no secret desires in her heart and no hatred in his. She walked to the rattan table and chairs by the corner window and sat down. "Did you sleep well?"

"Well enough." He hadn't slept a wink. It was irritating the way she looked so glorious and rested. He sank negligently into an overstuffed chair across the room.

"I'm glad. Sometimes that's difficult in a strange bed." She rushed on to cover the awkwardness between them, but, of course, she didn't cover it at all. If only he would quit looking at her like that. "I suppose you've already seen the children?"

"Yes. They're with their tutor now. You must see them soon. They're worried about you and filled with questions."

She laughed lightly. "I can imagine. They're not used to their mother showing any weakness. In the forest, I was scarcely my usual serene self."

"Your usual serene self? That's certainly a new one." His soft voice mocked her.

She merely laughed at his jibe and continued with her chatter. Alexander stared at her, scarcely listening. She wasn't going to show any signs of her true feelings about last night, he realized. Had she been badly hurt, shocked? Was she resolved now, as he was, that it had long been over between them, that such tactics as she'd employed were useless on him? Or was last night no more to her than a bit of untidy emotional refuse to be hastily swept aside and forgotten now that it was obvious it had served no purpose? He wished he could forget it as easily as she, but the sight of her in that wildly dramatic gown, her feminine curves enhanced by the bright soft silk, affected him. Nor could he stamp out the memory of the light from the windows outlining too clearly the shape of her body. His blood was still beating violently from that first vision.

A knock sounded, and Liz called out a cheery welcome. Maria stepped inside carrying a tray with coffee, marmalade and two servings of warm *bolillos,* a hard Mexican bread. The better Liz's humor, the worse his grew.

"You'll join me, I hope, darling?" Liz invited her now-scowling husband with the sweetest of smiles.

"I've eaten," came his terse reply.

"Then I hope you don't mind if I do?" she said, buttering a bolillo while she sipped her rich black coffee. "I'm starving. You may remember I always am in the morning when I've been enormously excited the day before."

"Enormously excited!" He lifted a dark eyebrow in irritation. How dared she skirt that sore subject so cavalierly. It goaded him that she appeared so unruffled, indeed so bold, as if that disgusting episode last night had given her immeasurable confidence.

She completely ignored his dark frown. Indeed, she seemed to thrive on his bad humor. He watched her smear a dab of marmalade on a slab of bread.

"I'm afraid this is going to be a busy day once I get started," she continued in the same bright voice.

"They've all been clamoring to wake you for hours, but I wouldn't allow it," Alexander replied testily.

Startled by this unexpected thoughtfulness toward

her, she glanced at him. His cutting gaze slashed her. Whatever softness had motivated him was scarcely apparent.

"There seems to be a bit of confusion downstairs," Alexander said, "that only you can resolve."

"That's putting it mildly, I'm sure. You see, Alexander, the water tank on the roof flooded my doll factory yesterday, before you came. But enough of my problems. I know you didn't come to Mexico without some purpose. It's time we got down to what brings you here. What do you want from me? Why have you come?"

She crunched off a bit of bolillo.

"I've come because of the children."

She swallowed the tasteless, half-chewed bit of bread crust in her mouth. "Of course, but what does that mean—specifically?"

He shot her a dark look. "Specifically—divorce and custody rights."

She dropped her fingers from her bolillo and clasped them together. She did not like the businesslike way he spoke of the children, as if they were just another profit-and-loss statement to be analyzed, another game that he could play and win.

He continued with savage intensity. "Our marriage was a mistake from the beginning. We were only together two months."

"Twelve weeks," she corrected faintly.

"And separated seven years. Not much of a marriage. We have no choice but to legally end it. Naturally I would prefer sole custody of the twins, and I'm willing to make a generous settlement if you agree. You can go on living in whatever bizarre lifestyle you're currently caught up in, but the children will have stability. I will give them the best schools. They can spend their summers in my villa in Sardinia or one of Maman's châteaux in France. Liz, you've scarcely managed to teach them a smattering of French. They're growing up with illiterate Indians."

"They're only six, and they speak both Spanish and English fluently," she retorted coldly.

She was seething. "Bizarre lifestyle," he'd said. How could he refer to Esmeralda and Maria as illiterate Indians? Didn't he see that they had loved her and cared for her when he had thrown her out?

Her voice was dangerously low, poorly concealing her anger. "I'm sure you've discussed this with the children."

"Why should I?"

"You mean their wishes would have no impact upon you?"

"I did not say that."

"Did it ever occur to you that it might do them irreparable damage to be separated from me? You cannot manage children the way you manage employees in your factories, Alexander. You say you will give them the best schools. Children need much more than that. Your mother, for all her dull ability to be everlastingly proper—a trait, I thank God, I lack—"

"Leave my mother out of this!"

She sprang to her feet, her hot temper flaring. "I won't! All she gave you were the best schools, those glorious villas you're throwing up at me, châteaux, and money. That's why you're hard, Alexander. That's why you could throw out a woman who loved you without a qualm. You turned your back on me when I needed you the way she turned her back on you when you were a child. You didn't care that I was hurting! I won't let you ruin my children the way your mother ruined you!"

Alexander leaped to his feet and crossed the room. He towered over her.

"Stop it, Liz. You're hysterical."

"I'm not hysterical! I'm angry! A while ago you

called Esmeralda an illiterate Indian. I'll tell you something that you in your insufferable narrow-mindedness will never believe. Esmeralda's a far more compassionate human being than you are."

"Are you through?"

"No. I would not have opposed a reasonable custody arrangement until you said these things to me this morning. Yesterday I saw that it was a grave error on my part to take the children so far away from you despite the hostile circumstances of our separation. I was sorry for that."

"And now?"

"I wish you'd never come here." She whirled away from him, her fists clenched against her stomach as she stalked toward the windows. She heard his heavy footsteps right behind hers. Was there nowhere to hide?

When she turned to face him, he was directly in front of her. The ruthless set of his jaw was grim with purpose.

"If you try to take the children from me on a permanent basis, I'll fight you. You can't buy me or my children the way you buy everything else in your life, Alexander Vorzenski."

"I suppose that's because you've already sold yourself to Jock."

Liz slapped him. She was so furious, so deeply insulted by his bitter, hateful remark, she did so without forethought of the consequences, and she instantly regretted her action.

He stood silent and unflinching, but she sensed the violent emotions surging beneath his taut features. Her own hand stung with pain; she could see the imprint of four slim fingers upon his cheek.

She'd gone too far. Too late, she knew it. Liz tried to escape him, but before she could manage one step, his large hands lashed out and seized her forearm in a viselike grip, hauling her against the muscular wall of his chest.

"You shouldn't have hit me," he growled as she gulped for air. "You invite like violence on yourself."

Her fragile bones threatened to break under his crushing hold. His fingers wound painfully into her thick hair, pulling her head back so that the curve of her neck was exposed clear down to the rising swell of her breasts. It was a seductive pose that awakened fully his marauding male instincts. His head moved closer and she could feel the heat of his suddenly irregular breaths against her skin.

"I'll scream, Alexander," she cried, "if you don't let me go." Her heart was fluttering against her rib cage like a trapped bird beating itself to death in a cage. "After last night, I don't want you to touch me ever again."

"Don't you? And last night it was you who wanted this."

When Alexander had first seized her, he had no thought other than bending her to his will, but her nearness was provocative. The scent of her, the feel of her body pressing close intoxicated him. Even the passionate fire of her anger aroused him. He lowered his head toward hers instinctively.

In a frenzy Liz tried to twist away from him, but her hair, caught in his hands, was yanked painfully. His mouth came down brutally on hers. His kiss was ravaging and frightening in its hard demand. His arms pressed her body against his thighs and made her intimately aware of his driving male hunger.

"I'll hate you forever for this." She gasped out the words beneath the smothering pressure of his mouth.

He released her lips. "Do you think I care? Stop fighting me, Liz."

He jerked her even more tightly against himself, knocking the breath from her lungs. His arms wrapped around her; his hands molded her curves to fit the hard contours of his torso and thighs. He kissed her more deeply than before. His anger and passion raged with the force of a wildfire swept by a savage wind, consuming everything in its path.

She screamed, the sound stifled against him, as the insolent plunder of his lips made her completely his. His hands moved beneath sheer silk and caressed the warmth of her. He was shaking as if overpowered by the storm of his own emotions. Fierce, unintelligible endearments were whispered against her ear. His mouth evoked wild pagan feelings she'd never felt before. Her arms went around his neck, and her lips trembled in wanton response.

Something melted within Alexander, gentling the angry tide of emotion. Rage and the desire to hurt no longer ruled him. The bruising force of his embrace changed subtly, and the hands that wrapped her so closely exerted tender mastery instead of punishment.

Perfectly attuned to Alexander, Liz instantly sensed the difference. His embrace was more dangerous than ever. Sensual longing flamed under the wanton expertise of his mouth, beneath the intimate exploration of his hand gently kneading her breast. She felt her resistance ebb. In another moment she would be lost. He would carry her to bed. A repetition of her surrender last night would be the final, unendurable humiliation. She had to stop him before it was too late. Her tattered pride gave her the strength to wrench free and stumble backward.

She felt empty and terribly alone. Her back was to him. She couldn't bear looking at him. His roughly carved face was too dear. She longed to be in his arms, and to assuage that need she wrapped her body tightly with her own. Her heart beat in wild longing. She couldn't let him know how shatteringly vulnerable she was.

From behind her his voice came, husky, gentler. "Liz—"

This new softness from him was more than the disturbed state of her nerves could handle. Liz turned around. His amber gaze startled her, compelled her. His hand reached toward her, not in anger this time but in—

She was never to know what would have happened had they not been interrupted just as his arms slid around her waist and shoulders in hungry possession.

She felt herself drawn intimately against him; his lips seared her brow in the tenderest of kisses. There was an embarrassed cough from behind the half-opened door. Her cheeks were flushed as she called out shakily, "Yes?"

Alexander drew a sharp rein on his own emotions as Juan stepped inside. To Liz's amazement, Alexander did not release her, and Juan accepted their embrace as perfectly natural between man and wife.

"Señora, you must come at once to the doll factory. We need your help, and that of the señor too, if he is willing."

"I don't think the señor is particularly anxious to help me," Liz snapped hastily. "He came here to—" She felt Alexander's fingers tighten on her skin and thought better of completing her sentence.

Stung because he was feeling extraordinarily loving toward her, Alexander responded without thought. "Of course I'll help!"

Liz stared at them both in helpless confusion, suddenly realizing the trap in which she'd been caught. Without meaning to ask for Alexander's help, she had, and now that he'd said he would, she had no choice but to accept. The very last thing she wanted was him running things in his high-handed fashion in her factory. It was bad enough that he was determined to make trouble about the children. Bad enough that she was in constant danger of letting her own needs for him humiliate her.

When Juan left, Liz said hotly, "You don't have to, you know."

Alexander dropped his arm from her shoulder with a pregnant emphasis. It was evident that he was now in control of the physical desire that had mastered him only minutes before.

"I said I would."

"But—"

"Leave it alone, Liz. Maybe it's for the best. It's obvious when we try to have any sort of reasonable discussion about our personal situation, things get out of hand."

"They wouldn't if you—"

"Liz, stop it. Get dressed in something that isn't—" His eyes ran over her body. The gown clung to every curve. He still wanted her. He wanted to make love to her as wildly as he had the night before.

Damn her! Why was she so beautiful? Even in anger she was magnificent. She had the most extraordinary eyes when she got mad. He had never seen eyes so brilliant in any well-bred woman's face before. They reminded him of the way she was in bed, all softness and fire, hellcat wildness and demure loveliness.

He wanted to touch her again, but he didn't dare. He'd just learned once again the foolhardiness of that. When he held her, his need for her became unbearable. He was determined never to give in to his weakness for her again.

She was so bold and completely determined not to be dominated. No other woman besides, of course, his mother ever opposed him. He was so used to getting his way with women, he wondered if he knew how to fight her. He had forgotten how to handle Liz—if he had ever known.

She was as damnably difficult as ever. He didn't know how he was going to get around her. But there had to be a way. He was determined the children were his and his alone.

Now all he had to do was convince Liz.

Chapter Seven

I won't have you turning my factory over to Manuel Rodriguez!" Liz said heatedly.

Alexander endured her temper with the infuriating calm he'd shown all week. There had been many tantrums since he'd started trying to avert the disaster her factory was headed for.

"Why not? He's the best man for the job."

"It's my factory! I suppose you think nothing of telling me I'm not running it properly."

"Nothing at all," he replied cheerfully. "You have absolutely no managerial talent, Liz."

"No managerial talent!" she shrieked. "I built this factory from nothing."

"Lower your voice, my dear," he said, suppressing a smile. "I'm sure you don't want to be heard in the furthest market stall in the village."

"I don't care who hears me," she shouted louder than before. "Nor in what market stall."

"That's becoming all too obvious. Whether you like

it or not, you need my help, darling. You've gotten yourself into a hopeless muddle."

She crossed her arms across her chest and glared at him, detesting his smug attitude. "Well, I don't like it. You're destroying everything. First you ruin morale by firing Juan."

"You should never have hired him in the first place, my love. He's all wrong for his job. He drinks. He has a negative attitude. Besides, I'm nearly positive he's been stealing."

She was trembling violently now. "And then you threatened to fire anyone else who didn't show up for work. Alexander, these people have land to plow."

He shrugged. "You have a factory to run, and you can't run it with the chronic absenteeism you've been tolerating."

"Then you started paying overtime, which I can't afford."

"Yes, you can once we get things organized and running efficiently. Look, Liz, actually it's amazing how well you've done considering your deplorable disorganization. The only thing that's pulled you through this far is your bullheaded determination and the unique charm of your dolls."

Bullheaded determination! "I'm glad you think I've done something right!" she snapped.

"Well, damn little. Your dolls are underpriced. Your machinery is dilapidated. New equipment would save labor costs. You have no distribution system. Shopkeepers just come here with a basket over their arms and collect what they want. Yes, I know Manuel has made a few calls on some stores in Texas and California, but that hardly counts. Then you went to New York and got your first real break, but that was the sheerest accident.

"You have a good product, but without the right publicity and a sales force, you're doomed. I can start

Manuel on the road to straightening all this out. The guy's really talented at getting the maximum out of your employees. He understands them. He knows when to be hard, and you don't."

She was infuriated at him for criticizing everything she'd been proud of. The most unforgivable of all was that in her heart she knew he was right.

"Liz, don't you see, without the factory to manage you'll be free to do more research and create more dolls. That's where you should focus your time. You're a designer, and I'm beginning to believe you're a good one." He admitted this last reluctantly.

His compliment, delivered in such a manner, did little to mollify her.

"All week you've been criticizing me and counter-manding my decisions," she cried angrily.

"Have you grown so stubborn and strong willed here in Mexico without a man's guidance that you can't listen to reason?"

"Of all the chauvinistic things to say. The last thing I need is a man's guidance, especially yours. A woman is equal to a man in every way."

"Not in every way, surely, darling?" A grin stole across his features, and his gaze drifted pointedly down the curve of her long neck to where her breasts spilled out from beneath woven silk. "That would indeed be a most lamentable state of affairs."

She blushed furiously. Her skin beneath her blouse felt as if it were on fire. "You're deliberately twisting my words."

"I was merely trying to understand your meaning," he replied innocently. His eyes lingered like a hot caress on her body. "You were saying?"

His manner was excessively polite. Irritatingly so. He kept looking at her in that warm way of his, disrupting her train of thought.

"I-I was saying," she stormed, "that you've ruined

everything. My employees, even Manuel, now look to you as the boss. The señor can do no wrong. They think I should be pleased. They constantly praise you to me. If I say what I think of you, I'll appear shrewish. I have to go along with your decisions because everyone else approves of them."

He lifted his eyes to the sky as if seeking divine assistance. "Ah, the ingratitude of woman. In one week I've cleaned everything up and held a disaster sale, raising more capital than even she believed possible. Everyone here but her is thrilled with the reams of fabric, yards of lace and satin ribbons, dainty braids, and the thousand tiny buttons I ordered. As if I like playing with dolls."

"And as if the exorbitant prices were nothing," Liz added grumpily.

It was true that everyone was grateful for what he'd done. They said it was a miracle the way he'd obtained the sewing machines she had been unable to get. That rankled. No one objected to his hiring twenty skilled seamstresses from Mexico City temporarily. They explained when she questioned the wisdom of this extravagance that she had said the New York orders had to be filled. In short, he'd taken over her world, and everyone except her was pleased. Even the children turned to him now before they turned to her.

In public Alexander treated her as though she were his beloved wife. He was affectionate and courteous. His hand would linger at her waist as he helped her to sit down at dinner. His gaze brushed her lovingly, and always when it did, her pulse leaped before she remembered he was pretending. She hated herself for craving his attentions, for seeking to be near him when others were present so she could enjoy his lavish little gestures of kindness. She would not have minded his taking over her world had he genuinely wanted to make a place for her in it.

When they were alone, however, he was even colder and more remote than ever. The hot anger he'd shown her in the beginning was concealed, and she almost thought she would have preferred it to the icy wall of reserve he had erected between them. When she grew angry about the way he had usurped her power in her own household and factory, he laughed. When she said he was too strict with the children, he merely continued doing as he pleased. Once when she tried to explain she believed too many restrictions would curb the children's natural initiative, he laughed. "So that's your excuse for letting them run wild."

As always, any criticism from him stung. "But that's the way children learn!" she'd cried defensively.

At just that moment Samantha burst into the room holding a snake behind the head. "Is he poisonous, Mommy?"

"Good Lord, Samantha!" Alexander gasped.

"No, darling," Liz calmly replied, examining the snake. "You're carrying him beautifully, dear. Where did you find him?" Liz had proceeded with a zoology lesson while Alexander gaped. "Why don't you show him to your father, dear. He's positively bug-eyed with curiosity."

"Not with curiosity, love," came the deep voice.

Liz realized that he did not approve of her child-rearing methods.

Alexander refused to be drawn into quarrels or any real intimacy with her. Why was he staying, then? Since their argument about the children, he'd said nothing more about divorce and custody.

Not only was Alexander running her factory, but he conducted Dazzle's business over the phone. He drove into Mexico City and dealt with the local Dazzle distributors. Liz knew there was a crisis in Paris, but he did not confide in her. He just stayed on at the hacienda as if he weren't the head of an international company, as if he had nothing better to do than to concern himself with the shape and cut of a doll's wig and the yardage required for a miniature ball gown.

Liz knew that Alexander was running her factory to occupy himself while he was here, until he did what he'd come to do. She felt like she was living in a state of limbo. Every day that he remained she felt more drawn to him, and yet more terrified.

The sound of his wife's laughter floating up from the courtyard came to Alexander as he poured over Liz's account books. He was expecting a phone call from Paris or he would have already joined Liz and the children for lunch. It was the siesta hour, and the workers who lived nearby had returned to their homes for the two-hour interval. While Liz and the children waited for him below, they were playing games in the courtyard.

Alexander shut the ledger and strode out onto the balcony to watch them. He leaned heavily against the black grill railing. It was a brilliant day. Beneath, the exotic trees were bedecked with splashes of reds, oranges, blues and yellows.

Laughing wildly, Liz threw a ball to Samantha, who squealed with disappointment when she missed catching it. Alex scampered to it and picked it up as it rolled past, but Alexander was not watching his son. He was gazing instead at Liz.

Her exuberance matched that of the children. Never had his mother played with him when he was a child, Alexander thought. Liz's black eyes sparkled with excitement. Her cheeks were flushed. Her hair was parted in the middle like a Mexican señorita's. Narrow golden loops glimmered at her earlobes. She was wearing tight jeans and a thin blouse. When she moved, he watched her breasts swaying full and unrestrained beneath the fabric. His skin flamed at the sight of her, and he forced his gaze toward his children. But his thoughts remained on his wife.

Despite the problems at Dazzle, Alexander had decided to give himself a few days to decide what to do about Liz and the children. After his quarrel with her about custody, he had chosen to avoid a snap decision. He could not afford to make a mistake where his children were concerned. The last thing he wanted was to drag them through a lengthy court battle and the inevitable publicity such a trial would bring. So for one hellish week he had lived with his wife in order to spend time with his children. He had thought he could ignore Liz by concentrating on the problems of her doll factory, the impending crisis at Dazzle and the children; but she had haunted his thoughts night and day.

He had tried everything he could think of to put her from his mind. Even when he worked so hard that he collapsed in his bed in a state of exhaustion, he lay alone, thinking of her.

Every time he looked at her, he stripped her in his mind. The memory of her breasts, her long slim legs entwined with his, and her wanton responsiveness drove him wild. A thousand times a day he wanted to take her in his arms. When she smiled up at him so innocently, he wanted to kiss her violently even if it was in the middle of the afternoon. At night he dreamed of her. In his sleep she came to him and placed her slim hot body over his. Her tongue and mouth ran crazily over his skin until his passion for her would jolt him into consciousness. He would awaken in a hard sweat, his breathing ragged, his anger against both himself and her, savage due to the torment she caused him.

How many nights had he sprung from his bed aroused by the vision of her soft, scented loveliness, consumed with the mad intention of going to her room and taking her by force. Instead he would pace the balcony barechested in the cold night air, pausing to stare at the moonlight slanting across the jagged black mountain peaks, waiting until his sanity returned.

Was he crazy—wanting this woman after what she had done to him, this woman who should be abhorrent to him?

Yet in the daytime, when he was not goading her about the mistakes she had made in the management of her doll factory, she was the last thing from abhorrent. He goaded her often, though he considered it a poor revenge for the torment she had unknowingly caused him. She, however, always treated him kindly. She had given him the most attractive rooms in the hacienda. She personally kept his rooms and clothes clean and orderly. His favorite dishes were prepared. Despite his desire to keep her at a distance, he found he relished being with her in front of others. Only then did he allow himself to "pretend" that he felt toward her as he would toward a cherished wife. Then he could touch her lightly without fear of the possibility of his caress deepening. When he was alone with her, he forced a coldness in his manner because he was too conscious of the forbidden intimacies he desired.

He watched her constantly, searching her personality for the faults that should have warned him long ago of her deceitful nature. But to his amazement, he saw nothing but sweetness and courage in her.

One afternoon when they were talking about the factory, she had explained the terrible dilemma the villagers had been in when she first came to Mexico. With an ever-increasing population, there was not enough land. Many families had to move. Some went to nearby Mexico City, where their plight was desperate in a city already choked by the multitudes of unskilled laborers pouring monthly into the capital from every part of Mexico. Other villagers migrated to the United States. Still others worked as *braceros,* temporary farm workers, in other parts of Mexico and the United

States. This meant that the men were separated for long periods from their families.

There was poverty and overcrowding in the schools. Liz had seen how talented the villagers were. She had marveled at their handcrafts in their markets. There were velvet paintings, pottery, silver jewelry, onyx ashtrays, handwoven blankets, embroidered clothes, leather sandals, bullwhips and carved wooden animals.

One morning in a market stall, as she fingered an exquisite obsidian statuette of a rain god, she had envisioned her doll factory. At first the factory was a barely formed dream, but it was something she could not dismiss. She'd felt alone; she'd desperately needed something to do. She wanted to help these people who had been so kind to her.

When she recounted the initial thrill of her idea, Alexander had felt awestruck. From nothing she had started a business that could expand into a giant. Her factory had grown every year, employing more villagers at higher wages.

Alexander learned from that afternoon's conversation how to make her accept his proposed changes, which she had been fighting. If he used the argument that to follow his advice would insure a more rapid growth and thus a greater benefit to the villagers, he could always win.

He thought of Liz more often after that discovery. How could she be so compassionate to these people when she had been so treacherous to him?

To the children, Liz was warm and loving and patient. No matter what she was doing, she allowed the children to interrupt her. She rarely scolded them, and they loved her. To his amazement, he had discovered a framed picture of himself in each of their rooms, and he'd learned that she had taught them to love him. That was why they had instantly accepted him.

When he took the twins on outings without her, they

talked constantly of her, asking him why he had not brought her along, begging him for money to buy her some little gift, and all too often he found that he was missing her himself.

He loved watching her with the children. When she knelt over their beds to kiss them good night, he would stand in the doorway. When she took them horseback riding in the forest, he would trail behind them, but that was partially because her stallion, Villano, was so unmanageable.

When Liz first mentioned Villano, Alexander had commented suspiciously, "Villain. I don't like that name."

Liz had tilted her head in that defiant way of hers and laughed recklessly. "You won't like the horse any better."

And he hadn't.

Leave it to Liz to own the most dangerous animal that galloped on rusting horseshoes. One thousand pounds plus of irascible, unpredictable, neurotic horse-flesh. Villano had a fiendish dislike of saddles, bridles and riders. He had innumerable phobias, especially of fire. At the whiff of a cigarette he went insane. The only human who could gentle him was Liz.

Thus, whenever his family went near this prancing black demon, Alexander accompanied them, and all too often he found himself enjoying himself—because he was with Liz.

Never having known the joys of family life before, Alexander found that this need in himself to be part of a family gave his wife an ever deeper power over him. He was beginning to see that it would not be possible for him to separate Liz from the children. He loved them too much to deprive them of the mother they loved.

Much to his surprise, he had discovered that Liz hadn't seen or spoken to her father since she'd run away. If she had stolen the formula for Roger, why were they now estranged? Roger had come to him once in London after Liz had run away, and begged him to tell him where Liz was. At the time Alexander had not trusted Roger enough to believe he did not know where his daughter was.

Alexander saw no easy solution to the problem of custody. A sacrifice or a compromise would have to be made.

At just that moment Samantha threw the ball wildly and it headed straight toward Alexander. He reached out to catch it, and as he did the weight of his body jammed hard against the railing. There was a ripping sound of metal grating against tile and stucco as a rusty bolt loosened.

Liz screamed. She was a blur as she raced up the stairs. He felt himself falling, and he grabbed wildly for the stucco pillar.

He pulled himself back onto the balcony just as Liz reached him. "Oh, Alexander," she said in relief. "I'm so glad you're all right." She threw her arms about his neck, and he felt her shaking. Alexander pulled her to him. The forbidden comfort of her embrace was treacherously pleasurable.

Looking past her shoulder, he saw the hard square Saltillo tiles beneath. He had narrowly escaped a serious accident.

The scent of her came to him, lavender soap mixed with jasmine. Her firm body against his own stirred all his old, unwanted yearnings. Breathing heavily, he set her roughly from him so that she fell against the white stuccoed wall.

"I should have repaired that railing a long time ago," she said shakily. "You could have been killed."

For an instant he almost believed she cared.

He regarded her for a long moment, carefully masking his emotions. "Look on the bright side," he said cheerily at last. "You would have been a very rich widow."

She paled, and he saw the glimmer of tears in her eyes before she dropped her gaze and turned, then descended the steps slowly to join his children in the courtyard. She did not see the involuntary reaching of his hand toward her before he stilled it.

He pivoted abruptly, went inside her office and kicked the door shut. The memory of her face would not leave him, her black eyes filled with pain and yearning.

He slammed his hand hard against the wall. A shaft of pain stabbed clear to his elbow.

Damn her! Damn him for wanting her! And damn the world for being what it was!

The phone began to ring. It was Paul. The news from Paris was devastating. Alexander was suspected of having caused the fire in Dazzle's lab himself, but when Paul demanded that Alexander return, he refused. Before, it had been uncharacteristic of him to put anything before Dazzle. Now it was suicidal.

The hacienda was jammed with revelers, the courtyard filled with the sound of guitars and marimbas as amateur village musicians played Mexican folk music. Juan and Manuel sat at a small table.

"Despite what you and Liz say, Manuel, I do not trust Juan," Alexander said. "He has been making threats against us in the village plaza when he has been drunk on pulque."

"He is a braggart. He will do nothing."

"I'm not so sure. You know I didn't just fire him. I offered him another job, but he felt he was being demoted and quit. He threatened me, and I had to throw him off the place."

"Forget Juan. He took advantage of your wife's gentle nature. He will do nothing but drink more pulque and shout in the plaza." Manuel smiled. "Why should he be the only one to have that pleasure? Join me in another *copa de tequila.*" He leaned across the table and tilted his bottle toward Alexander's glass.

Alexander nodded. Perhaps Manuel was right and he should forget Juan. He drained the glass with one swallow.

"It is good, no, *mi amigo,* the tequila?" Manuel asked, mixing the Spanish linguistic structure with his English. "A man can forget his problems."

"Then pour me another, my friend." Alexander's swarthy face split in a slow white grin as his gaze fell upon his wife dancing beneath bright paper-shaded lights in the courtyard. He lifted his glass in a mock salute toward Liz. "To the end of my problems." Alexander drank deeply.

The fiesta was in celebration of the village's patron saint. There had been a parade in the village streets.

Liz was dancing with Alex. Her hips swayed in sensual rhythm to the Latin beat.

The tequila was not working, and then Alexander's thoughts twisted cynically, and he knew it was working too well. His head was swimming, and yet after the long days of constant tension, it felt good to relax. His only problem was Liz. He knew he should not watch her. He should concentrate on what Manuel was saying, but her every movement was so gracefully provocative that he could not drag his gaze from her. Surely there was no other woman on earth who moved like that. He thought of the way she moved beneath him in bed, and he wanted her with a tearing ache that made him reach for the bottle of tequila.

She was dressed in a gown of lavender lace that was cut like a peasant dress, exposing her slim shoulders, enhancing the curvature of her breasts. The silvery sound of her laughter came to him. How could she laugh, when she put him in hell?

"The Mexican people, we love fiestas," Manuel was saying, the tequila making him loquacious. "In our village we have fifty-two fiestas a year, *mi amigo*, each lasting three to four days. There are the barrio fiestas, where each barrio celebrates its patron saint. Then we have the holy days of the Catholic church. Naturally we can go to the fiestas of other villages and towns outside our *municipio*. . . ."

Alexander was not listening. He was watching his daughter. Beneath the broken piñata, Samantha was scrambling with a horde of children for the best prize. She looked wild and untamed, a miniature version of her mother as she seized several pieces of candy and grabbed for more.

His daughter was going to be a handful when she grew up. She would need a father's protection.

"You know, *mi amigo*, you're a smart man except with women," Manuel said, interrupting Alexander's thoughts. Manuel would never have dared so personal a remark had he not been very drunk.

"You think so?" Alexander muttered.

"I know so. You watch your wife as a man who wants no other man near her. But if you don't mind my saying, your wife is not the kind of woman a man should leave for seven years."

The tequila dulled the glimmer of Alexander's rage. "It was her fault we parted," he retorted coolly.

"But how will you accept it when your coldness forces her to marry the other Frenchman who sometimes comes?"

"Damn you in hell!" Alexander exploded, leaning across the table. "Don't talk about my wife and other men!"

Too late, Manuel saw the danger of the subject. "Easy, *mi amigo*, I meant only that a man must guard that which he wants from those who would take it. She loves you, and she has taught the children to love you.

Your wife, she make everyone happy here. She bring us the factory. She love the children. If anyone in the village have a problem, he comes to the hacienda because he know she will help. But no one can help her. She has been sad. I see it often in her eyes. But when you came, she started smiling."

Alexander shrugged and sank back in his chair, pouring himself another tequila. Out of the corner of his eye, he noticed that Alex had joined the romp beneath the piñata. Liz was leaning against a tree, watching the children, her slippered foot tapping out the beat of the music.

"Excuse me, my friend," Alexander muttered. He was tired of listening to Manuel, and the tequila had loosened his iron control regarding Liz. "I haven't danced with my wife in a very long time."

Manuel merely smiled.

Alexander knew it was crazy of him to go to Liz when he'd been drinking. He was sure he would regret it, but he could not stop himself.

She did not hear his approach because of the music.

"Liz—"

She started. He saw the flashing light of her black eyes in the shadowy darkness beneath the tree.

"Dance with me, Liz." It was crazy, asking her to dance when his need for her was pounding in his blood. His hand touched hers.

"No. Please."

She was tense, ready to run from him, but he pulled her into his arms.

She forced herself to meet his gaze. "Alexander, please let me go."

"Darling, don't you see that I can't." His arms tightened around her body, and he began to dance. She moved in time to the music with the fluid ease he remembered so well. He did not hold her close, not at first, but he was aware of her body, tantalizingly near. It took the most terrible control not to crush her against himself. Her fingers brushed the skin beneath his collar; her other hand was folded tightly in his. He breathed deeply, liking her touch, needing it with a fierce hunger he was not sure he could continue to deny.

She sighed, and he realized she was even more nervous than he was. They danced without talking, and slowly their bodies eased together. Her head lay against his shoulder, her hair an amber cloud, sweetly scented against his cheek. For song after song they swirled together in the darkness, far from the others, wrapped in each other, neither daring to speak.

At last he stopped dancing, but his hand lingered on hers and he pulled her further into the darkness. They walked up the stairs and along the balcony until the drumbeats of the music were as faint as heartbeats.

He paused, forcing her back against the wall. He placed his hands on the stucco beside her face and leaned toward her, his weight on his arms so that she was imprisoned by his body. Her face was tilted up toward his, her lips lush and innocently inviting, though her lashes were lowered. He wanted to kiss her, to make wild, violent love to her, but some last shred of sense restrained him.

"You've been drinking, and I think a great deal," she said warily. "Too much."

"Tequila. They say it turns a man's blood to fire—like a woman can." His husky voice was suggestive.

"Do you think it wise—to drink so much?"

"No wiser than to allow the wrong woman to fire one's blood." With his thumb he traced the softness of her cheek, then the curve of her lips, urging them open. He groaned when her mouth parted and she accepted the gentle invasion of his fingertip.

Her heart began to pound under the exploration of his fingers.

In a low voice he said. "You see, my love, I can't keep my hands off you."

"You shouldn't drink if it makes you do things you regret."

"You sound too much like a wife. I'll drink as much as I please, damn you."

She flinched, but her voice was soft. "Alexander, I don't know what you want, why you danced with me, why you're talking to me like this, touching me like this."

A muscular denim-clad thigh inserted itself between her legs, and she was arched against him. She lifted her head, subconsciously inviting his kiss. His mouth hovered near hers.

She felt the tantalizing whisper of his breath against her lips. "I don't want to feel this way. I don't know how in the hell I'm ever going to get you out of my system." One of his hands slid down her throat and brushed the tip of her breast.

She squeezed her eyelids shut with pain from what he said, even as her nipple hardened from his light, casual touch.

His mouth closed over hers in plundering demand. He lifted her body against his. She gasped as his mouth trailed from her lips downward to scorch her breasts through thin gauze with hot damp kisses. Her legs felt weak and unable to support her, but he was holding her and it didn't matter. Nothing mattered except the dizzying sensations his lovemaking evoked.

At last he drew away. He stared at her, his eyes fierce, his body pulsing with unwanted desire.

She choked back a half-sob, so intense was her longing for his love and not just his passion.

Her hand reached tentatively toward him, and she curled her fingers into the smooth darkness of his hair.

"Alexander, oh Alexander, what in the world are we going to do?"

The sadness in her voice reached him and stayed his passion.

"We need to get out of each other's lives," he muttered. "But that seems more and more impossible."

"What do you mean?"

"I mean that our children need both of us. They love you, and they need you. But they need a father as well. They need more discipline. I want to resume our marriage. Come back with me to London." His voice was cold. He did not speak of the hot insanity that thrummed in his blood.

"But you don't love me."

"Love is not the only basis on which a marriage can be made," he went on, still in that cold tone she hated. "Men and women choose to remain married for practical considerations every day."

Practical considerations! That was a euphemism if he'd ever heard one to describe the taut fire in his loins.

"But I don't want that sort of marriage," she said.

He made the mistake of looking at her again. Her throat was naked and slender. His gaze trailed lower to the thrusting bloom of her breasts above her lace gown. "Do you think I do?" he said hoarsely. "The children need both of us, and I must admit that I want to watch them grow up. I've already lost six years. It confuses children to separate them months on end from one parent so they can be with the other."

She bit into her lip and said stubbornly, "It would not be a real marriage."

"It would not be without advantages to you. I would help you with the children. As long as you were discreet, you would be free to do whatever you wanted. I will help you with your factory so that the work you have started will continue. And, Liz, you will be home, in England." He didn't say "home with me," but he thought it. It took all his willpower not to drag her into his arms and convince her with his mouth and body.

But would it feel like home, she wondered desperately, when he was so set against her? He had said that as long as she was discreet she would be free. Nothing he could have said could have brought her more pain. She would be his wife in name only. She could not live with him, loving him, if she meant nothing to him.

"Alexander, what you ask is impossible." She flung herself away and ran, her slim form disappearing into the darkness.

From the courtyard beneath came the gay music and the sound of laughter and dancing.

She was right, of course. A marriage between them would be a living hell.

He stormed down the stairs, illogically angry at her for her answer. He remembered the softness of her, the scent of her. God, did he ever think of anything else? He'd forced himself to speak to her coolly, formally. The whole time his desire had been a hot, electric force barely under control. He'd said he wanted her because of the children. That was a laugh. Every time he looked at her, she aroused in him an avalanche of passion.

What he needed was another drink and a woman in his arms. He asked Esmeralda to dance, and then he asked every woman at the fiesta. He drank and he laughed and he swore, and still the vision of a flaming-headed goddess lingered on the fringes of his inebriated mind to taunt him with her forbidden beauty, to remind him that it was a tall, slim body he desired and not short, brown, rounded ones.

It promised to be a long, hellish night.

Chapter Eight

$\mathcal{A}$ dog barked outside the hacienda. Liz lay awake, listening to the sounds of the night. She'd scarcely slept since she ran from Alexander all those hours ago. She'd thrown herself upon her bed and sobbed for all that they had lost. Eventually she had gotten up and undressed for bed and fallen asleep, but a short while ago some noise had aroused her.

She thought of the children and, remembering the noise, a vague unease crept into the back of her mind. She decided that before she tried to go back to sleep, she would check on them. She slid from the bed and pulled on a thin robe, then tiptoed silently across the room out onto the balcony.

Her hand floated lightly along the balustrade as she made her way toward the children's bedrooms, which were past Alexander's. She was almost past his shadowed door when she heard a low male chuckle.

Her heart stopped.

Alexander was leaning nonchalantly in his doorway,

his chest bare. In one hand he held a bottle of tequila. The hot scent of the alcohol came to her. Too late, she remembered the times she had heard him pacing outside on the balcony.

"So you can't sleep either?" His voice was lazily slurred, and she realized uneasily he must have gone on drinking after they'd parted. He stepped into the moonlight, baring his teeth in a smile. An aura of danger surrounded him.

"I was going to check on the children," she said tautly.

"Ever the virtuous mother? Perhaps it's time you played the role of wife as enthusiastically." His eyes were fixed on hers. They were hot, and darkly intense.

She shrank against the rail as he loomed nearer. He wasn't going to let her pass. "I wanted to make sure they were all right."

His hard eyes swept her insolently. "And I was flattering myself that it was me and not the children you were coming to see."

"You're very drunk. Go to bed before you do yourself some harm," she said, her voice harsh because she was afraid.

"Always thinking of others, my love?" he taunted, moving so near she could smell the tequila on his breath, and also his warm male scent. His black hair swung loosely across his forehead. "I can see you're disgusted because I've been drinking, but it was you who drove me to it."

"Don't blame me because—"

"Who else?" he rasped. "I thought only to drink until I could forget you, but I want you more than ever." He held the bottle up. "Betrayed—even by the bottle." He laughed softly and turned back to her.

The passion in his voice sent an odd shiver through her. She did not try to prevent him when he slid his arms around her shoulders and held her tightly against himself.

Seeing her unexpectedly in the darkness had tapped all the feelings he had been fighting to contain for the past weeks. He'd come out onto the balcony because he could not sleep for thinking of her. And now she was here, in his arms, arousing in him an uncontrollable white-hot blaze of passion.

"I want to take you to my bed and make love to you." His voice was a husky whisper in her hair. "Every night I lie awake thinking about you, about your breasts, your long legs, about your silken skin. I want to touch you, to kiss you. Damn you, Liz. No other woman—"

Her hair fell over her shoulders like a net of fire. It was an act of instinct, of terrible hunger that drove his fingers deep into the soft, shining thickness to bring her face closer to his. His mouth hovered inches above hers, burning her lips, caressing them with his breath before he brought them even closer. Against his chest he could feel the warm touch of her breasts, their quick rise and fall, the rapid beating of her heart.

"Alexander—"

His hard kiss cut off her words. His tongue plunged into her mouth, boldly, intimately, exploring, tasting the inner sweetness of her. When at last he released her, she stumbled back toward the safety of her room.

He swayed unsteadily, but his eyes were alert, dangerous. The moonlight shone upon his face, revealing his turbulent passion. She turned to flee, but he ran after her. He caught her just inside her door. He gripped her arms so hard, she knew they would be as bruised as her lips, which his mouth possessed again and again with savage hunger.

He forced her back against the doorframe, his muscled body pressing into hers, and he kissed her so hard and so long she thought she would faint. His hard mouth coaxed hers into parting, permitting the entrance of his tongue. Again he tasted the honey sweetness of her mouth. Her breathing quickened in arousal, her mouth moving under his, her heart pounding as his fingers explored her body, caressing the length of her spine.

His hands fumbled with the fastenings of her robe, removing it, so that it fell rippling from her shoulders in a pool at her feet. He was sliding her nightgown off her shoulders, his palm cupping her breast. Dreamily she twisted her body, her softness absorbing the hard structure of his hips, the long columns of his thighs.

"Alexander, someone might see—" There was an eagerness in her own voice that betrayed the scorching desires of her body.

"No one will see, my love."

He lifted her into his arms and kicked the door shut behind him. She clung to him, wanting him with the same driving need that possessed him.

"You are my woman. You have always been my woman. There has never been anyone except you."

"Someone once told me that you were a despoiler of women," she said with a giggle. "I'm beginning to believe—"

In the darkness he laughed. "A myth, my love. There's only one woman I want to . . . despoil."

His lips sought hers, and she was desperately willing, mindlessly in want of despoiling.

He laid her upon the bed, and stripping quickly out of his trousers, he settled himself on top of her, his knees on either side of her hips.

His hands trembled against her skin as he removed her gown. He kissed her everywhere, his tongue and mouth moving along her throat, beneath her hair, to her breasts and then lower down to her more sensitive flesh, flicking along the inside of her thighs. His kisses were slow and hot now that she no longer resisted.

"Oh, Alexander, don't kiss me there."

"Despoilers don't take no for an answer. Love, I'm determined to live up to my infamous reputation."

His mouth nuzzled, and shivers of excitement coursed through her until her whole body tingled with erotic quivers. When she thought she could bear no more of the exquisite, pulsing rapture his tongue and mouth evoked, he pushed her down on the bed and covered her body with his. His desire raged out of control and his hands moved over her, arousing her to new heights, carrying her with him into a whirling world of dark desire.

With his hand, he made sure of her readiness before he entered her. Then he could contain himself no longer, and he took her with the shattering force of a man too long starved for the one woman he wanted.

Afterward he lay with his body still pressing into hers. His hands cupped her face, and he bent to kiss her perspiring brow.

He wanted to talk to her, but he could not find the words. He could only stare at her in speechless wonder and watch as she fell asleep in his arms, exhausted, clinging to him, too emotionally spent for anything other than sleep.

He lay in the darkness, thinking, and as his passion ebbed, the enormity of what he had done to her crashed down upon him. He remembered his violence toward her on the balcony. She had not wanted him. He remembered the way he had run after her. He had forced her because he'd been crazy with drink and desire. It didn't matter that in the end her passion had matched his.

He had taken Liz, his sweet and gentle Liz, with anger. He had used her against her will. He had overcome her with sheer physical strength. Then he'd carried her to the bed, and after that she had not fought him. He'd been an animal with no thought but for his own need, and he hated himself for what he had done. How could he possibly face her when he could not even face himself?

Slowly he slid his arm from beneath her head, carefully so that he did not wake her. He smoothed her hair upon the pillow, brought the sheets over her body, and then the sarapes. Quickly he dressed, and then he strode from her room back to the comfortless solitude of his own.

"Mommy, but I saw him!" Samantha cried. "It wasn't a dream!"

"Why would Juan come into your room in the middle of the night?"

"He was looking at me like he was mad, and he smelled awful, too. Then there was a noise on the balcony, and he ran away."

From outside Liz's office came Esmeralda's voice. "Samantha?"

"*Aquí,*" Samantha trilled, dashing outside to join her brother and Esmeralda for breakfast beneath the papaya trees.

Feeling slightly worried, Liz watched her daughter bound out the door. The child was subject to nightmares, but she had been more adamant than usual about this one. Of course, like all the others, this dream was no more than a product of her overly active imagination. At least it was not so terrifying as usual.

Liz returned to the stack of invoices and opened her checkbook, but it was impossible to concentrate. She thought of Alexander, hoping that things would be different between them.

She remembered him as he had been last night, his eyes hot, his expression dark and sensual as his strong arms had pulled her tightly against his masculine body. He had wanted her terribly. The memory of his excitement made her shiver. How would he act when he saw her? What would he say? What would she say to him? He'd been wild and angry, not the indifferent stranger he'd seemed for the past week. His embraces had been hard and demanding, but they had stirred the deep carnal desire in her. Afterward her sleep had been the dreamless sleep of complete fulfillment. But now . . .

She'd been up for hours feeling crazily mixed up. She felt shy with excitement and anticipation at the prospect of seeing him again. She felt thrillingly expectant, and yet at the same time terribly afraid.

At the swish of soft cotton skirts and a soft, *"Perdóneme, señora,"* Liz glanced up and blushed.

It was only Maria entering her office with her breakfast and coffee on a tray.

When the woman left, Liz poured herself a cup of coffee. Again she tried to work, but she was far too agitated, so she just sipped her coffee and waited. When at last she recognized the heavy tread of Alexander's footsteps, she froze, her heart fluttering. Hot color scorched her face. She did not dare to look up even though she was aware of him standing in the door, hesitating as though he felt as awkward in her presence as she did in his.

Her stomach knotted. Why didn't he say something? Didn't he know that he was killing her with his silence? She remembered the violence of his lovemaking, and a thousand doubts formed in her mind. Was it to be even worse than before?

His rough voice broke the silence.

"I'm sorry, Liz, about last night. I was half-crazy with tequila. I swear I never meant for that to happen, and it won't again."

Her gaze shot up. Did he regret— His eyes were remote, unreadable. Guilt and self-loathing made him look grim and angry, and Liz's heart began to beat fearfully.

"I—" Her throat was too dry for speech.

"I'll be returning to London tomorrow. We'll have to work out a custody arrangement and the details of our divorce later. You'll never have to see me again."

"Of course," she managed.

She continued to look at him, scarcely able to think for the despair and hopelessness tearing at her.

Alexander wanted to tell her that she had never looked more beautiful to him than now when she was lost to him, that the thought of leaving her forever brought him the most unbearable pain. He had thought he hated her, but he had been wrong. He had never stopped loving her, and the last thing he wanted to do was hurt her, no matter what she had done to him. He hated himself for last night, and he was determined to leave her so that he could inflict no more anguish upon her, even if it killed him.

He longed to lean forward and curve her body against his. More than anything he wanted to explore again the sweetness of her mouth, to feel the glory of her response, to know the exquisite delight of her hands and lips running wild over his body.

He said only, "I'll be with Manuel in the factory if you need me this morning. And later I'll tell the children."

"All right." How did her voice sound so calm, when she felt that she was flying to pieces inside?

When he had gone, Liz blinked against the tears that betrayed the ravaging grief in her heart. What a fool she had been to hope. It was obvious he despised himself as well as her for what he had done. If he hadn't been drinking, he would never have come to her.

She buried her face in her hands and wept. She still wanted him, shamelessly, hopelessly. No matter how hard she tried to put him and her desire for him aside, she couldn't. She had led him on, tempting him with her dancing, with her laughter, with her kisses. All week she had dressed for him, worn her hair the way it pleased him.

Everything was her fault. If she had not been so forward, perhaps none of this would have happened, and he would have stayed longer. Perhaps somehow she would have found a way to reach him. Until he came, she had never realized how much the children needed him. Who was she trying to fool? She had never realized how much she still loved and wanted him. And now it was over. As this thought sank remorselessly in upon her, she began to sob more passionately than ever.

Things grew worse as the day progressed. She couldn't concentrate on her work. After Alexander talked to the children, they ran screaming and crying into her office, blaming her, begging her to make him stay. As if she could.

"Daddy is going away without us!" they cried.

"I know, my darlings," she said, her voice leaden.

"You must stop him. If you would only tell him you don't want him to go, he would stay," Samantha said.

"You don't understand." Liz could think of no words to explain that it was because of her that he was leaving, and not because of them. "I can't ask him to stay," Liz said woodenly.

"Are you going to divorce him?" Alex asked.

"Yes."

"But why?"

"Because he wants to, and it's for the best. We haven't lived together for seven years."

"You haven't tried. Neither of you have," Alex hissed in disgust, sounding older than his years. "The least you could do is try. That's what you always tell us."

"I know, darling, but this is not the same. Not the same at all. Someday when you are older, you will understand."

"I'll never understand!"

The hours dragged. The children blamed her, and they were solemn and tearful as they followed their father around like frightened puppies.

Alexander avoided her. When she visited the factory, he left, and no matter how long she stayed, he did not return until she departed.

She took no pride in the hum of fifty sewing machines working simultaneously, nor in the hum of the industrious hairdressers, cobblers and stitchers busily at work at their tables. In a daze she watched her sewers plunge their hands time after time into boxes of silky blue and gold fabric, run gathering threads on their machines so that the miniature garments bloomed like flower blossoms into Cinderella ball gowns.

Feeling useless and out of sorts, she wandered through the factory, past boxes of brown felt elf shoes for Peter Pan, gauzy white aprons for Alice in Wonderland. Other cardboard boxes were marked "Pearls for Elizabeth I" and "Wands for Fairy Godmother."

Carlos, her hatter, and his three apprentices were in a room by themselves, twisting straw into perfect miniatures of Edwardian bonnets. In another room Imelda was busy making her tiny ruffled parasols. Her daughter Lucinda was rolling small stockings rightside out for a thousand small feet.

Liz realized Alexander had worked wonders in the short time he'd been there. Despite the flood, never had the factory run more efficiently.

For once she did not care about the factory. Her thoughts were concentrated solely upon Alexander. This was their last day together, and he wouldn't come near her. Her heart was breaking from his coldness, but pride kept her from going to him. She was terribly conscious of his every activity. She knew that he took his lunch with Manuel in the factory and his dinner with the children in the room she had set up as his office.

Alexander took innumerable overseas calls, handling them with a calm ease that maddened her. How could he conduct business as usual when she was an emotional wreck? That evening he took the children into Mexico City without her.

After watching the last curl of dust behind her red Fiat, Liz returned to her design room, but she listlessly eyed the fabric samples and the model she was constructing of a new Hawaiian doll. A dozen research books were piled beside the model, and she decided to try to make a few sketches for the doll's costume. For an hour she sat, sketchbook and pencil in hand, without drawing a single line.

At last she gave up and went to the living room, where she sank down on her favorite chair and stared out at the darkening sky. She switched on the television, and Mimi Camille's husky purr filled the room, bringing back more powerfully than anything memories of Roger and the time Liz had spent with him in France. It was one of Mimi's early French films, with subtitles. Mimi played the part of a demonic woman with the face of an angel. Liz turned the set off abruptly, as always the mere sight of Mimi affecting her negatively. The last thing Liz needed was to think of Roger. Later it began to rain gently. She went to bed, but she was still awake when the Fiat chugged into the drive.

Alexander and the children came upstairs. The children's voices were sleepy, his gentle and reassuring. Esmeralda helped him put the children to bed, a ritual which Samantha made as long as possible. She cried that she was afraid, and begged for glasses of water. This was the way Samantha frequently acted when she'd had a nightmare the evening before, but because her father was leaving in the morning, she was even worse than usual.

At last the children were quiet and Liz heard the sound of Alexander as he walked to his room, the shutting of his door, his movements from within, the creak of his bed when he lay upon it. She wanted to go to him, but she did not. She lay miserable and lonely, never supposing that he might be as miserable and lonely as she.

How was she going to stand living without him for the rest of her life?

"Mommy!" Samantha's cry was a thin wail of terror that jolted Liz awake.

Liz jumped out of bed and ran outside. Moonlight flooded the balcony and courtyard. Beneath she heard a muffled sound on the cobblestones.

The cry came again from Samantha's room, and Liz ran more swiftly, her thin nightgown clinging to the shape of her body, the tile floor freezing cold under her bare feet.

Alexander's door opened, and he stepped outside wearing only a pair of jeans.

"It's Samantha," Liz said, unconsciously reaching for his hand, and he ran with her to their child's room.

Samantha was sitting up stiffly in her bed, bundled in her innumerable sarapes. Alexander swept her into his arms, cradling the shaking child against his chest. Liz leaned over and stroked Samantha's tangled hair.

"What is it, Samantha?" Liz asked gently.

"He came back!"

"You had your bad dream again?"

Samantha's black eyes were wide in her white face. "No! This morning I told you it wasn't a dream, and it wasn't!"

"What are you two talking about?" Alexander asked.

"I told Mommy that Juan came into my room last night, and she wouldn't believe me. She said it was a dream, but he did come! I knew he did, and tonight I bit him on his hand when he put it on top of my mouth."

"That was very brave, Samantha," Alexander said soothingly. "What happened then?"

"I told him I would bite him again if he didn't let me go. He dropped me back onto the bed and ran out."

In a voice of steel, Alexander said, "Liz, hold Samantha while I check on Alex."

He left them, returning almost instantly, his handsome face dark with alarm.

"Alex is gone. I think Juan took him."

"Oh, no! Juan wouldn't—" Liz bit back her cry of anguish. She remembered Juan's terrible anger when Alexander fired him.

"I'm going down to tell Manuel. First we must search the hacienda. If we don't find Alex, I'm going after him."

"Send for Esmeralda. I want to go with you."

"No."

"But I think I know where Juan might have taken Alex if he has him. He has a *jacal* on the edge of his plot of land on the other side of the forest. It's a little cornstalk hut where he sometimes stays when he's drinking or when he doesn't want to walk home from his field to the village. I don't think he'd take Alex to the village. We'll have to take Villano." She looked at Alexander pleadingly. "You've got to take me with you!"

The wild, desperate look in her eyes broke his iron resolve to refuse her. He knelt beside her. "Alex is all right, Liz. We'll find him." He took her hand in his.

"Go get dressed." To Samantha he said, "I'll wait with you until Esmeralda comes up."

Liz dashed to her room and dressed in the darkness, pulling on jeans, a wool sweater and a Mexican poncho. When she reached the courtyard, Alexander called her.

"Liz! Over here!"

Alexander was leading Villano by the long reins of his bridle. Sensing something was wrong, the black horse snorted and pranced skittishly upon the uneven stones.

Liz wished she had a mango to give him, and she began talking soothingly in Spanish. *"Villano, por favor. Cálmate, mi querido."* She reached up and stroked his neck as Alexander jumped onto his bare back. The horse tried to nuzzle her hand in search of the fruit she usually brought him. Alexander reached down, grabbed Liz by the shoulders and swung her roughly up behind him.

"Hang on," he ordered, and she obeyed, circling his waist with her arms, lacing her fingers together against his belt buckle and burrowing her cheek tightly into his back.

Alexander dug his heels into Villano's sides, and Villano neighed, backing sideways, before he jumped forward, plunging into the darkness in a mad gallop.

"Take the first dirt road to the left," Liz cried. "Juan's jacal is at the end of the road."

The moon was hidden by the black mountains, but its silvery light peeped over the jagged peaks. Hooves pounded upon the hard road, and loose stones flew in all directions.

When they headed up the twisting mountain road, so overgrown it was scarcely more than a path etched between fields and forest, Villano ran more slowly, the weight of two riders and the steep incline draining him. Suddenly, when they rounded a curve to enter a patch of forest, the horse jerked his head wildly. Alexander urged him forward, but Villano reared.

"Damn fool—" Alexander jabbed his heels more deeply into the horse and slapped his neck with the reins.

"I smell smoke," Liz screamed. "It's no use whipping him, Alexander. Villano is terrified of fire."

"Naturally." Alexander leaped to the ground and helped Liz down. Her body slid along the length of his.

"We might as well let him find his own way back to the hacienda," Liz said. "He'd only hurt himself if we tied him here."

"How much further is it?"

Liz peered into the darkness. "Just ahead where that orange— Alexander!" She gripped his sleeve frantically. "Juan's jacal is on fire!"

Their gazes touched in mutual terror. Then they ran toward the billowing glow, Alexander quickly outdistancing Liz.

Liz reached the flaming jacal in time to see Alexander push a drunken Juan to the ground and dash inside the inferno. She waited in an agony of suspense.

It seemed an eternity before Alexander reemerged, carrying the limp child in his arms. Liz screamed in horror. The back of Alexander's shirt was on fire.

"Alexander!"

Ripping off her poncho, Liz ran to them and began beating Alexander on the back. When the flames were out she flung her ruined poncho onto the ground.

"Alexander, are you all right?"

He stared at her, the lines of his face grim, his mouth a grimace because of his pain. "It's Alex," he muttered, "that you should worry about."

"Is he—" The fear inside her choked off her words. Feeling more helpless than she ever had in her life, she stroked the brow of her unconscious son. "Alex, can you hear me? Darling, Mother's here."

Alex's face was terrible in its stillness and waxen pallor.

"His pulse is very weak, Liz," Alexander said gently. "We have to hurry and get him to a doctor."

From behind her came Juan's drunken voice, muttering brokenly, "Fire no on purpose, señora. The cigarillo, I dropped him. I never hurt the niño. I only want to scare the señor."

Alexander was too concerned about Alex to express his rage. He turned his back on Juan and strode down the road that led to the hacienda.

Liz ran to keep up with him. The long walk home on that rutted road was interminable. Alex never regained consciousness.

Liz watched Alexander lay her child gently upon the couch in the living room, and in the light of the lamp she saw for the first time how pale he was. There was an angry bruise across his jaw, and she wondered if Juan had struck him.

"Stay with him while I get the car," Alexander commanded. "You'll have to give me directions how to get to the nearest hospital."

While he was gone, Liz held Alex's limp hand in hers. He felt so cold, so lifeless.

For the first time she wondered if her child was going to die.

Chapter Nine

The doctor worked slowly, slicing Alexander's shirt from his back. The immaculate blue-tiled treatment room seemed an oasis of peace in the overcrowded hospital. In the hall outside, the emergency waiting area was packed with a throng of families and patients. Babies cried, mothers tried to corral small children, nurses scurried with trays of medications, and doctors were summoned over the p.a. system.

As the scissors flashed, Dr. Gomez spoke of Alex's injuries. "The boy's had a severe shock, señores. He received a concussion. The burn on his arm is serious. He suffered smoke inhalation, but he will recover."

Liz exhaled in relief. Then she looked at Alexander. Her husband's dark face was pale. He winced as the doctor examined his injury, and Liz realized he must have been in pain for hours.

As the doctor pulled the last strip of cloth from Alexander's back, Liz bit into her bottom lip. "Oh, Alexander, I didn't realize you were hurt so badly," she

said in a choked voice. Gently she took his hand in hers
as she gazed at the blackened welts and blistered flesh.

Alexander gripped her slim fingers instead of reject-
ing them. The doctor gave him a shot for pain and
began to cleanse the wound. Alexander went whiter,
and the pressure of his grip increased.

"You are going to have to change your husband's
dressing every day, señora, so this burn will not become infected. He will be on antibiotics, but the
nursing care he receives is very important. He needs to
take it easy for four or five days. By then I should be
able to release your son from the hospital, and the
worst will be past for both of them."

When the physician left the room, Alexander said,
with a weak smile, "Well, I guess it won't be so easy for
you to get rid of me after all."

"I don't want to be rid of you," she admitted softly.

His golden eyes met hers, and for once they did not
gleam with cynicism at her kindness. "I could return to
my hotel and hire a nurse."

"Alexander, please, stay with me."

"I never thought I'd hear you ask me to stay with you
again," he said, his voice almost caressing. Again she
felt the increased pressure of his strong fingers around
hers.

He smiled at her, and an odd, thrilling sensation
swept her. For no reason at all, just being with him like
this meant everything to her.

"Funny how things work out," she murmured, and
she turned away, too proud for him to see that her face
was illuminated with joy.

She didn't know how deeply her concern touched
him, how fiercely he fought the wave of tenderness he
felt toward her.

The hour was late that night when Liz and Alexander
returned to the hacienda. They had both been reluctant

to leave Alex alone at the hospital even though he was doing well. Finally they had compromised and returned home, but only after Esmeralda had been summoned to stay with the sleeping child.

Liz helped Alexander get ready for bed. He said his back was hurting despite the pain-killer shot, and he held himself stiffly, watching her as she pulled back the sarapes and sheets of his bed. She flushed as she felt his eyes upon her. The simple things she did to the bed, plumping the pillows, smoothing the sheets, seemed to take forever under his piercing gaze.

It wasn't what she did that interested him, but the swaying motion of her hips when she walked, and the invitation of their upturned roundness when she bent over the bed. She suspected his thoughts with a discomfiting accuracy that annoyed her.

"Well," she snapped when she was done with the bed. "Are you just going to stand there watching me, or are you going to undress and get into bed?"

"I would definitely prefer the latter," he said with sparkling eyes and a devilish white smile, "providing you join me."

"I—I didn't mean *that!*" she cried hotly. "I meant I'm dead tired, and I think you should be thoughtful and accommodating for once and go to bed like a good patient before we both collapse from sheer exhaustion."

"It's a good thing you avoided the nursing profession," he said dryly. "Your bedside manner leaves something to be desired."

She bit back the angry retort that sprang to her lips. "I suppose you're right there," she agreed grimly. "I haven't the patience to be a nurse."

"Ah, but you have other talents, my love, that more than make up for that lack." His voice was pitched low and was deliberately suggestive.

She knelt and poured him a glass of bottled water, in

her fury splashing more onto the table than into the glass. Then she shook a pain pill out of its bottle with an explosive rattle and set it beside the glass on the bedside table. Without looking at him, she said, "I'll leave you to undress if there's nothing else you need."

She was at the door, anxious to make her escape, when his husky voice stopped her. "Who says there's nothing else I need?" She cocked her head defiantly, and he went on. "Liz, I hate to ask you, after all you've done, but would you help me undress?"

Her eyes lifted to the golden brilliance of his. She regarded his grave face with suspicion, and she thought she detected the trace of a smile at either corner of his lips. Like hell he hated to ask! Her nerves gathered in weary knots. She was about to refuse.

"I'll understand if you won't, of course, since you don't have the sensitivities of a real nurse," he said smoothly in his softest, most provoking tone, "but it hurts like the devil every time I move, Liz." At her doubtful look, he groaned. "It really does, but I don't want to bother you further. I'll sleep in my shoes."

He really sounded quite pitiful and humble—so pitiful, in fact, she suspected a trick. Still, he had saved Alex, and the thought of him sleeping in his shoes was more than she could stand. If she allowed that, she *was* heartless!

Liz walked warily toward him. "What do you want me to take off?"

"Everything."

The one, hoarsely uttered word was provocatively dangerous. Her heart began to hammer wildly.

Was he really in such pain? The doctor had given him a shot that should have left a giraffe reeling. But if he were, she couldn't bear the thought of leaving him.

Liz walked slowly toward him. The room was charged with the primal force of their sexual tension.

As if in a trance, she took his hand and led him to the

bed. She knelt beside him and with shaking fingers began to work the laces. Fumbling, she clumsily knotted them.

Alexander watched her, misinterpreting her distress as distaste for him. No doubt, that was a result of his rough treatment the previous night. He felt guilty; nevertheless, his senses reeled at her sweet-scented nearness. He saw the movement of her breasts against her sweater. He longed to drag her into his arms and use her as her womanliness was made to be used.

Odd that he felt so drawn to her even after this hellishly long day. Maybe it was just that he'd been afraid for Alex, and now that the danger was past, he was still keyed up. He remembered her sweetness in the hospital, and he knew that, whatever the reason, he wanted her more than ever.

He ached for her, his injury and the long night having done nothing to quell his desire. Every muscle in his body tautened with suppressed desire.

She jerked the laces free at last and removed his shoes. He felt the softness of her fingers against his calf and ankle as she rolled the first sock downward. Then with the same tantalizing slowness, she peeled the other sock off. When she was done, she hesitated, a small sigh of relief escaping her lips.

She glanced into his eyes, then quickly averted her gaze, but not before he saw that her cheeks were flushed. Each knew that he could release her, if only he would.

Glancing down at her bright, demurely lowered head, he said mercilessly, "You know I always sleep in the nude."

Her voice was a whisper. "Yes. I remember."

"Undress me," he ordered, his voice ragged.

She jerked herself upward and too briskly attacked his belt buckle.

"Gently," he cautioned with a tight smile, whitening.

She instantly regretted that she'd hurt him.

"I'm sorry," she said in a low, muffled tone.

His brown hand cupped her chin, and he tilted her face. He saw his own passion mirrored in the luminous glitter of hers. Slowly and tenderly he lifted her lips to his, which were blazing hot with desire.

"Alexander, you're hardly in the condition for this sort of thing."

A hot, pulsing fire hardened in his loins. "I think I'm, er, a better judge of my condition than you, love," he said on a vibrant chuckle.

His mouth moved to each corner of her lips in turn. Then he explored her eyelids, the lush curl of her closed lashes, the winged arch of her brows. He nuzzled the curve of her silken earlobe.

Just as an uncontrollable shudder made her shiver, he removed his mouth. She moaned with suppressed longing as he pressed her into his body, burying his face in her hair.

They clung to each other, their bodies hot and shaking. She could feel his pulse thundering at the same mad tempo as her own. Silently they held one another. It was their first moment of mutual tenderness in seven years. At last Alexander put her from him.

"You were undressing me," he said as if nothing had changed between them, though everything had.

She unbuckled his belt and unfastened his pants. He stood up, and she, still kneeling, lowered his slacks over his hard, muscular thighs. He groaned as her hands trailed over his legs.

His briefs came next. Trembling fingers moved beneath the elastic waistband. She lowered them slowly. At the sight of his exposed maleness, she never faltered as she removed this last, most intimate item. When she finished, her hands lingered caressingly once more upon his body until he was breathless with unbearable need.

Then her lips followed the path of her hands, gently exploring his thighs until, at last, her mouth claimed the satin hardness of him in a passionate, damp nuzzle of complete possession.

He clasped the back of her head, prolonging this moment of complete intimacy. She kissed him until his breathing was harsh and ragged.

"I love you, Alexander," she murmured. "I always have, and I always will. Can't you please believe me?" He felt the heat of her breath against his aroused flesh.

He wanted to believe in her love, but he could not.

His failure to answer her brought tears to her eyes, tears which she quietly suppressed. She was too proud to go on pleading.

When she rose, he said gently, "Sleep with me tonight, Liz. More than anything I want to fall asleep in your arms." His voice changed, and she heard the hint of humor as his hands moved over her. "Not quite more than *anything.*"

He'd rejected her love. He wanted only her passion. But, though he didn't believe her, she'd caught an inflection in his voice that was almost tender. It wove a spell around her that she could not resist.

"All right," she murmured uncertainly.

Hot golden eyes watched her every movement as she stripped.

She moved into his arms, and the fusion of their warm bodies was heaven.

"Alexander," she whispered as he drew her down onto the bed beside him. "You're forgetting your pain pill."

"I won't be needing it with you in my arms," he said as he positioned her beneath him. "Ever the diligent nurse," he mocked as his body slid provocatively against hers.

"And I thought you didn't like my bedside manner."

"There's nothing I like better than your bedside manner. Unless it's your in-bed manner."

"Alexander, you said that it hurt like the devil every time you moved."

"Perhaps I exaggerated the pain just a trifle, my love." At her frown, he grinned sheepishly. "But that was only to win your sympathy." His grin broadened. "And to win your kisses and the pleasure of your sweet, warm body."

Before she could protest, his mouth closed over hers, and he moved his body erotically over hers, crushing her in a tight embrace and thrusting deeply inside her until their passion built to shattering ecstasy.

The next morning Liz awoke buried beneath the warmth of Alexander's body. Maria was tapping lightly on the door.

"Ahorita, vengo, Maria," Liz whispered, careful not to disturb Alexander, who was at last sleeping deeply.

Alexander's head lay against Liz's white shoulder. Her legs were entwined with his, and she felt warm and safe and happier than she had in years.

Carefully she disentangled her body from Alexander's, and brushing the rumpled darkness of his head with a kiss, she rose. She dressed hurriedly and went to the door. Casting a lingering look at Alexander, she felt a curious protective feeling toward him. His rugged face was abnormally pale. There were gray circles beneath his eyes.

Alexander was infinitely precious to her. She would have to tell Maria that he was not to be awakened. Stealthily, Liz opened the door and slipped outside, closing it behind her.

Maria began speaking rapidly in Spanish.

"Señora, the other Frenchman, Señor Rocheaux, is downstairs."

Remembering the enmity of the two cousins, Liz felt a wave of alarm that Jock had come while Alexander was there. Her husband must not confront Jock while he was still injured.

Liz said coolly, "Please tell Señor Rocheaux I will be down in a moment."

Ten minutes later, Liz swept into the living room where Jock was having tea and bolillos. Jock chuckled when he saw her. She wore satin harem trousers edged with gold-threaded georgette flounces, and a ruffled blouse. The material was diaphanous, and the graceful outline of her body was revealed beneath the softly flowing, richly incandescent fabric.

At the sight of her at the door, Jock rose and crossed the room to join her. He lowered his golden head and kissed her hand. This old-fashioned gesture was typical of Jock, who radiated charm with the fire of the sun god. All his life women had chased him, and Liz knew he was fickle, never dating for long any of the beauties who clamored for his attention. She had been the only exception.

Jock was more classically handsome than Alexander, whose piratical look made him appear dangerous. Jock, on the other hand, fit the image of the urbane man-about-town. His was a complex personality. He was suave, brilliant and cultured; his tastes ran to the eclectic. He was a race car driver, an opera devotee, a womanizer, an artist and a gambler. Despite his charm and sophistication, it was an unwise man who underestimated Jock. In business he was ruthless.

Jock had perfect, chiseled features, indigo blue eyes, and golden skin. There seemed nothing hidden nor mysterious about him. He was tall, though not as tall as Alexander, and smooth in manner and temperament, unlike her more volatile, strong-willed husband.

Jock's blue eyes slid over Liz. "You're looking like—" He paused, searching for the right word in English to describe the whimsical quality she inspired in him. "Like some exotic, Arab, forest naiad."

"An Arab—with red hair? And a forest naiad as well?" Liz laughed lightly, deliciously. "I'm not sure that hodgepodge of images is altogether flattering."

He smiled in that open, easy way of his. "Like all women, you seek compliments."

"Naturellement," she replied in her French, which was every bit as atrocious as her Spanish.

Trying not to wince at her flat accent, he squeezed her hand. "Ah, *chérie,* you deserve them. You are unique. Beautiful, flamboyant, courageous. Most of all, you are fascinating."

"Stop!" she cried teasingly. "I feel positively stuffed on compliments now." The gilt clock on her desk chimed. "My goodness, I didn't realize it was so late." Liz chattered rather frantically, but while she did so, she wondered why Jock had come without warning. He usually wrote or called.

He let her rattle on for a while, and suddenly he broke in, his low voice serious. "You're different, Liz. There's a radiance about you that I thought you'd lost forever when Mikki threw you out seven years ago. He is here now, isn't he?"

Her still face told everything.

"I thought so."

"You can't see him, Jock. He's hurt, and—"

"And you're concerned about him?"

"Yes. He was injured carrying Alex out of a burning hut last night."

"Don't worry, Liz, I have no wish to see him. I merely wondered if he was here. Dazzle is in a state of absolute chaos, and for three weeks the president has been out of the country. There are even rumors now that he was personally involved in the explosion at Dazzle's lab in Switzerland. Rumors that have not been quieted by his lengthy absence. Damned peculiar. Preposterous behavior for a chief executive. I've known Mikki all my life, and I decided there was only one thing in the world that could make him shirk his mammoth responsibilities. That one thing is you, Liz. Does he want you back?"

"No. He came here because of the twins. He still believes that I'm guilty of stealing Paul's formula and giving it to you seven years ago."

"I can see you're determined to change his mind."

"Yes."

"That may be more difficult than you realize. Mikki is stubborn. This whole thing is as crazy as that time he accused me of having something to do with Sasha's death. Hell, the guy drove over the cliff himself. He was trying to force me over it. It was either my life or his. It was a choice I made in a split second, but Mikki wouldn't believe me. Sasha was after me, Liz."

"Why?"

"I never knew. Sasha had always resented my closeness to Mikki. Mikki and I were once the best of friends, you know."

"What happened to change that?"

"A long time ago we made the mistake of falling in love with the same girl. Mikki and I were participating in a regatta at Deauville, and we met an enchanting woman-child named Rochelle in a seaside café. She was an exquisite little thing, with blue eyes. Her skin was olive gold, her hair as black as a raven's wing."

"She must have been beautiful."

"More than beautiful. Unforgettable. She was solemn and passionate, quite different from the girls we had known before her. We both courted her, but when it came time for her to choose between us, neither of us could bear the thought of losing to the other. We were two young, callow, egotistical fools. So we dropped her, each of us loving her, neither of us thinking how she might react."

"What happened?"

"She wrote us a desperate love letter, and we

realized we'd broken her heart. Mikki said it was foolish for all three of us to be miserable when two of us could be happy. We decided to let her choose. Rochelle was a very sensitive girl. We went down to Deauville to tell her, but we were too late. Two days before there had been the most terrible accident. Rochelle had been found dead one morning, having swallowed a handful of sleeping pills that proved a lethal combination with the alcohol she'd drunk at a wedding party the night before. We blamed ourselves, and the guilt over Rochelle was the first wedge in our relationship. After that the easiness between us was gone. Then there was Sasha. Now we've been enemies so long I can scarcely remember when we were not. But I didn't steal that formula from Dazzle. Why should Radiance steal a perfume when we can develop our own fragrances? I believed that formula was ours, developed by our chemists, when I launched it. I didn't know you were married to Mikki, or I never would have gone on and used your face or your name with our launch. That made me look quite absurd when everyone found out you were married to the president of Radiance. Roger nearly fired me. When accusations were made that Radiance had pirated Dazzle's formula, Radiance's reputation suffered immeasurably, not to mention my own. Roger withdrew the product from the market immediately, and he refused to discuss his decision or to let me investigate the matter further. But I've explained all this to you before. Your marriage was a secret then. You told no one."

Liz had turned her back to Jock, and she was staring at the awesome majesty of the purple mountain.

"I told one person."

"Who?"

"I'm still not ready to reveal that."

"Why not? Maybe it would shed some light on all this. Maybe I could help you."

Liz was very pale when she turned from the window and faced him. "No one can help me, Jock. Alexander believes that I deliberately tried to destroy him. I have always believed that I was the victim as well. I think it's time I return to London and Paris to find out what really happened and confront the person I believe is responsible."

"Sometimes innocence is impossible to prove."

They regarded one another in silence.

"You know, Liz, you never ask about your father or Mimi when I come."

Liz stiffened. She did not want to think of Roger and Mimi.

"They would give anything to hear from you, *chérie*."

Liz hesitated. "How are they, then, since you are so determined I should ask?" There was no warmth in her question.

"They miss you terribly. They don't understand your silence. They want to talk to you, to see you again. They are curious about the outcome of your pregnancy. Roger wants grandchildren so much. It's senselessly cruel of you to deny him the twins."

"What have you told my father?"

"Nothing."

"Good."

"But—"

"Jock, leave it alone."

"It's been hard on Roger, Liz," Jock persisted. "Mimi's been in the hospital several times the past few years."

"I didn't know."

"Roger kept her illness out of the papers, but he's been alone a great deal. He needs you."

"No! He doesn't!"

Jock had never been able to understand Liz's unreasoning coldness toward her father. When Liz had first discovered Roger was her father, there had even seemed to be a deep, instantaneous affection between them.

Jock knew the whole story, of course—that Liz's mother had been Catherine Carruthers, the famous American movie star in the fifties who had become the mistress to globe-trotting Roger Chartres, the French perfume magnate who owned Radiance. When they conceived a child, Roger had refused to marry Catherine. In desperation Catherine had married Ashley Killigen, a member of the English gentry. They had gone to live at Killigen Hall in Cornwall, where Catherine had given birth to Liz.

Catherine had always remembered Roger as the grand passion of her life, and she did not bring the scholarly Ashley much happiness. Catherine was a restless, lost soul, and the only real love Liz had known as a child came from the gentle Ashley, whom she adored. He was a famous archeologist, and he had taken Liz on digs all over the world. When he died, her mother had run off with a younger man. When Catherine put Killigen Hall on the market, Liz became permanently estranged from her mother.

Liz had felt bitter and adrift. She had had her shop, her career as a designer, her lifelong hobby of collecting dolls, but nothing else. There had been no one she could turn to. For a time she'd run away to Argentina and Brazil, living in the Andes with Indians. When she returned she went to work in her shop. It had been then that her real father, Roger Chartres, had come into her life, astounding her with the news that he was her father, that she was his only living child and his heir. He had invited her to France, brought her into Radiance, settled a fortune upon her, introduced her to Jock and tried to convince her of the wisdom of marrying Jock.

Ironically, Liz had repaid Roger's generosity and

trust by marrying his greatest rival, but Jock knew that Roger had forgiven his daughter.

Roger had been enraged when he learned that Mikki had thrown Liz out. Six months later, when it was apparent she had totally disappeared, Roger grew so desperate that he humbled himself and went to talk with the son-in-law in London he detested, despite the bitter dispute over the formula.

What transpired between them behind the locked doors of Mikki's office, Jock never knew, but after that Roger never spoke ill of Mikki again. Even now, when the newspapers hinted that Mikki had had a part in the explosion of Dazzle's lab, Roger defended him. "The journalists are crazy. He didn't do it."

Jock knew he should let the subject of Roger and Mimi drop; Liz's mind was completely closed against her father. But for some reason he did not.

"Liz, do you resent Mimi so much that you have decided to have nothing to do with your own father?"

Liz trembled. It wasn't that she resented Mimi. Her feelings were more complex than mere resentment. "I don't resent Mimi. In my short acquaintance with my 'real' father, I realized he is the kind of man who will always have a beautiful, smiling face before him. My mother once fulfilled that role. Now he has Mimi."

"There is much more to Mimi than a beautiful face or a smile."

Liz shivered. Maybe that was what had always bothered her. Mimi was not the person she presented to the world.

"Mimi's real story has never been published," Jock said. "She grew up in Marseilles on the waterfront. She clawed her way from the pit of her hellish birth and degrading poverty to the dazzling pinnacle of world stardom. She is a very strong lady who knows how to get what she wants."

"You mean she sleeps with rich men now as indiscriminately as she once slept with poor."

Jock shrugged. There seemed nothing more he could say. As always, Liz refused to listen to any defense of her father. There had always been some difficulty between her and Mimi. It was not like Liz to be bitter and unfair. As always, he wondered why.

"So there's no chance for us?" Jock asked at last, changing the subject. His voice held resignation. "I can feel the difference in you. Mikki—"

She moved into the circle of his arms because he was a dear and cherished old friend, and he was French and expected her to.

"It's always been Alexander, Jock. I wish things could be different. I really do. If only it were you, and not Alexander." She kissed him gently then on the lips in parting.

"Yes, if only," he murmured, aroused by the warmth of her lips. He released her mouth reluctantly. "Will you tell Mikki I came?"

"I don't think so. It would only upset him to know that we've been together, however innocently."

Neither of them knew that someone was watching them.

Chapter Ten

It was a beautiful evening with lavender skies and an orange sunset. A week had passed since the night of terror, a week in which Juan had been arrested, a week of constant togetherness between husband and wife that had deepened the bond of love Liz felt toward Alexander.

Alex had come home from the hospital the day before, and though the child was pale and listless, he was improving.

Liz enjoyed tending to Alexander. She hoped that by showing him kindness, he would feel her love.

That particular evening Liz stepped into Alexander's bedroom to collect his supper tray and saw that he was sitting barechested at the writing table. Without his shirt, he exuded a primitive maleness that made him seem even more dangerous than ever.

His supper tray was untouched.

"Alexander!" He looked up and met the challenge of

her gaze. There was warmth in his eyes. "You haven't eaten your soup like I told you to."

He eyed her stiff form. "Obeying orders is not my strong suit," he said easily. "I'm tired of eating chicken soup."

"But it's so good for you. You delight in being deliberately difficult."

"If wanting to eat something for dinner besides chicken soup is being difficult, then I'm difficult. This is the third night in a row."

"Alex is eating his soup. He's six, and he's much easier to take care of than you are, Alexander. He does what I tell him."

"Perhaps, my dear, you should use different tactics on a man than with a child. Maybe he likes it when you're bullying and hard with him. I don't."

"I'm never bullying and hard with him," Liz cried. "I have to tease him and tempt him with things he likes."

She moved into the room, her skirts swaying over her hips as she began straightening things. Golden male eyes gleamed with new intensity as they trailed over her curves. "Perhaps I could be persuaded to eat too, if you were soft and teasing. If you tempted me—with things I like," he said in a beguiling, silken tone.

The back of her neck went hot. She flushed scarlet and felt shivery because his words and his voice stirred her senses alarmingly. She avoided looking at him while she brought herself under control.

"I might even eat cold chicken soup for the third night in a row," he murmured devilishly. "Why don't you come over here and tempt me?"

She snapped the stem of a flower she'd been adjusting in the vase by the window. She whirled around to glare at him. "Frankly, I don't care if you do starve." Those were just words. Her heart was pounding like a startled bird's as he rose and moved nearer.

His mouth twitched with suppressed amusement. "That's obvious. If you really wanted me to eat, you'd bring me a steak or some tantalizing French dish with a rich sauce."

There was something in his manner that alarmed her.

"All right! I'll bring you a steak or veal swimming in cream and mushroom sauce. Whatever you want. Right now."

"I don't want a steak or veal—right now."

"What do you want?"

"Why do you always ask questions when the answer's so obvious?"

When he moved toward her, she felt like running, but he caught her arms. His mesmerizing gaze told of loneliness and overwhelming need, of hopelessness and of desire. She saw as well a flicker of his old warmth and regard.

If only . . . if only he could love her again.

His hands moved slowly over her body, making her skin tingle. Very gently his fingers slid along her throat under her chin, and he tilted her face for his inspection.

"Liz, it would be so much easier if I could hate you."

She scarcely breathed. In the hushed silence she was aware of his rough fingertips moving against her flesh, in her hair, over her body. He knew too well how to touch a woman. He lowered his black head to hers with a suppressed groan, and she closed her eyes as his mouth covered hers.

The contact was intimate and sensual, bringing the thrill of sexual arousal. She trembled under the force of the earth-shattering emotions that shuddered through her.

At last his mouth released hers, but his hands on her back continued to press her into the angular contours of his body. His voice against her lips was a husky tremor that told her he was as shaken as she.

"Liz, Dazzle is in the midst of a crisis I need to resolve. I've got to go back to London immediately, but I want you and the twins to come with me even though I can't—" He hesitated. He didn't want to hurt her.

She opened her eyes and looked into his and saw his doubt and desire and compassion.

"Make promises that you can't keep," she finished.

Her skin was flushed with the blooming, soft warmth of a velvet rose. He buried his face in her hair. "God help me, Liz, I can't go back without you," he muttered raggedly. "I ache for you. I burn for you. The board will lynch me, but when I think of those seven hellish years—"

The pain in his voice ripped her emotions and filled her with guilt to know that she caused him such torture.

"I don't know how I feel about you," he said. "I need time. But the children want to come, and I don't want to leave either of them, especially right now, not with Alex convalescing, not with the possibility of Juan's relatives seeking some sort of revenge for my having pressed charges against him."

"How can I leave the factory when so many people here have come to depend on me, Alexander?"

"Liz, I can help you improve the managerial structure of your factory so that we can oversee it from abroad."

"It won't be easy for you, Alexander, if I come back. Your family, everyone at Dazzle believes I betrayed you."

"No," he agreed, "it won't be easy—for either of us. But think about it, and give me your answer tomorrow. I want to leave the next day."

She thought of the long, empty years that had separated them, of the gulf of misunderstanding that still separated them. Quiet tears filled her eyes.

"I don't need to wait until tomorrow to tell you," she

answered huskily, knowing she would do anything, promise anything in order to stay near him. "Alexander, I'll come back with you."

"Thank you," he said softly, brushing her lips with his fingertips.

His expression was grave, and when she read the doubt in his eyes, she began to sob.

"Don't cry about it, Liz. Just let me love you now," he whispered hoarsely as he possessed her lips.

Liz clasped Alexander, careful of his bandaged back. She clung to him in wild, dizzying abandon, withholding nothing, giving herself totally.

Her mouth moved from his lips to touch every intimate place of his body. No woman had ever made love to him as she did in that long wild night.

At one point he said, "You're a talented little despoiler yourself." She merely laughed.

Trembling fingers stripped his clothes from his hard body and caressed him until he was feverish and shaking with male need. The scorching, featherlight fingertips were followed by the molten, seductive tracings of her flicking tongue.

Where had she learned to love a man like this? he wondered as her silken tongue slid over his skin, arousing blazing, shivery sensations. He had not taught her. Yet she had said there had never been anyone else.

As she kissed him, her wanton tenderness was like a flame licking at the thick block of ice that had encased his frozen heart for seven years. Something inside him melted with each stirring kiss, with each velvet caress, until the pleasure of that moist tongue was too exquisite to be borne. He dragged her into his arms once more.

He pulled her down on top of himself, cupping her breasts with each of his hands, plunging deep within the warm bonds of her flesh as her hair spilled in a sweeping mass over his face. He plunged again and again, wanting to lose himself in her, wanting to love her forever. They soared like the blaze of a comet's path across a hot, star-filled sky over a wild, restless sea. Alexander brought her to peak after peak of sobbing surrender. Trembling waves of excitement washed her body, leaving her breathless and shattered, limp and softly, breathlessly loving as she tenderly kissed his damp cheek. It was that last gentle kiss that pushed him over the fine edge of control. When the curl of pink tongue licked his earlobe caressingly, he could hold back no longer, and he took his satisfaction in a shuddering burst of glory.

Afterward, as he lay in her arms, he experienced a feeling of total fulfillment and contentment, and he knew that even in the darkest hour of her betrayal, he had never stopped loving her. He cradled Liz gently in his arms.

Feeling ridiculously happier than he had in years, Alexander awoke the next morning and reached for Liz only to discover she was gone. Then he heard her voice drifting up from the patio. Her Spanish, which was always atrociously ungrammatical, was even more so when she was excited. No one could murder the beauty of a Romance tongue more enthusiastically than Liz. She was arguing passionately with Manuel over the solution to a problem in the doll factory. Alexander listened to the fervor in her voice with a lazy smile, recalling her wild sensuality of the night before. This morning she was equally impassioned. He longed to see her, to kiss her again, to press her against his body, to hear her ardent voice change into husky whimperings and moans.

This morning he was hungry to see her again. He thrust the sarapes aside and got out of bed. He stripped and strode into the bathroom. When he discovered the hot water was off, and he was going to have to shower and shave without it, he cursed Liz and Mexico and everything he could think of in a loud, roaring voice that could be heard clear to the doll factory. Fortunately this abusive storm was in French, and only Liz, who doubled over in laughter, understood him.

"Is it a national pastime to turn off the burners of the hot-water heaters everywhere in Mexico?" he railed. He was still grumbling to himself and dressing hurriedly because of the chilled air when Samantha skipped into his room. Behind her Maria carried his breakfast tray. He glanced at them both with annoyance because his hunger for his wife burned in him savagely. Maria spread out the sumptuous meal and laid a copy of the *Excelsior* beside Alexander's plate while Samantha chattered brightly. Alexander felt trapped and out of sorts, yet there was nothing for it but to eat breakfast. Samantha would be crushed if he left without eating.

Samantha sat opposite her father at the table and watched in silence as he ate *huevos rancheros* and sipped his coffee while he skimmed the financial section of the newspaper. She did not understand his mood. Usually he was so attentive. Today none of her usual gambits entranced him.

"How's Alex?" Alexander asked absently, his thoughts really on his wife.

Samantha felt his lack of interest, and she pursed her lips. It was a look that spelled trouble. "He's still sleeping," she said.

"Don't you wake him," Alexander admonished without looking up.

Samantha did not like to be given orders. Bored and feeling ignored, Samantha shrugged and everything on the table jumped.

Alexander caught his glass of orange juice before it fell over.

"Samantha!" This time he glanced up, but only briefly. Radiance had made the financial section of the *Excelsior*, and he was trying to read the article.

"I'm sorry!" the child said in a low, disgruntled tone. She sank back down on her chair, and then, forgetting the need to be still, she leaned forward on the table, tilting it.

Alexander looked up, and she guiltily lifted her elbows from the table too abruptly. The table straightened, sloshing juice and coffee.

Samantha would have done anything or said anything in that moment to get his attention. Suddenly her agile mind seized on the most disturbing topic she could think of, something she'd been bursting to tell for nearly a week. Before Alexander could return to his newspaper, Samantha spoke importantly. "If you leave tomorrow, I'll bet you'll be sorry. 'Cause you know what? If you leave, Mother's going to marry Uncle Jock."

This time he did look up, and he stared straight into her eyes with a fierce look.

"What? Where in the world did you get an idea like that?"

Samantha clammed up with fear. "Nowhere."

"Tell me what you're talking about this minute, young lady."

Samantha was momentarily too intimidated not to answer. "He was here again, and I saw him kissing Mother!"

Alexander's face darkened. "What do you mean?"

The words rushed from the little girl in a panic. "Uncle Jock came the morning after Juan burned Alex. You were still asleep, and Mother said I couldn't come upstairs till you woke up. That's how come I saw them kissing."

"Are you sure you didn't imagine this?"

"Why don't big people ever believe me?" Samantha cried, stung by his doubt. "I didn't imagine Juan in my bedroom, did I? And I didn't make up Uncle Jock kissing Mother either. Take us away, Daddy, please, before he comes back and kisses her again." Samantha jumped out of her chair and leaped into her father's steely arms. "I don't want Mother to kiss anybody ever again 'cept you, Daddy." She considered. "And me and Alex."

Alexander swallowed the bitter bile clogging his throat, his emotions raging in turmoil. Jock here. Liz kissing him when she knew how Alexander, her husband, felt about Jock? Was his wife such a skilled liar, such a skilled lover that she could go from one man to another? She had said Jock was not her lover, and like a fool, he had believed her. Liz had not mentioned Jock's visit.

He realized his anger was sweeping aside his ability to be fair-minded. Had Samantha misinterpreted what she had seen? Shouldn't he give Liz the benefit of the doubt and the chance to defend herself? But why should he? There were too many reasons for him to distrust her. She knew how he felt about Jock, and she had seen him anyway.

No, he would not confront her. That would only set her on guard. If he wanted to learn the ultimate truth about her character and the reasons behind her betrayal, he would have to ride her with a loose rein no matter how deeply she cut him with her treachery.

He set Samantha firmly on the floor. "Go outside and play," he said, not wanting to inflict his grim mood on the child.

She ran from the room, and he sat back and stared unseeingly at the article about Radiance. The warm desire to see Liz had left him, and his heart felt hard and cold.

Alexander was still gripped in his abysmal mood an hour later when his older half brother, Paul, called from Paris. Paul skipped the amenities.

"A most unpleasant rumor has come to my attention, Mikki."

"What, precisely?" Alexander drawled, feeling irritated at the hysteria in his brother's voice.

"That the reason you have been gone so long is that you have found Liz and have reconciled with her."

"What if I have?"

"It's the end of your career at Dazzle."

"Why?" Alexander's voice was low and dangerous.

"How can you ask the obvious, Mikki?" Paul shrieked.

"She is my wife."

"The board cannot forget she almost ruined the company."

"That was never proven in a court of law," Alexander stated coldly, wondering cynically himself even as he did why he was bothering to defend Liz.

"We have evidence that one of the employees from your office visited our Swiss lab, supposedly on your orders, the night before the explosion. We're not sure yet if the purpose was to incriminate you or steal something vital."

"I know. Michelle."

"You know?"

"What does all this have to do with Liz?"

"We suspect Michelle is connected to Radiance. Liz is Roger Chartres's daughter and his chosen heir to Radiance. She sees Jock on a regular basis. But, of course, you cannot be ignorant of that fact. Jock was in Mexico visiting her not six days ago. Don't tell me he managed that without your knowledge? What is going on with you, Mikki, that you can lie to me about the reason you're in Mexico and then entertain Jock Rocheaux?"

"I did not entertain Jock."

"Then it was your accommodating wife who welcomed him so warmly. There was a time when you would not have stood by—"

"Shut up, Paul, damn you."

"Not before I give you some big-brotherly advice. Forget Liz. She's trouble. Disaster. You will not be able to keep the presidency of Dazzle unless you come back to London without her. For once, where she is concerned, do the smart thing."

"And my children?"

"Get custody."

"Liz won't give them up. Besides, they need her."

"If you bring Liz home with you, no one here will trust you."

"Not even you?"

There was a long silence before the line went dead, and Alexander had his answer.

So, at least part of Samantha's story about Jock having visited Liz had been confirmed. Did all of Europe know that his wife received Jock's attentions even when at the same time she made the most passionate love to her husband?

Alexander replaced the receiver and strode downstairs to the garage. He would take Liz's car and drive into Mexico City to wrap up a few business problems he'd planned to leave in the capable hands of his subordinates. Now that the last thing he wanted was to spend the day with Liz, he decided he would handle these matters himself.

Alexander was easing the car out of the garage when the soft sound of his name being called stopped him. Liz was in the drive, looking beautiful in a gauzy dress.

He braked, and she came to the car and leaned into the open window. The scent of her assailed him. The sight of her entranced him and made his stomach quiver with an odd pain despite the fresh evidence of her treachery. Alexander looked at her, his face twisting with conflicting emotions.

"Where are you going in such a hurry that you didn't even say good morning?" she asked in her husky, bedroom voice that stirred hot, sensual memories.

"I have something to do in Mexico City," he said curtly. His lonely, black despair had closed around him, smothering him, and he ruthlessly and deliberately shut her out.

"Oh." Her courage faltered, but still she managed to ask, "Alone?"

"Alone," he replied grimly.

"Be careful," was all she said in a tiny, forlorn tone as she retreated from the car.

"Your concern overwhelms me," he snarled, his voice harsh because his own pain was acute. He accelerated and the car whipped past her. Liz stared after him, stunned.

"Alexander," she murmured in bewilderment, chewing the edge of a nail as she watched the Fiat jolt around the bend in the rutted dirt road. She buried her face in her hands.

Had everything come to this? She'd tried so hard. She'd been kind, patient, even when he'd been rude and difficult, and slowly she'd sensed the beginnings of a change in him. Last night . . . Deliberately, she suppressed the glory of his lovemaking. It was too painful to think of now. She sobbed desperately. Was it all to come to nothing?

After a few moments, when she had managed to calm herself, she turned to go back into the hacienda. For the rest of the day she agonized over his departure. She couldn't understand why he had left so abruptly. Why had he deliberately wanted to hurt her, when this week he had begun to treat her at times with kindness and even tenderness? Now he was angrier at her than ever.

Chapter Eleven

Liz and Alexander ate dinner in the dining room that night. When she entered the room, he glanced at her warily. Liz's hesitant smile was soft and warm and beautiful, and Alexander was caught for a moment in the spell of it before he reminded himself she probably smiled just as warmly for Jock.

Liz's joy at seeing him was instantly dashed when his dark, brooding face hardened with contempt. When he returned from Mexico City late that afternoon he had not sought her out. She suspected he had avoided her all day because he regretted their closeness of the night before. Now his harshness confirmed her worst fears.

She wore a long black strapless gown. The dress was cut daringly low in the back, the tantalizing vee crisscrossed with silken black lacings. His eyes were hot and dark and ravaging, but his scowl only deepened. It maddened him that he had only to look at her to feel bewitched by her beauty.

He bowed stiffly and helped her into her chair. As

she sat down, his eyes ran down the creamy length of her bare back, the warm, smooth skin tempting his hand. He almost touched her, but he managed to stop himself in time. He balled his hands into fists and clenched them tightly until the pain of his nails biting into his palms distracted him.

The *carne asada* might as well have been burned cardboard. They ate in awkward silence, but they were keenly aware of each other. Liz felt the heat of his eyes frequently upon her, but when she glanced toward him, he deliberately looked away. It was only when dessert was served that Liz dared to speak.

"What time should I have the children ready tomorrow?" she ventured.

"As early as possible," came his terse reply.

"I'm looking forward to going home," she said shyly, trying to make light conversation, thinking that perhaps she had been wrong to humor him with silence.

He shot her an odd look, his heavy-lidded gaze cynical. "Really? Why?"

"There are so many reasons."

"I'm sure there are." That cutting, sardonic edge she hated had crept into his voice. He wondered if she was thinking of Jock, who would be more accessible to her when she was in London.

"For one thing, Alexander, I want to come home because of you—to try again."

"To try again." The words hung in the air between them, husband and wife interpreting their meaning differently. She meant she wanted to try to save their marriage, and he wondered if she meant she was determined to destroy him this time.

"To try what, my love?" He flashed her a look of deep bitterness.

"Alexander, I don't understand why you're so angry," she began uncertainly. "What have I done?

Please, don't close me out like this. If you would only tell me."

"I will tell you nothing," he growled. "And I will take you with me only on one condition."

"What condition?"

"You are not to see or even to speak to Jock again. Nor do I want you to communicate with your father, at least for now."

"I see."

"But will you promise me?" he demanded.

"I promise," she said, agreeing only because she felt forced to do so. "But why, Alexander? What have I done?"

She started to push back her chair from the table, and he was beside her at once, helping her. When she stood up, he towered over her, his eyes studying the arresting beauty of her still face. The tenderness and pleading in her eyes moved him much more than he wanted them to. His gaze wandered to her upturned red lips, lips that taunted him with their sensuality.

She felt faint under the intensity of his dark stare.

"You ask what you have done?" his harsh voice mocked her gentle question as his hard brown hand moved beneath the curve of her chin and lifted it. His other hand caressed the smooth skin of her neck, but there was something threatening in his light touch. "What have you not done to destroy me would be a better question, my love. Once you nearly cost me my career. Are you such a witch that you demand my soul as well?"

"All I've ever wanted is your love."

"Then we are at cross purposes, my sweet. All I require of you now is the pleasure of your voluptuous, talented body in my bed." His gaze roamed insultingly over her soft curves to where the bright sheen of black silk plunged between her breasts.

Shame scorched her. "Alexander, please don't deliberately humiliate me," she begged quietly. "I don't want to destroy you. I love you."

Though he did not want them to, her velvet-soft words stirred him. He lifted his eyes and studied the becoming flush that tinted her ivory complexion with delicate color. She looked vulnerable and innocent. He watched her pink tongue nervously wet her lips, and he felt a wave of intense desire.

"My beautiful Liz," he whispered as he gathered her in his arms, despising himself for his weakness. Like the Sirens of mythology, whose song lured men to their destruction, she lured him. Nothing mattered but his need. He could almost forget that she probably offered herself just as shamelessly to Jock.

Liz was just as affected by him. She trembled from his embrace, from the heady nearness of him, the male scent of him hanging heavy in her nostrils. He crushed her to him fiercely, possessively, seeking to obliterate the image of her kissing Jock from that black corner of his mind where it lingered.

She slid her arms about his neck; she could feel his heart pounding against her breast. His powerful body was shaking as he leaned down, and his mouth closed over hers savagely in a forceful, demanding kiss. They clung together, each hoping for a clue to the other's heart.

Alexander kissed her long and deeply, his tongue plunging into her mouth before he lifted her into his arms and strode out of the dining room, across the patio, and inexorably bore her up the stairs to his bedroom. She held on to him, frightened yet eager, clinging, her mouth responsive beneath the suffocating pressure of his.

He laid her upon the bed and sank beside her, his fingers deftly unfastening the zipper of her gown and then the intricate network of lacings. The touch of his hands sent rivulets of fiery sensation radiating across her skin.

Black silk peeled, revealing the warm lush fruit of her opulent female flesh.

"Delicious," he murmured, sucking the nipple of her breast until it stood erect, pouting temptingly beneath his lips. He sucked its thrusting twin, and then let his tongue nibble the entire globe as though he were starved for the sweetness of her.

Sliding the dress downward until it fell in a pool at the foot of the bed, his hands wandered over her body, cupping her breasts, sliding over the curve of her belly, caressing her waist and hips, running the length of her slim legs and then returning to touch the velvet dampness of her womanhood with slow, gentle strokes. He lowered his head to kiss the soft folds of flesh.

She gasped and tried to push him away, but he subdued her easily, her puny efforts at resistance proving futile against his superior strength. With one hand he pinned her wrists to the bed and continued to have his way with her, returning to taste her tart nectar.

Much later his lips sought the pleasure of her trembling mouth again, and he kissed her long and insolently until she was weak and shaking from his hungry kisses.

"You are beautiful, my wanton, treacherous witch," he stated in a low voice before he left her briefly to shed his own clothes.

She watched him strip, his brown fingers jerking roughly at the knot of his tie, then ripping the loose, dangling ribbons from his neck, shrugging out of his suit jacket, unbuttoning his shirt. He ripped the shirt off, and with it came the last remnant of civilization. His bare chest and shoulders were bronzed and rippled with muscle. To Liz he seemed a primitive male, dangerously relentless and all-powerful.

Her senses clamored in response to the power of his

pagan male appeal. Hurriedly he unsnapped his trousers and slid them down. When he came to her again, she gasped as he fused her body to his dark, virile length, the warm hardness of his naked flesh against her own, rocking her senses.

She longed for some shred of gentleness in his lovemaking, but he gave her none. He was determined to use her body and ask nothing from her soul and heart. Though his lips explored her with ruthless thoroughness, and her blood pounded in her veins, she felt the loss of something infinitely precious. She wanted love and tenderness and commitment, and he gave her only hedonistic sensuality.

She realized he was deliberately humiliating her. She hated that part of herself that reveled in his touch, and she began to struggle in the futile effort to save for herself some last remnant of pride.

"Don't do this to us," she begged. "Please, Alexander, you must stop this mad, destructive course you're determined to take. If you can't love me, let me go."

He laughed that soft, cynical laugh she hated, that low male sound that mocked them both. "How can you sound so naive when you don't want my love any more than I want yours, my tantalizing witch? All you want is this. Doubtless any man would do." He was thinking specifically of Jock.

He was about to lower his mouth to hers when she cried out in fury and lunged to slap him. He caught her hands in one swift movement and held them in his iron grip as he wrenched them behind her and lowered her back on the bed.

"I'm your wife," she murmured desperately, "the mother of your children. Have you lost all respect for me?"

"Respect?" He laughed at that. "I told you, you have only one thing I want now." He lowered his mouth and kissed the satin button tip of her pink breast, punctuating the point he was making with the whirl of his tongue against her nipple. "You are my wife in name only." His tongue licked again, leisurely, expertly, and a series of shivers radiated inward from the moist, sensitive surface of her skin. "I intend to use you as a mistress, nothing more. And that, my dear, is much much more than you deserve. I'm a fool not to throw you out."

She felt wretched with heartbreak. "Then I'll not let you," she said tonelessly. "Just because I love you, that doesn't mean I have to allow you to rob me of my self-respect."

"You can't stop me, love." His eyes were dark and merciless, but his hands were gentle on her body. He knew so well how to touch, how to caress, how to inflame. "You don't even want to stop yourself," he whispered. "Your own body betrays you."

Violently she kicked at him, and he laughed at her and she knew he enjoyed her struggles, the feel of her soft warm skin twisting erotically against his. When she jumped at him fiercely in one last burst of energy, he avoided her blow by twisting aside. His grip on her wrists slackened, and she jerked free and lunged toward the opposite side of the bed.

He caught her and pulled her back, rolling on top of her writhing body, pinning her arms beneath her, forcing his hot mouth on top of hers, kissing her again and again until her anger gave way to another, equally powerful emotion. Desire made her ache as his tongue thrust deeply inside, slowly, lingeringly and, in the end, gently.

At last he released her. "You belong to me," he murmured. "At least in bed. Tell me that you don't want me, and I'll let you go, Liz."

In the dim light his tanned skin seemed even darker, his hair even blacker than usual. There was a blazing wildness in his eyes. He looked like a primitive Indian or an ancient warlord, noble, proud and savage. He was shaking, and she knew that passion raged within him.

The will to stop him had left her. She stared up at him with a drowsy, voluptuous, yielding look. She existed only in a blurred world of sensation and carnal desire. He had won. She wanted him with such violent intensity that she could not deny her feelings even for the sake of her broken pride.

He lowered his lips and kissed her again. His hard mouth ground her lips against her teeth in a kiss that bespoke domination and mastery. She was his, hopelessly, desperately his. She was his for whatever casual, meaningless pleasure or use he wanted to make of her. It was useless to struggle or to ask for more than he was willing to give.

Wild pagan needs throbbed in her blood beneath his ruthless, expert caresses until she thought she would die without physical release. His fierce embraces gentled. He teased her with his languorous, slow lovemaking, withholding that which she craved with every fiber in her body as if to torture her as he was tortured by his own pulsating need of her.

She was quivering, begging him to take her even when some inner force screamed that she had lost all pride to allow herself to be so humbled by her love for him. But what good was pride, if she lost even this last glimmer of the fire that remained of their love? She loved him, and he wanted her. It was the one bond that still held him. If she denied him her body, he was lost to her forever.

For love of him she had no choice but to risk her heart, and soul, and pride.

Alexander's lips sought all the erotic places of her body, using his mouth to bring her the most exquisite sensual pleasure, until at last she moaned his name in ardent, mind-shattering surrender.

Her soft crooning made his passion rage out of control, the male in him satisfied that at least he could drive her as wild as she drove him, and he carried her with him to peaks of blazing ecstasy that left them dazzled by the volcanic glory of their union.

He took her again and again that night. He used her brutally, forcefully, and yet there was rapture in his fierce embrace, which ignited a mutual fire that devoured all save their desire one for the other.

When it was over, they lay on the soft mattress amid tangled sheets, plump pillows and scratchy sarapes, their moist bodies still touching, neither daring to speak.

He had conquered her, but in so doing she had conquered him. Neither was conscious of victory; each only of defeat.

Chapter Twelve

A gray slanting rain was falling when the Vorzenski jet touched down in London's Gatwick Airport. Alexander and Liz had flown to New York and spent the night there on their way to London so that Alexander could talk to Jon and Philippe, two of his cousins on the Dazzle board.

Liz felt weary and wrinkled from the flight. The children were tired and irritable. A customs official waited at the gate. Several journalists stood in an agitated cluster beside him, all of them jostling for a favorable position on the rain-slick concrete runway. There was a television crew with cameras.

At the sight of the crowd, Alexander swore to himself. Publicity was the last thing he needed; he had hoped to avoid it until he had made the board accept his reconciliation with Liz. Alexander stepped outside, his dark face a mask that revealed nothing of his misgivings as he smiled and invited the customs official on board.

When the press clamored to be admitted as well, he told them that he regretted there was not enough room to invite all of them inside the jet.

Once the passports and luggage had been cleared, Alexander called airport security to find out if his pilot could radio George, his chauffeur, to drive to the gate in order to avoid a scene with the press. Permission was granted, and when he saw the Vorzenski Rolls, Alexander helped Liz and the children disembark. They were instantly surrounded; microphones were thrust in front of their mouths. Flashbulbs popped in their faces as rapidly as the reporters' questions.

"I'm from the *London Times*. Prince Vorzenski, is it true that you have reconciled with your wife? That you have only recently discovered you are the father of twins?"

"Prince, do you consider that your marriage represents a conflict of interests? Will you continue as president of Dazzle when your wife is connected to Radiance? What do you have to say about your name being linked to the bombing at your Swiss lab?"

"Look this way, Princess, and give our readers a big smile!"

"Princess, do you plan a return to your career as a designer? Is it true that you have been manufacturing dolls in Mexico?"

To all these questions, Alexander replied curtly, "No comment, gentlemen." He whispered to Liz, "Smile, darling. Wolves bite harder if they think you're frightened of them."

The boldest journalist, an aging, obese man, jumped in front of Liz. He leered into her face. "Princess, why did you run away seven years ago? Is it true that you married the prince to steal Dazzle's formula? Isn't it a fact that you're still determined to ruin him?"

Liz's expression froze. An odd, frantic feeling built inside of her. Was this what everyone really thought of her? That she was a monster? She felt defiled by his insinuations, and she wanted to run, to be alone, to escape even Alexander.

Seeing the desperation in her face, Alexander realized how close she was to hysteria, and he felt intensely protective toward her. He stepped between Liz and the man, grabbing the burly fellow by the lapels. "Leave my wife alone, do you hear? What kind of man are you to bully a woman?"

For an instant a breathless hush descended on the crowd as everyone reacted to the dangerous aura of Alexander. His tawny gold eyes had changed to fierce black glitter in his hard face. The powerful leashed force within him that he always fought to curb was barely held in check. Effortlessly, Alexander lifted the man onto his toes.

The man's eyes bulged with fear as Alexander set him down, but a hundred flashbulbs burst at once. Liz flinched as she realized that by trying to help her, Alexander had only worsened things for himself. The press would crucify him now.

To Liz, Alexander whispered reassuringly, "It's almost over. Get in the car and let me handle this." He guided her gently toward the door.

She smiled at him gratefully, his touch and the proximity of his tall, muscular body imparting comfort and security.

The door of the silver Rolls swung open and Liz stepped thankfully inside, the wide-eyed twins and Alexander right behind her. The children climbed into the back seat and stared out the rear window, gaping at the journalists.

"I'm afraid that you made headlines when you grabbed that reporter," Liz said softly after Alexander shut the door. "And all because of me."

He regarded her pale, anxious face warily as he sank into the seat beside her. For an instant a strange feeling of excitement and happiness twisted his stomach before he reminded himself what a hypocrite she was. These were the hardest moments of all for him—when Liz pretended caring and concern.

"You're probably right," he replied in a low, tired tone. He was already angry with himself for the way he had acted. Normally he was cool in his dealings with the press, never showing any irritation even when he was furious. The trouble this afternoon was that he'd gone insane when that man had been bullying Liz and she'd looked so frightened and lost. Nothing had mattered to him in that moment except protecting Liz. When he thought of his behavior he considered it irrational, and himself a fool.

"It seems that I make things worse for you without even trying," she said in a small voice.

He laughed softly in his taunting way as he regarded her white, beautiful face again.

"I never . . ." She broke off, realizing the uselessness of defending herself.

"Always innocent, aren't you, my dear?" His gaze dropped insolently to her body. "When will you realize you can stop playing that part with me? It's not innocence I want from you." He looked away, but the gesture did nothing to rid her of the scorching shame of her humiliation. "I'm sure you realize, Liz, that the scene at the airport was nothing compared to what will take place when I face the board tonight."

"Tonight?"

He nodded grimly. "My enemies are going to demand my head on a silver platter, and likely as not, they'll get it."

"Because of me?"

"You're one of the reasons."

She flinched. "Oh, I almost wish I hadn't come."

"But wasn't that why you came?" Glinting gold eyes swept her solemn face in cold amusement. "It's a pity

you won't be there to witness my execution, love. You
would enjoy it."

She gasped.

"What, love?" His voice was deliberately cruel.
"Haven't you the stomach to see the blood you've
spilled? I'm surprised."

How could he believe that? Her gaze dropped to her
lap, and unconsciously she fingered the amethyst pen-
dant she was wearing, feeling completely dejected by
his coldness.

"Alexander," she murmured in a choked tone,
"please, don't believe that about me." It took all her
courage to lift her face and look at him.

He loomed closer beside her, dwarfing her, forcing
her to tilt her bright head back to meet the angry glitter
of his gaze.

Their eyes met, and the luminous concern in hers
made him feel guilty for his harshness before he
reminded himself that she was probably acting and that
he would be a fool to trust any show of kindness from
her. Unthinkingly, Liz reached for his hand, and his
shook when she touched him.

"Alexander, please. It is so difficult for me to fight
for us when even you are against me."

He was staring at her slim hand on top of his own,
which was still shaking. He was appalled that her
slightest touch could make him tremble as though with
a seizure. Good grief! he thought, despising himself. I
want her love so desperately, I could take on the world
if she truly cared. It wouldn't matter if I lost Dazzle, if I
lost everything, if only I could have her. Without her, I
will be nothing even if I win at everything else.

Aloud, he said deprecatingly, "There's no need for
you to distress yourself, my love. I'm sure you're much
closer to victory than you realize. Content yourself with
the thought that your wantonness binds me to you and

makes me capable of the most self-destructive behavior. There's scarcely a chance of you failing." His eyes stripped her, ravished her, branding her with the fire of his unwanted desire.

Her face turned ashen when she caught his meaning. Their bodies were close. Against her shoulders, she felt the heat of his curved arm stretched across the back of her seat. He moved slightly, and the granite-hard muscles of his thigh pressed against hers.

His thoughts plunged him into an utterly black mood, and he wrenched his hand from hers and forced his gaze to turn away. Never had London seemed more dismal to him, as the rain slashed against the hood of the speeding car. Much later he roused himself and began to point out the sights to the children when they reached the Chelsea Bridge and crossed the Thames, the limousine threading its way in the thick traffic of Chelsea Bridge Road and Sloan Street.

The noise of London was extinguished as the Rolls sped toward the townhouse that Alexander had leased in Belgravia for the past six years from Gerald Grosvenor, duke of Westminster, the richest landlord in London. The house was on a quiet back street a short distance from Hyde Park and the gardens of Buckingham Palace. The residence would be convenient as well to Isobel's, Liz's shop in Knightsbridge.

Liz didn't care about the house, nor about the excitement of returning to London; she couldn't care about anything except surviving the next few hours and retaining the courage to go on.

She couldn't give up. But when she dared a glance at the immobile, dark figure of her husband, and felt so cut off from him, she was afraid. She was determined to find a way to save her marriage no matter how great the odds were against her success. She loved him. He'd been hurt because of what he considered her treachery, and she couldn't blame him for that. Wasn't she at least partially responsible because she hadn't told him that she was Roger Chartres's daughter? She'd been a fool to run away seven years ago. That had merely convinced everyone of her guilt. Now she was determined to fight no matter how much it hurt her. She had to do something, and quickly. If only he hadn't made her promise not to contact her father.

As the Rolls passed Belgrave Square, turned down a side street and pulled up in front of the house, Liz had her first clear view of Alexander's home. It was remarkably like its aristocratic neighbors on the street, enormous and grandiose with a classic stone exterior, like so many houses in London. The only difference was that a tangled wisteria vine ran up the grilled ironwork and the face of the stone building. The house was sedate and private, like the street, and Liz was thankful for that untamed vine, which lent rustic charm and a bit of wildness to the otherwise forbidding and austere building.

Alexander helped Liz from the car. As George unloaded the bags and the children scampered up and down the sidewalk, Alexander held Liz's arm. He didn't release her when he allowed the others to precede them into the house, and she was keenly aware of his towering presence. The scent of him made her conscious of a dull, unhappy ache inside her. If only . . . if only he would show some sign of affection outside the bedroom.

If only. Those two words said it all.

Inside the mansion, the rooms were grandly proportioned, with large windows to let in the sun when it chose to shine. The house was furnished with antiques, rare French rugs and paintings, the paintings belonging to the fabulous Vorzenski collection.

Samantha was jumping up and down in excitement,

and then she whispered something devilish into Alex's ear. The boy let out a yowl of delight just as Mrs. Benchley, Alexander's portly, staid housekeeper, stepped into the hall to greet them.

"Whose children, Prince?" She gaped as Alex ran his toy car along the top of a polished table that had once graced a Scottish castle centuries ago, and Samantha watched, fascinated.

Doubtless the table had received worse treatment during the past two hundred years by rough Scots, but that was no comfort to Mrs. Benchley. She had a peculiar reverence for antiques, if not for children, and her round face couldn't have puckered with more horror if the twins had been a stampede of wild orangutans.

"The children are mine," came the deep, familiar baritone that brooked neither disapproval nor unwanted questions. "We will need to interview a governess. In the fall they will attend school, but they will still need to be supervised in the afternoons. You will see to that, won't you, Mrs. Benchley?"

"Of course, my lord." Mrs. Benchley's eyes widened as she watched Samantha streak past a Rodin sculpture to yank Alex's hair because he had stolen her doll.

Alex screamed, but he dropped the doll. Not in time, though, to avoid Samantha's revenge. Another yowl erupted when she pinched him sharply on the arm.

"I don't believe you've met my housekeeper, Mrs. Benchley, Liz," Alexander began, introducing an embarrassed Liz in the midst of the hubbub while Liz tried in vain to subdue the children. Liz felt nervous, and Mrs. Benchley's disapproval only made her feel all the more so. Alexander's hand remained possessively on his wife's elbow as the two women exchanged courtesies, and somehow it gave Liz the courage to smile at the staid housekeeper, who was doubtless marveling at the necessity of introducing his wife of some seven years and his two six-year-old twins. An odd turn of events, to say the least.

Ana Lou, the upstairs maid, appeared on the stair. "Why, what precious children, my lord."

The entire staff referred to their prince as "my lord" because he would not allow them to use his title.

Mrs. Benchley gaped at her maid. Ana Lou was the oldest sister from a family of seven, and she had a way with children.

"I can see they don't know what to do with themselves after a long day of travel," Ana Lou said with understanding. "You poor dears. It must have been terrible to be all cramped up for hours and hours." She came down the stairs, her young face warm and friendly. "How would you like some biscuits and milk, and I could tell you stories. Later we could explore the garden."

"In England biscuits are cookies," Alex said wisely.

"Oh, tell us stories," Samantha cried, unimpressed by her brother's attempt to show off. "About monsters and snakes."

Ana Lou laughed and took them each by the hand. "I know some giant stories," she began.

Neither child objected to giants, and Ana Lou led them away. At their departure, all was as silent and regally grand as before.

Liz wondered if it would be possible to fit herself and her two lively children into Alexander's elegant and well-ordered household. She was beginning to fear she had made a dreadful mistake returning with him. The housekeeper's next words did little to cheer her.

"Your brother, Mr. Paul Rocheaux, has been calling all afternoon, my lord," Mrs. Benchley said. "He says it's urgent that you return his call at once."

Liz felt Alexander's fingers tense on her arm. She raised her eyes uncertainly to his, but he deliberately avoided her gaze. She had known they would have no time together, no period of adjustment, but she hadn't really let herself believe it would begin the minute they stepped inside the house.

"Thank you, Mrs. Benchley." Alexander's level voice betrayed no emotion. "I will attend to that at once. Mrs. Benchley, will you show my wife to our room upstairs and send someone to assist her in unpacking?"

"Of course, my lord." She nodded and was gone. Orders were barked crisply and servants scurried, gathering pieces of luggage.

Alexander looked at Liz. "So you have survived your first encounter with the indomitable Mrs. Benchley. I advise you to take the upper hand with her from the first. Though she can be stubborn at times, she is an excellent woman. I would hate to dismiss her."

Liz realized he had remained at her side to help her during what he knew would be a difficult time for her. Not only that, but he was making it clear that the house was hers to run and that he would stand behind her. A little of her tension subsided. It was curious the way his protectiveness was at war with his determination to be cold and aloof. She never knew what to expect from him.

"I wish there were something I could do to help you, Alexander," Liz said impulsively in gratitude.

An arrogant brow arched in his aristocratic face to mock her. Once again his features hardened. She did not know that this happened because he wanted to mask the softness he felt. "Help me, my dear? Perhaps you would like to attend the board meeting tonight so you can wield the axe and gloat when my head rolls?"

She began to tremble, conscious of his searing eyes relentlessly fastened upon her. A startled cry of pain broke from her lips, and she whirled free of his grasp to mount the stairs and escape him.

"Liz—"

She ran even faster, and rather than make a scene, he watched her fleeing form disappear into the upper regions of the vast house before he turned and stalked down the hall to his study to call Paul. Alexander wanted to forget her, to immerse himself in the crisis at Dazzle. But he could not.

Seven years had not separated him from her even when he'd been determined to hate her. She had conquered even his fierce, stubborn will. There was no use running from her any longer. She was a part of him, albeit an unwanted part, and when he hurt her, he hurt himself. Damn it to hell! He loved her. He would have gone down on his knees and told her if he hadn't been sure that would only increase her contempt of him as well as her feeling of power over him. He wanted to forget her, but the vision of her stricken face remained with him long after he'd left the house and driven to Dazzle's offices.

Damn her. Damn himself for wanting her. Was that to be the perpetual circle of his thoughts?

Chapter Thirteen

The shades were drawn and the elegant silver room was dark and silent except for the blare of the newscast. Liz Vorzenski's ravished white face filled the screen before the camera was jostled and Mikki Vorzenski's face shielded her from view. Another camera caught the scenario of the prince dramatically protecting his wife from an overly zealous newsman.

The person on the brocade sofa in the dim room leaned forward tensely, hands clasped on knees, brows furrowed in determination to catch every word. When the newscast ended, the set was switched off by gloved fingers that shook with an overpowering emotion.

The sudden silence was startling, but the person in the room did not note it.

Liz had come back. She didn't look as radiant as she had as a bride seven years ago, so all was not patched up. But there must obviously have been some sort of reconciliation between Liz and Mikki, or Liz would not

have returned with him. The twins were adorable, but
that was something that didn't bear thinking about.

The person in the room felt like God. Hadn't the
Vorzenskis suffered enough? Seven years? Should
they now be allowed a normal lifetime of joys and
sorrows?

The mere thought bit like the pain of a dagger in an
unhealed wound and brought the stifling feelings of the
old madness and hatred. The possibility of any happiness between Mikki Vorzenski and Liz was as endur-
able as it had always been.

"Never! Never will I allow it."

Gloved fingers reached for the telephone and dialed.

The buzzing phone seemed as agitated as Liz's
thoughts, but she did not answer it because she remembered that in Alexander's house the phone was always
screened first by the staff.

Alexander's lavish suite included two bedrooms, two
baths, two dressing rooms and a sitting room between
the bedrooms. If Liz had not been so upset she would
have thought the rooms beautiful. As it was, the
subdued, elegant charm of the apartments scarcely
made an impression. Bleakly she observed that her
battered luggage had been placed on a pair of oak
luggage racks, and a maid had hung her clothes in the
massive closet that contained Alexander's.

Liz removed her heels and tiptoed across the soft
Aubusson carpet to the dressing table with its gilt-
framed, beveled mirrors. Her face was a stranger's face
with haunted black eyes and a drooping mouth. Her red
curls were a riotous, untamed mane. I look like an
unhappy clown, she thought dismally, without my
painted smile. She rummaged through her purse for a
lipstick.

In the mirror she could see the bed, which was

covered with a blue damask spread that matched the blue and gold brocade drapes. How long would she share Alexander's passion in that bed? She thought of the power of his bronzed body, the way he had clasped her so tightly to him only last night in New York. How long would she have even that? Desire without love to sustain it was bound to fade. She jerked her gaze from the bed, and her eyes flickered over the room and its furnishings.

A rich gold paper had been hung between lustrous wainscoting. In the bathroom there were fleecy towels monogrammed with golden, sloping Vs. Beside the fireplace in the sitting room were a white velvet sofa and two matching chairs. Everything down to the smallest detail was perfection, and Liz was reminded that Alexander was content only with the best.

This perfect suite for the not-so-perfect couple. How long would Alexander endure being half of a marriage that wasn't working?

The lipstick dropped from her shaking fingers and rolled across the dresser toward the wall, then tumbled over the edge noisily, so that it would be impossible to reach without summoning two men to move the heavy antique dresser from the wall. The lipstick hardly seemed worth that effort.

She paced restlessly. She didn't know what to do with herself in this grand, orderly house. Ana Lou had taken over the children, and for the present Liz was relieved about that. The flight had stretched her patience with Samantha's liveliness to its limit. But Liz would need something to do. In Mexico she had had the factory to run and the hacienda to manage.

She glanced at the phone beside the bed. After seven years she couldn't call old friends. They would be curious, and she wasn't ready for that. Her shop was closed for the rest of the weekend. She wondered if Ya

Lee, who'd been managing the business, would resent her now that she had returned. She would have to tread warily there too.

Liz's thoughts returned to Alexander. An hour ago she had stood forlornly at the windows and watched the rain spatter his ebony hair and the expensive coat covering his broad shoulders, as he leaned down and stepped into the Rolls. He'd never looked up or given a thought for an affectionate caress or good-bye kiss from his wife. She'd burst into a frenzy of tears.

Why couldn't she accept their marriage for what it was? She was the wife of a powerful and wealthy man, a man who desired her, a man who was a conscientious father. Doubtless many wives had less. As she'd watched the Rolls disappear in the blur of rain and traffic, the truth had come to her. She might never be able to prove her innocence. Her life might be filled with such cold departures silently viewed from upperstory windows. Alexander might never stop hating and resenting her for what he believed she had done.

The gold walls and drapes closed in upon her as suffocatingly as a prison. She couldn't stand the feelings of hopelessness much longer. Alexander had said he would be crucified by his family and the Dazzle board tonight because of her. Was there nothing she could do to improve her situation? What if she went and pleaded with the board in his behalf?

What could it hurt? Perhaps someone on the board would believe her. Surely his own mother couldn't be utterly heartless.

A glance in the mirror told her that a bit of color had come back into her cheeks. Her black eyes blazed with new courage as she rummaged through her clothes in Alexander's vast closet for something appropriate to wear. Though she didn't know it, in the eyes of the conservative board members, anything she wore would be wildly inappropriate.

She was pulling out a satin jacquard skirt and a velvet bodice and bolero with its billowing sleeves, outlandish garments of her own design, when a knock on the door and Mrs. Benchley's muffled voice from the hall interrupted her thoughts.

Liz opened the door, and the sternly disapproving Mrs. Benchley said, "Mr. Jock Rocheaux is on the phone, madam. I told him I did not think the prince wished you to be disturbed."

The gossip surrounding the enmity between Jock and Alexander had not escaped the housekeeper's ears. Liz remembered her promise to Alexander and knew she should say sweetly that, of course, her husband was right, that she was resting and could not speak to anyone this evening. But the thought of Alexander exacting such an unreasonable promise still angered her.

"Nonsense, Mrs. Benchley," Liz said with a sharp note of defiance. "Of course I'm not too tired to talk to Jock."

The thin mouth sagged alarmingly as Liz's hand touched the receiver. For a minute Liz thought Mrs. Benchley was not going to allow her to speak.

"As you wish, madam," Mrs. Benchley replied stiffly, relenting. "May I ask if there is anything else you require?"

Liz extended an armful of rumpled velvet and satin. "Would you have these pressed. I'm going out—immediately."

When the door shut and the hall outside was silent, Liz lifted the phone. Her hand was shaking.

"Jock!"

"Hello, Liz."

"Jock, Alexander made me promise never to speak to you."

"Really?" Jock did not sound in the least worried about this pronouncement. "Don't you think that's carrying the jealousy bit a little too far, even for Mikki? I'm surprised you're willing to let him play dictator, *chérie*. After all, you were raised in England, and there are more uppity women on this insignificant island than anywhere else in the world."

"I don't exactly have a choice right now."

"You always have a choice, but I did not call to discuss Mikki. I must see you at once."

"Jock, I can't. Alexander would never forgive me."

"Mikki be damned! Your father wants to see you, Liz. He saw you on television, and he has asked me to bring you to Paris."

"Oh."

"Liz, the man's brokenhearted. He said you believe he is responsible for wrecking your marriage to Mikki. He wants to explain and to apologize for what happened."

"So he admits he's responsible?" Liz asked dully.

"Not in so many words. You know Roger is hardly the kind of man to lay his feelings out on the table for my perusal. But, yes, he feels responsible."

"Jock, I made up my mind a long time ago that I didn't want to have anything more to do with a man who destroyed the one thing in my life that mattered to me. Even if he is—" Her voice broke. "I can't see either of you because I promised Alexander I wouldn't."

"Liz—"

"Good-bye, Jock."

She sank down upon the bed, buried her face in her hands and gave into a burst of frenzied anguish. She'd refused to see her father, and to what purpose? She did not have Alexander either.

Liz was already dressed and in the foyer waiting for a cab when the stony Mrs. Benchley came to her and told her that Jock was on the phone again.

"Please tell him I'm not at home."

Mrs. Benchley opened her mouth to say something, but Liz had already run out the door, a flurry of bright hair, black velvet and opalescent satin.

Alexander sat at his desk, which was piled with mail, contracts and reports. Michelle, his secretary, was trying to explain the chaos.

Finally he stopped her in midsentence and snapped in his deep, thundering baritone, "Save your breath, Michelle. You may need to explain this to the new president if I'm sacked tonight."

"Surely they won't do that, Mr. Vorzenski."

Michelle did not use his title because Alexander would not allow it.

Alexander glared at Michelle, wondering if in truth she worked for the competition. "I'm not so sure." Slowly his hard expression softened, and he managed a smile, which deepened the wolfish slashes beside his mouth. "Run along, and type that one report I asked for now, if you don't mind. I need to organize my thoughts before the meeting."

Alexander lifted his gaze thoughtfully to the portrait of his grandfather. The painted eyes of Philippe Rocheaux, who had founded Dazzle Ltd. ninety years ago, met his. Alexander felt responsible for Dazzle, and he knew that the company was headed for certain disaster if he were ousted from the presidency. Ruefully Alexander thought of the company, of its history and the components that had made it a great fragrance company.

Dazzle was not as ancient as some French houses of perfume, but its name stood for excellence. Like his grandfather, Alexander was dedicated to the preservation of Dazzle's eminent reputation as well as to his company's financial well-being. The company's motto was that quality counts in everything—from the design of the stopper of a flacon to the perfection of an essence.

Alexander's grandfather had begun Dazzle in the nineteenth century. A chemist who'd grown bored with his soap and candle business in rural France, Philippe Rocheaux had sold everything and moved to Paris with the intention of developing delicate scents for ladies' soaps. Quickly he'd moved into perfume.

With the launch of his first scent, Empress, in 1906, and then Paradise in 1908, Philippe Rocheaux proved himself a giant, one of those rare talents in the perfume industry.

Within a decade, Philippe proved his undisputed right to be classed among the great perfumers, with Francois Coty, the creator of Guerlain's Shalimar; with Ernest Beaux, who did Chanel #5; and with the prodigious freelancer Edmond Roudnitska, author of Christian Dior's Eau Sauvage.

Philippe's business expanded into one of mammoth proportions. Dazzle had six Parisian shops as well as subsidiaries in eighty-five countries. In France and Switzerland alone there were four Dazzle factories. The major laboratory was in the Paris suburb of Colombes; another was in the Swiss Alps, where the explosion had occurred.

Paul Rocheaux was Dazzle's perfumer now, and he was the sole creator at the house of Dazzle. He was, like his grandfather before him, a genius.

Alexander found his brother Paul infuriatingly difficult to deal with. Paul could putter in his lab for three or four years, making hundreds of changes in one creation alone. Other perfume houses would launch one scent after the other while Alexander and everyone else on the Dazzle board waited for Paul.

During the years between creations, Dazzle had no

new product to launch. Few perfume companies still operated in this old-fashioned way. Instead they relied on flavor and odor companies for new fragrances. That was why the stealing of Paul's formula seven years before had been such a disastrous occurrence. It had represented three years of perfectionism and arduous work.

Alexander chafed with impatience during the empty years between creations and their launches, but Paul, for all his slowness, had never created a flop. Paul gloried in explaining himself to the press during every launch. With an affected wave of scented sample papers, he would say, "I start with a basic note like a composer. I stay within a certain key signature, *messieurs*."

Alexander smiled to himself as he thought of his brother's ego at such times. Paul lived for those brief hours of glory, and when he spoke, he was always dramatic and metaphorical. He would wave his hands wildly with the pompous excitement of a conductor. "Then I blend scents, like the blending of notes into chords. I build harmonies and fugues of odors. Always I add and I subtract, changing the relative strengths on a delicate scale, until I realize the achievement of the ultimate scent I consider worthy of putting before the public."

In the shadows in the back of the room, away from the lights, the glitz and the clamor, Alexander, who always hired the best publicity people in the business to stage these media events, would watch and listen to his brother with great pride. It was in between these moments of dazzle and pomp that the brothers found it difficult to deal with one another.

The intercom sounded, and Michelle informed Alexander that Paul was outside.

"Send him in."

Paul Jacquard Rocheaux stomped angrily into the room. He was smoking one of his expensive Monte Cruz cigars, and the curling whisps of gray trailing his agitated motions increased the impression that he was spouting like a tea kettle ready to bubble over with rage. He came toward the desk and ground the stub of his cigar into the Wedgewood ashtray on his brother's gleaming rosewood desk.

"Hello, Paul," Alexander said blandly. "It's good to see you."

"Is that all you can say?"

"It seemed appropriate for starters," Alexander replied, still in the same imperturbable tone. "You've been so upset by my absence, I'm surprised you're not overjoyed to see I'm back."

"You come back to London less than two hours before this board meeting, and you're surprised I'm not overjoyed."

"Did you expect me to hurry back for my own hanging, Paul?" Alexander lounged indolently in his chair, but his eyes were alert.

"For a man about to be hanged, you don't look too upset, Mikki."

"As a matter of fact, I'm not—any longer. Thanks to you."

"And what is that supposed to mean?"

"All in good time, Paul." Alexander shrugged negligently.

Paul reached across Alexander's desk for the silver lighter that stood beside a group of elaborately cut crystal flacons filled with exotically scented ambers and golds. Paul lit another cigar. The acrid scent of the cigar soon warred with the chaos of sweet odors, but neither of the hostile men, both famed for their sensitive noses, noticed it.

Paul sighed impotently. He hated fights; they overwhelmed his delicate nature. "Mikki, you picked one hell of a time to disappear."

"Ah, but I didn't pick it. It picked me. I would never have left if the circumstances had been anything other than extraordinary. Thank you, Paul, for filling in for me."

"Damned inconvenient for me and inconsiderate of you."

"I'm sorry, but you seem to have handled things. Besides that, I just read the report about your new fragrance. Frankly, I was overwhelmed with relief. Dazzle needs a new launch. It would give us the kind of positive publicity we must have."

"You can't mean that you intend to prepare for a launch at the same time we're having to contend with this police investigation in Switzerland! Your own name is being dragged into the mud. Who knows how long you'll even remain president? I thought in six months, when all this blows over, we could launch."

"I want to begin now. There are times when you've got to take aggressive action to turn the tide of events in your favor. I want a media campaign bigger than any we've ever had."

"Sometimes I think your enemies are right and you're nothing but a damned privateer who'll be the end of Dazzle."

"Everyone expects us to knuckle under and assume a low profile, but that's exactly what we've done too long. I want to get out there and slug it out. Things couldn't have worked out better if I'd been home running the company myself."

"I didn't come in here tonight for praise."

"I hardly thought you did. I know that look of bulldog purpose. What's on your mind?"

"I saw the evening papers. You brought Liz back with you."

"She is my wife."

"An unfortunate mistake that belongs in the past. Why don't you divorce her?"

A tiny line had formed between Alexander's dark brows. "Because I don't want to."

"Why are you so determined to make a fool of yourself over that woman a second time?"

"Because . . ." How could a man defend the pull of his heart and soul when he scarcely understood the intricacies of that process himself? "Because . . . Damn it, Paul! I don't have to explain my feelings for my wife to you or anyone else!" Alexander's hand slammed down on the desk, and then he dragged it wearily through his rumpled hair.

This exchange was followed by a silence just as lengthy and just as tension filled.

A pale gray light slanted against the rich paneled walls of Dazzle's executive suite. Alexander wore an expression of fierce determination and weary exasperation.

Though they resembled one another, Alexander was the bolder and more charismatic of the two. Paul had inherited his sensitivity from his father, who had been a concert pianist as well as the princess's second cousin, and his "nose" from their grandfather Philippe Rocheaux. Both brothers regarded one another gloomily, each knowing the futility of further argument.

The funereal atmosphere was broken when Michelle knocked and came into the room, announcing, "You told me to tell you when everyone was in the boardroom, Mr. Vorzenski."

Alexander smiled. "We'll be there in a minute, Michelle."

Michelle handed him the report.

"Ready?" Paul asked, rising.

"As ready as I'll ever be, I suppose." Alexander rose. "I met with Philippe and Jon in New York yesterday, and not too successfully. Paul, you haven't told me whether you're for me or against me."

"You already know the answer, Mikki."

"I do?" Alexander was filled with doubt. Paul had never seemed more hostile.

"No matter my personal feelings over your stupidity regarding your wife, I am always for Dazzle. You're still the best man to run the company."

"Thank you, Paul."

"Don't thank me, Mikki. I don't really have a choice."

Alexander smiled genially despite Paul's barb. He realized Paul's attitude reflected the view of the board toward Liz. All Alexander had to do to win them over was to reassure everyone he would acquire a discreet divorce.

If he did that, the presidency was his, and his family would once more be on his side. If not . . .

Chapter Fourteen

The rain that had slanted in sheets in Belgravia gentled abruptly to a soft, weakening patter as Liz's taxi slowly threaded its way between red double-decker buses and black taxis onto Piccadilly. The Ritz Hotel was coming into view.

Wet asphalt and concrete glistened. The stone buildings loomed against a sky washed by the afternoon's showers to the palest of lavenders. Soft clouds stirred in the wet breezes, and a low orange sun painted their underbellies with a golden glow. It was a beautiful evening, had Liz been in the mood to enjoy it.

Instead she leaned forward on the edge of her shabbily upholstered seat and stared out the window at the familiar landmarks with dread. Through the open window a freshly rinsed London bombarded her. The smell of exhaust and diesel, the odor of fried food from a thousand restaurants, the scent of dogs, and cool, wet air. There were the hoarse shouts of street vendors, the whir of tires, the screeching of brakes, police whistles.

Everything was the same as it had been seven years ago—the plane trees in the parks with their enormous leaves that fell in the autumn to cover the earth with crackling gold, the row upon row of somber buildings, the traffic, the constant rush of people in their dark raincoats on the sidewalks beneath a roof of umbrellas, this eternal bustle that was London—yet she felt she no longer belonged.

Once England had meant Cornwall and Killigen Hall to Liz. Oh, the comforting antiquity of that house, that superb feeling of being part of a family that had endured for generations. Those illusions had been stripped from her by Ashley's death, but she still remembered her former home. She remembered cavorting on the sloping green lawns. Cornwall meant the rush of waves against cliffs, the scent of salt spray, the shrieks of gulls and ravens as they skimmed low above golden sands. She could almost smell the tang of cooking over furze fires on summer evenings when she and Ashley had camped out and lain beneath the stars, and he'd told her stories of knackers and tin miners.

In those years there had been Ashley and Mother. Her world had been filled with love and warm security. How fragile are the things we build our lives upon, Liz thought with a pang. But how precious. She was flooded with an aching nostalgia.

That peaceful world was gone forever. Funny, how she'd taken it for granted. She'd lost Ashley first. Then her mother had run off to France with her young man, in the futile search for her lost youth and beauty.

Liz swallowed the dry lump in her throat. Usually she never looked back because remembering brought too much pain. But she'd wanted to remember that time of love and security. She had the feeling that if she fought hard enough today, and if she could win Alexander's love, she might be able to give that kind of life to her own children and to Alexander. She longed to share that kind of deep happiness with Alexander, the kind of happiness that, for all his sophistication and success, he had never known.

Without his love, her future and that of her children were bleak and uncertain. What if she failed? She clenched her hands. She had to fight because she was fighting for her soul.

At the thought of braving the Dazzle board alone with Alexander against her, a wave of new terror made her stomach knot into a hard, queasy ball. What could she possibly say? How would Alexander react? And how would she even get into the building? She would have to lie smoothly and plausibly to get past the guard, and she wasn't a good liar under the best of circumstances. She could say that there was an emergency, that she had to see Alexander. It would have to have something to do with the children. The taxi driver braked sharply and began yelling to another driver to his left. The wall of taxis and buses in front of them had come to a standstill.

"What's going on up there?" the driver cried.

A dramatic shrug of hands and a violent curse from within the other taxi was the only answer.

When Liz realized that the traffic ahead where Regent Street and Piccadilly converged was impossibly jammed, she tapped on the glass behind the driver. "Let me off here," she said, handing him three pounds for the fare and tip. "I've decided to walk the rest of the way."

The damp air was refreshing after the stale cab. Liz walked past elegant boutiques and shops toward the gleaming white brick building that housed Dazzle's London offices. She saw little of her surroundings; she was only vaguely aware of the frustration and clamor of the stalled traffic.

In front of the Dazzle building a Volvo had crashed into a bus on Regent Street, and the bus had plowed into a building. The smashed car was abandoned. Water from a broken fire hydrant sprayed fifty feet into the air, and the streets and sidewalk were flooded. Liz had to tiptoe in her velvet shoes, and finally she was forced to step through deep puddles.

"Now isn't that a shame, lovey," a grandmotherly woman behind Liz said crisply. "You've ruined your shoes. I seen it happen, you know, the accident. Almost looked as if the man in the car did it on purpose, the way he ran into that bus. He ran off the minute it happened. Didn't stay around, not him that done it. A foreigner, if you ask me. Too many of them in the city these days, and not one in ten that knows how to drive proper like."

Liz nodded, and the woman began speaking to another pedestrian.

Bobbies ran about whistling and barking orders. Pedestrians crammed the streets between the blocked cars to view the wreckage and the impossible tangle of cars. A carnival atmosphere of excitement pervaded the area. Florid-faced men with wide smiles stood in the door of a pub across the street.

When Liz walked into the Dazzle building, no one was at the desk in front of the lift to question her. Everyone from security was down the hall in the office helping the police make telephone calls. Over the squishing of her wet shoes, she could hear the babble of voices. With her pulse racing for fear they would come out and discover her before she was safely inside the lift, she decided to take the stairs instead.

Once inside the stairwell, Liz sank against the wall in relief. She heard the sound of high heels skittering on the concrete stairs high above her, sharp, panicked beats like the pounding of her own heart. A door opened and closed, and then there was silence. Slowly Liz began to walk up. With every flight her stomach felt queasier than ever.

When she reached the top floor and stepped outside, the hall was abandoned. She was almost there. Almost. And it had been incredibly easy. Too easy, she would have realized had she not been so nervous.

She marched purposefully toward her husband's office. If she could only get into his office! She knew that it opened directly into the boardroom.

Her heart jumped jerkily when she turned the knob and let herself inside Michelle's office. The outer office was empty, but a cup of tea marred with a lipstick ring steamed on Michelle's desk, indicating this wouldn't be true long.

Liz opened the door to Alexander's office and stepped inside. The rich paneled walls were the same as she remembered, as were the wine-colored wool carpet, the long windows, the cathedral quiet, the sense of power and pampered luxury his office had always exuded.

On one wall hung the painting she had given Alexander so long ago. She went to the picture. She could not resist reaching up and touching the gilt frame. The wood was as smooth as polished gold beneath her fingertip. The painting depicted the granite cliffs of her former home plunging to caress golden sands and the wild surf of that Cornish sea. It had been her favorite view, and Ashley had commissioned a famous artist to paint it for her twelfth birthday.

On her wedding night, Liz had bestowed this greatest treasure of hers on Alexander. "A piece of my soul," she had whispered when he undid the wrappings. He had taken her in his arms, and they had not spoken for a long time.

Odd that he had kept it, that it still hung where they had placed it together. Her eyes misted, and Liz forced herself to look away from the painting in the vain hope of putting the past back where it belonged. But Alexander's office was too filled with other, unhappier memories for her to succeed.

This was where . . . The thought trailed off and then came back with renewed power. A pain as sharp and painful as a blow in the stomach hit her, and she leaned against the door for support. Seven years were swept aside, and she recalled that morning so long ago when she'd let herself inside this room in a state of joyous anticipation to tell Alexander she was pregnant.

She'd been wild with happiness. He was standing at the window looking down upon Regent Street, and he turned when she called to him from across the room. But instead of smiling as he always had before at the sight of her, his face had blackened with rage, and before she could say anything, he accused her of marrying him only to steal Paul's formula. Then she hadn't wanted to tell him about the baby. She thought she'd wait until the awful misunderstanding was cleared up.

The happiness they'd known had been destroyed within a half hour in the quarrel that erupted. He refused to listen to her. She'd run from him. There had been nowhere, no one to whom she could turn.

Despite the support of the door, she felt faint. For a moment she lost her courage. The memory of Alexander's anger and her own sorrow overpowered her present purpose. All she had to do was walk out the door and return to the house in Belgravia. Perhaps she could find some easier way to patch things up. Her backward footsteps toward the only avenue of escape were involuntary. Then a choked gasp from the darkened corner behind Alexander's desk snapped her rudely back into the present.

"How did you get in here?" Michelle asked in a shaken voice. The secretary stepped into the light. Something told Liz that usually the girl had a cool blond beauty when her blue eyes weren't wide with fear. Michelle clutched a sheaf of papers beneath her breasts as if her life depended on them.

Curiously, the girl's fear lessened Liz's. "I came to see my husband," Liz said, moving slowly toward the door of the boardroom. "I'm Mrs. Vorzenski."

"I know."

When she reached the door, Liz lifted the handle soundlessly.

"You can't do that!" Michelle cried. The papers she'd been so carefully holding spilled onto the floor.

"I just did," Liz said with a bold smile as she swept like a glorious butterfly into the room on opalescent wings of satin and black velvet, albeit a butterfly rooted to the earth with squishy shoes. Behind her Michelle's voice grew outraged.

"Mrs. Vorzenski, you can't—"

In a glance Liz noted the opulence of the boardroom, the long, polished conference table, the leather upholstery of the chairs. What struck her with potent force was the heavy atmosphere in the room.

She was one—against so many.

Princess Vorzenski, the family matriarch, had been speaking passionately in French, and she halted in midsentence, momentarily too stunned to continue. She was silver and elegant, and rigidly upright in her chair. In her well-ordered world things like this didn't happen. She looked unbendable.

Everyone in the room gaped at the woman in black velvet whose red hair cascaded in a shower of unruly ringlets, giving her the untamed, exotic charm of a gypsy.

Everyone except Alexander. He was seated at one end of the table. His dark face had been bored and impassive until Liz walked into the room with that wildness blazing in her eyes that could only spell trouble. He smelled danger, but her presence lit a fire within him that had nothing to do with danger. Paul and his mother sat on either side of him. Alexander stood up slowly, his eyes bland and guardedly amused, and yet everyone in the room was instantly aware of his power.

The same thought was in all their minds. Unwelcome or not, the woman was Mikki Vorzenski's wife.

Never had Alexander seemed taller nor more nobly majestic and beloved to Liz, and never had his tenderness and love seemed more hopelessly out of reach.

Alexander said smoothly, "Ladies and gentlemen, may I introduce you to the lady we've all been so avidly discussing. My wife, Liz." He pushed his chair back from the table.

"A pleasure," said Liz, filling the gap of awed silence with the musically flowing irony of her voice. Her French, as always, was atrociously structured, her genders and pronouns hopelessly scrambled, but for once it was to her advantage. Her American-British accent made her seem less French, less Roger Chartres's daughter, and there was a certain charm and ingenuous creativity in her horrendous constructions.

Several members of the board forgot themselves and smiled. Even Paul looked less sour when Liz flung out *"par usuel"* in an overconfident burst. Only the princess, who considered the French language sacred, stiffened and groaned, *"Comme d'habitude."*

Satin rustled, velvet shoes squished, calling attention to the movement of Liz's slim wet feet as she strolled the length of the room. She knew she was leaving a trail of footprints on the expensive carpet like a swamp animal, but she couldn't stand still. Her courage would desert her completely if she did. She felt their eyes boring into her, assessing her, distrusting her, and she wanted to run.

Princess Vorzenski regained her tongue and attacked. "So this is your impossible wife, Mikki?"

"None other, Maman," he said in a tone of velvet steel.

Alexander came toward Liz, and when he reached her, his arms slid protectively about her waist. Liz could feel a hard tension in his grip that belied his negligent manner.

"How dare she come in here and break into our board meeting!" came the now-familiar high-pitched voice of the princess.

"Surely you would expect nothing less from such an arch criminal, Maman," Alexander said softly. "A woman with the courage to marry her father's enemy with the intention of ruining him can scarcely be expected to observe the proprieties, can she? Perhaps I should frisk her and see if she's carrying a gun."

This time it was Liz who shrieked. "No!"

Alexander bent his dark head to his wife so that only she could hear him. "Ah, love, delightful as frisking you would be, this is hardly the place." His hand, shaped against her waist, burned through the luxurious fabric of her gown. A hot flush stole across Liz's throat and cheeks. Aloud Alexander said, "Now that you're here, I'm glad you came, darling. The board couldn't have made an unbiased judgment of this matter without seeing you." His gaze left Liz and returned to his mother. "But, Maman, would you and Paul chair the meeting for a few minutes without me? I would like to speak to Liz in private."

Before the princess could answer, Liz replied defiantly, resisting the pressure of her husband's hand, "Darling, that won't be necessary. You see, I didn't come to talk to you, but to the board. We can speak privately later."

"What are you doing?" Alexander demanded in an urgent whisper. "Just this once, surprise me and resist the impulse to be suicidal." His hand on her body held her so hard it hurt.

"Is this the wife you promised us you would hide in the country, Mikhail, while you smooth everything over?" the princess persisted. "The wife who would keep a low profile and avoid publicity? This creature who storms in here dressed so flamboyantly and who flagrantly disobeys you? Doubtless she feels she photographs well in that outrageous costume. I wouldn't be surprised if she's called every newspaper in town. I knew I was right and that you should be removed from the presidency until you recover your sanity where this woman is concerned. Maybe now everyone will listen to me. For one month you abandoned your responsibilities because of her. Liz Chartres, you tried to destroy my foolish son once. I'll not let you succeed a second time. You must leave this room at once so we can decide what to do about you."

"Won't anybody here listen to me?" Liz cried. "Are you so sure I'm guilty that you won't even let me speak?" She turned on Alexander. "So, you've been planning behind my back to bury me alive in some country house where I can do no harm. Well, that hardly surprises me, but you don't know me. I won't go to the country. You can't make me take up sewing and gardening or tennis or whatever innocuous pastime you have in mind. I won't be turned into a dull and suitable wife. I'd rather be dead than become the boring paragon you want—some whey-faced little seamstress that hasn't the sense to stand up for herself."

It took Alexander an uncomfortably long time to banish his unbidden smile. He should have been furious, but he wasn't nearly so angry as he ought to have been. "It never occurred to me I could turn you into a dull and suitable wife, my dear, nor—how did you put it?—a whey-faced little seamstress, though as a designer even you must admit you do have a few talents with the needle. Perhaps I should have considered that possibility."

Was he trying to make a joke of it and thus render her harmless? Well, she would never never allow it. She flung off his grasp and whirled angrily on the princess and Paul.

"I know you're against me. I know you want Alexander to divorce me, but I love him. I never did anything deliberately to hurt him or you. It was reckless of me, I know that now, to marry him without telling him of my connection to Roger Chartres. But, you see, knowing who Alexander was, I didn't want to fall in love with him any more than he would have wanted to fall in love with me. I even tried to run away from him in France."

"A shrewd gamble," the princess said scathingly, "that a chase would only whet his appetite."

"But I did fall in love with him, and then I was too afraid of losing him to tell him the truth. I came here today not, madame, because I wanted to be photographed by newsmen. Not because I want to make more trouble for any of you or Alexander, but because I wanted to tell you that I am innocent. And so is he. I know that some of you think you can't trust Alexander to remain president of Dazzle if I'm his wife. You hold him to blame for what I was accused of doing seven years ago. I came here because I couldn't stand by and let his career be ruined because of me without at least trying to—"

"Make sure you destroyed him?" the princess finished. "If you're innocent, Liz Chartres, why didn't you come to the board seven years ago? Why did you run away?"

"Alexander told me he wanted me out of his life, and even though I was devastated, I tried, for his sake, to accept that. I was pregnant, and I thought if I stayed, there could be no clean break with Alexander. If I left him, maybe he would manage to save his career and return to his old life. I only wanted to help him. I thought he did not want . . . children from me, that he could not really love them." Her last sentence was a dying whisper. "But I was so very wrong . . . about everything."

"Liz—" Alexander's voice betrayed more warmth than he would have liked. Doubtless she was wielding the deathblow to his career, but it didn't seem to matter very much. All that mattered was Liz. He was losing the battle to suppress a startling tenderness that had crept through his expert guard.

"Don't try to stop me, Alexander," Liz said softly, speaking at last to him. "I'm going to find out for sure who stole Paul's formula and deliberately framed me, because I know you won't believe me unless I do. And, Princess Vorzenski if you have any feelings as a mother or grandmother, you would stand by your own instead of backing those who oppose him. You want to strip him of the presidency as a power play to make him divorce me."

"A fine speech that I'm sure you've rehearsed, young woman, grammar mistakes and all," the princess said coldly. Her pale skin was mottled with rage. "How dare you accuse me of not being a good mother! By your own admission you trapped my son into this impossible marriage with a lie, while I've given him everything! All I want is for you to leave Mikki in peace. There can never be any happiness in a marriage like yours."

"And is there in yours?"

A stillness came over the taut features of the princess. There was the fleeting glimpse of pain in her eyes, and then she said in low, measured words, "Why do you cling to a man who has already begun to hate you?"

"Hate—"

That one word destroyed the noble fury that had driven Liz. To hear his mother say it made it loom as a horrible reality in her mind.

Alexander was pale from the exchange between his mother and wife. Liz looked stricken. He said gently,

"Liz, you should never have come here. You've made yourself ill. I'm going to take you home." To the others he said, "I think that nothing more can be accomplished tonight. I'm sure everyone will agree we should resume this meeting in the morning."

Liz swallowed. Had she ruined everything? No one believed her. Had she embarrassed her husband irreparably in the eyes of the board? Would they agree with the princess that he should lose the presidency because of his impossible wife? Or would he divorce her? The glimmer of tears brightened her eyes.

"I'm glad to see that you have at least some shred of conscience," the princess murmured. "Give Mikhail up before you destroy him. Go back to Mexico and make your puppets again."

Black misery filled Liz's heart, weighing it down like a heavy stone.

She said in a dull, tired voice, "Princess Vorzenski, if you throw me out, you throw your grandchildren out as well. If I return to Mexico, I'll take them with me. Don't you have any curiosity about them? Not even a scrap of tenderness for them? Alex is very much like Alexander. He's six years old, and he was in a serious accident two weeks ago. He would love you so much. You couldn't help loving Samantha either if you would only give yourself the chance. She's so vital and irrepressible."

For a moment the princess could think of nothing to say.

"If you want to see them, you will have to come to me," Liz said quietly.

After an infinite silence the reply came. "I will never want to see any children of yours, Liz Chartres."

Liz's eyelids fell. She stared fixedly at a patch of rug that she'd stained with her damp shoes.

"You've made your decision then, I see," Liz said in a strained, low tone. "It's useless to talk further."

"I made it seven years ago," the princess replied, "and your coming here today has only confirmed that I was right."

"What you want in a daughter-in-law is a speechless nonentity."

"That would be infinitely preferable to what I have."

Liz could bear no more. She spun on her heel and dashed into the hall. Behind her she heard the excited chorus of voices, and the princess's strident voice overrode them all.

A hammer pounded inside Liz's brain. She'd been wrong to come. There was no chance. No chance at all.

Liz pushed the button for the lift and waited, her feeling of hopelessness building. Alexander came out of the boardroom looking weary and drawn, and at the sight of him Liz felt a stab of fierce longing. Despite the shadows beneath his eyes, his dark, virile handsomeness compelled her more forcefully than ever. She devoured the lithe power of his body as he moved toward her with his long, easy strides. If only he would fold her into his arms and say that nothing that had been said in the boardroom mattered to him. If only he would kiss her gently, comfortingly.

But, of course, he did none of those things.

"You shouldn't have run off like that when I said I'd take you home," he said grimly.

"There's no need for you to trouble yourself about me," she replied, cut more deeply by his coldness than by his mother's attacks in the boardroom.

She did not know that her own voice sounded even harsher than his. When she looked at him like that, with her face closed against him, Alexander was tormented by thoughts of Jock. Again he wondered what had really happened between them when Jock had come to Mexico. He was angry suddenly that she shut him out while behind his back she had welcomed Jock into her arms.

"Damn it, Liz. I want to take you home," he insisted stubbornly.

His tone made her feel defiant, and she said stupidly, "So that I won't get into more trouble?"

"Don't you think you've done enough for one night's work? You've certainly stirred up a hornet's nest here."

"That's not what I intended."

"I won't ask you what you intended, then."

"Alexander, I'm sorry I came. I shouldn't have provoked your mother. I'm worried that now she'll find it hard to forgive me."

He laughed shortly. "Maman does not have a forgiving nature. I had hoped to bring you two together under different circumstances. I wanted to introduce her to the children first. As it is, you met. You collided. Now we must deal with the consequences."

"I thought only to—"

He was determined not to let her pretend she had had his interests at heart. "Liz. Don't. I'm taking you home."

She saw that he wouldn't believe in her, and a demon of recklessness possessed her. "Maybe I don't want to go home—with you."

He blanched, but she was too filled with her righteous fury to care. The doors of the lift opened, but when she was about to step inside, he leaned forward. His heavy arms circled her to prevent her escape. When she struggled, his grip merely tightened. The doors closed, leaving them alone once more.

"Where are you going, then?" he demanded. "To Jock?"

"What if I were?" She said this very nastily because she was afraid she might burst into tears. "You don't care about me. You said you only wanted me now for . . . for . . ."

"This," he rasped in a goaded undertone. He pulled

her roughly against his hard, masculine body, his mouth crushing insolently down upon hers.

In that moment he did not care how he hurt and humiliated her. He was filled with resentment because she held him in thrall with silken threads of sensual bondage. She was in his blood. He needed to taste her, to feel her, to possess her, and these needs filled him with the savage desire to hurt her as well.

He forced her head back and pressed a ruthless kiss upon her upturned lips. She fought him, but she could not free herself. Her hands pushed in vain against his chest, but he was too strong and too brutally determined. Stubbornly, Alexander held her still and caressed her. His mouth moved upon her stiff lips and then moved lower.

A tongue of flame leaped from him to her like a charge of electricity, and Liz shivered. It was all she could do to restrain her arms from lifting to circle his neck. But even though a dizzying wildness tingled in her arteries, she denied her own desire in the futile attempt to thwart his.

Soon her passive submission was not enough to satisfy him. He forced her to return his kisses, parting her lips, filling her mouth with his thrusting tongue, slowly, lingeringly, killing her will to resist him until all too soon she felt dazed and hungry for much much more.

He forced her backward against the wall, his weight pinning her against the cool green tiles. The shape of his male body molded her curving slimness, and she felt his potent state of arousal. He was on fire, and so was she. She could feel the hammering of his heartbeats as crazily frenzied as her own, the disturbed unevenness of his breathing. He was no more immune to her sensually than she was to him, and this thought gave her a fleeting sensation of power until the ache in her heart reminded her of the lasting fulfillment she desired and could never have. She wanted his love.

Alexander's need was so grippingly elemental he was not troubled by rational arguments. He kissed her with ruthless passion; a wild, reckless abandon to prove his mastery over her drove him. Only when her body melted against his, and she trembled everywhere his lips and fingers played across her skin, did he release her.

Only then did he set her from him without uttering a word of apology. She was shaking with an overwhelming emotion that she wished fervently were unequivocable rage instead of the humiliating passion for him that it was.

"You are despicable," she cried. If only she believed that!

"So I've been told," he replied imperturbably, pleased to see she was as shaken as he. "Though not usually by a woman trembling from my embraces." The dark power that had driven him was once more leashed, though barely.

"Alexander, we can't go on like this, tearing each other to pieces one minute and the next minute making love."

"Do you dignify what just happened with the euphemism 'making love'?" he asked mercilessly.

On a sob she said, "Things only get worse between us every day."

"What do you suggest then?"

"I-I don't know anymore, Alexander. Look, I can't pretend that a while ago I didn't want . . ." She met the knowledge in his eyes with a shiver.

"Yes?" A black brow lifted sardonically.

She turned scarlet. "Why should I state the obvious, that I want you, that a minute ago I felt I'd die, I wanted you so much? Don't you know that you're killing me? I'm not cut out for the kind of marriage you want. I don't want to be a sex object you'll cast aside in a few months, when you tire of me."

"Is that all you really think you are to me?" he demanded quietly. "Don't you know—"

"All I know is that I can't go on with you like this, Alexander. And tonight I need to be alone, to try to think what to do. Please, let me leave, by myself."

"If you won't come home with me, at least let me see you safely inside a cab," he said wearily.

"Spare me your show of concern and gallantry. I can take care of myself, thank you. In case you don't remember, I've been doing it for the seven years since you threw me out."

"Damn you, Liz. It's black as pitch outside. London's not as safe at night as it once was. For those same seven years you were taking care of yourself, I was crazy wondering if you were dead or alive. I'll put you into a cab if I have to carry you over my shoulders to do it."

"I'm sure such caveman tactics are exactly the thing to appeal to a man of your baser instincts."

This remark enraged him as she'd intended for it to. He was reaching for her when the doors of the lift opened. Only their mutual awareness of the man standing in the shadows inside it brought the situation between Liz and Alexander under control. Instead of seizing her, Alexander let her walk stiffly past him. He had every intention of following her, but when he glanced at the man who moved out of the rectangle of light toward the doors, Alexander recognized his cousin, Jock Rocheaux.

As Liz stumbled into Jock's waiting arms, both men stared at each other in stunned surprise. The doors began to close. Too late, Alexander lunged toward the lift as the twin sheets of stainless steel slid together. For an instant he felt paralyzed by the thought of Jock with Liz. Then he rushed blindly toward the stairwell.

Inside the lift, Liz pressed her shaking body against Jock.

"You've quarreled," Jock said gently with his old-world courtesy.

"Terribly. Oh, Jock, it was awful. I'm so ashamed of the things I said to his mother."

"Don't be. Aunt Paulette deserves far more than you could possibly deliver."

"And then in the hall just now, I was even worse. I deliberately wanted to hurt Alexander. I even let him believe I was going from him to you."

"Dear me. You certainly wasted no time in throwing me to the most unpleasant wolf in the pack." He didn't look in the least worried. "And I thought you and I were friends."

"Be serious, Jock. Please. I've made such a terrible muddle of my life. I've hurt everyone—even you."

"You can't be in love without hurting people. I should know. I'm an old hand at hurting. Here . . ." He handed her his handkerchief.

She dabbed at her eyes. "Then we must be deeply in love, because we're both hurting. Jock, I feel like I'm dying!"

"Take it from an expert, *chérie,* when you feel like that, that's the surest proof you're not. You're wretchedly in love, that's all. It was almost pleasant to see Mikki again. I've never seen him so miserably enraptured." His voice changed, and there was an element of something in it that would have alarmed her had she noted it. "But Liz, seriously, do you realize the jeopardy I'm in because of you? I snuck inside Dazzle tonight to see you. I would have broken the doors down if they hadn't been wide open, or assaulted the guards if they'd been on duty."

He was joking, and yet he was not. His face had never been graver.

"Why, Jock?"

"Liz, we have to talk—now." His golden face was more urgent than she'd ever seen it. "You've got to come to Paris with me."

The doors of the lift opened, and a powerful arm reached inside and wrenched Jock bodily from Liz.

"Paris! If you think for one minute I'm going to let you sail off into the sunset with my wife, Jock, you are deranged," Alexander snarled in a breathless burst. Breathless because he'd dashed headlong down the stairs. "And I'll thank you to keep your filthy hands off her."

"Unfortunately you've got things all wrong, Mikki. Liz won't have me. She foolishly prefers you."

Four uniformed men surrounded Jock and Alexander.

Jock eyed the five men about him. "Mikki," Jock stalled. "I came because I have to convince Liz to come to Paris. What I have to say can only be said privately—to her."

"I never doubted that for a minute. Say it to me, you bastard."

The four guards hustled Jock down the hall toward a small office. Liz realized there wasn't going to be a chance for her to talk to Jock now even if she stayed. Alexander would prevent it, and she wasn't up to any more quarrels tonight. Liz seized the opportunity to escape.

It was raining again as she plunged out into the street. The wreck had been cleared, and the traffic was flowing smoothly. She hailed a cab and slid inside.

Within the building Jock was the first to notice that Liz had not followed them into the office.

"Where's Liz?" he demanded, his voice urgent.

"I don't know."

"Mikki, you've got to find her. It's a—"

Alexander had already run out of the office and down the hall into the rain. He didn't hear the end of his cousin's harshly expelled sentence.

"It's a matter of life and death."

Chapter Fifteen

Liz was trembling with fatigue and nervous strain as she mounted the wide flight of steps of Alexander's house. The hour was late, the air cool and sweet from the rain. Ana Lou let her in and, to her anxious questions, gave assurances that the children were fine, having gone to sleep hours earlier.

"And my husband?"

There was the briefest hesitation.

"He has not come home, my lady." Ana Lou averted her gaze out of kindness, but the gesture of sympathy betrayed her suspicions more than anything she could have done.

Liz trudged up to her bedroom feeling a stifling sensation of aloneness. She should be glad that Alexander had not come home. At least she would not have to face him, but the tumult of her emotions had left her drained and yet at the same time too stimulated to sleep. Nor had her lonely dinner at the Savoy or her long cab ride eased her tension. Her mind was still a jumble of remorse over what she'd done.

She took a long bath, but that did not relax her. She had told Alexander she needed to be alone, but now that she was, that wasn't what she wanted. She found herself listening to every sound in the house. For a woman who did not wish her husband's return, why did she long for the heavy tread of his footfall on the stair?

She combed her hair, tugging her brush through the hopeless tangle of curls. She paused frequently, her brush suspended and still above the bright fall of hair, while she strained to listen. Much later she went to bed, but it seemed hours before she fell asleep.

The room was utterly black when she awoke, but she was aware of someone moving about.

In the darkness, Alexander's voice came to her. "Liz, are you awake?"

She pretended to be asleep though his vibrant baritone stirred every nerve in her body.

He began to undress. She heard the thud of a shoe falling upon the carpet, the sounds of a belt buckle and zipper. He went into the bathroom and closed the door.

The bathroom door opened again, and he strode across the room. The mattress dipped, and he pulled back the covers and slid inside. She smelled the fresh male scent that was his alone.

She felt his warmth even before he touched her.

"Liz?" This time her name was a low murmur.

She didn't answer.

"Aren't you awake?" The sheets rustled and he folded her stiff limbs against his body. "Yes, you are. I can tell." His hand gently smoothed her hair from her forehead. "I don't blame you for not wanting to talk."

She began to cry.

"I looked everywhere for you," he admitted, his voice as low and comforting as she had wished it to be earlier. "I came home on the chance that you were here."

"I had dinner at the Savoy," she mumbled through her tears.

He sounded relieved. "Why there?"

"Some nostalgic homing instinct, I guess. You took me there on our first date."

"I remember."

"Tonight it was so different."

"I can imagine that it was."

"We were so in love that night."

"Yes." He hesitated, stroking her hair. "We were."

"It seemed like such a long time ago. It made me even more unhappy to remember."

"Sometimes there's an odd enjoyment in stoking the embers of depression by indulging in sad memories. I imagine you were in that sort of mood."

"Tonight, when I went to Dazzle, I only wanted to help you, Alexander, and I ended up hurting you." More tears fell.

"I've been hurt before. I'll survive." His voice was infinitely gentle.

"I guess now it will be difficult for you to convince the board you can manage me."

"Quite difficult."

"I'm sorry. Can you believe me when I say that I didn't mean to make things harder for you?"

"Honestly?" His hand in her hair was still.

"Honestly," she said.

"I don't know."

"Alexander, how can we go on like this, when you have all these doubts?"

"Because not going on would be so much worse. I learned that much tonight when you ran out into the rain." Again his warm fingers moved on her, this time in a caress upon her shoulders beneath the heaviness of her hair.

A thrilling heat burned in the trail left by his fingertips.

"I'm the wrong woman for you."

"In all ways but one." His voice was huskier now. She heard the hint of a smile in it, the beginning of the warmth she so longed for.

He spanned her waist with his hands. His touch brought the familiar ripple of excitement. Slowly she turned in his arms and tilted her face for his kiss.

"I'm sorry," he said. "Not really for kissing you in the hall. I couldn't help that. But for everything else, I'm sorry."

"So am I."

"Even about Jock?" she insisted.

"Even about Jock." He had tensed, but his voice remained easy. "I was . . . I am . . . jealous."

"What happened between you two after I left?"

"I threw him out without finding out why he'd even come. I haven't the patience to deal with Jock." He didn't say, "Because I know he was with you in Mexico, and you didn't tell me."

Liz's hand slid lower over Alexander's flat belly, deliberately stirring him.

"You have nothing to be jealous about." Her tone had deepened suggestively.

To that he said nothing. He wanted to believe her.

A varnished fingertip dipped inside his navel, and it was a decidedly pleasant sensation.

"I hate to quarrel," she continued, still in the low bedroom voice that aroused him. "It makes me feel so lost. After I left you I was silly and frightened in London on my own. I'm afraid I didn't sort anything out. I just missed you and wished we hadn't quarreled."

His arms wrapped her body fiercely. "I missed you too. God, what an understatement! The last few hours

have been a soul-searching hell." He'd never thought
he'd confess that.

"For me too," she admitted.

He held her in silence for a long moment, his mood
lightening.

"There's only one good thing about our quarreling,
Liz."

"What's that?"

"Do you really have to ask?"

"I'm afraid I do."

"Making up, my darling."

"Oh, that?"

"Yes, that."

The one word spoke volumes. She moved so that her
body slid erotically against his. "Making up, you say?"
she teased. "Like this?" She moved against his thigh
again. He gasped. Her leg brushed the length of his.
"And this?"

"You catch on fast, my love. What in the hell are you
doing with your toe?" She did it again, and his heart
slammed against his rib cage. "Where in the world did
you learn a trick like that? If you don't stop, my
curiosity will have me insane with jealousy all over
again."

She was laughing when he lifted her against his chest.

"Maybe it's time you showed me the one way you're
right for me," he taunted.

"You mean a home demonstration?"

He chuckled. "Go right ahead and demonstrate, my
love."

"My pleasure."

"No, love, mine."

Words became unnecessary. Within moments that
powerful force that was outside them both had taken
charge, making a mockery of their hatreds and distrust.
In that timeless, white-hot moment of shattering pas-

sion they were one, all that was between them melting into nothingness in the deluge of their shattering fulfillment.

Then it was over, and he drew her into his arms. They didn't speak. Each felt slightly ashamed for that loss of self.

The next morning she felt shy toward him, and he was moodily silent. It was still dark when Alexander switched on a lamp. As Liz was slipping out of bed, he glimpsed a tantalizing curve of leg and thigh before she managed to pull on her silk robe. Because of his warm look, she smiled drowsily at him with love in her eyes. A quiver of unwanted desire darted through him, and he looked away. He remembered her sweetness and gentleness last night in his arms and her wantonness in his bed. The old torment gripped him, and he wondered how long he could endure the conflict of emotions she aroused. She was tearing him apart inside. One minute he hated her, the next he loved her. He got out of bed and dressed quickly, anxious to escape her and bury himself in his work.

Later, from the bath, she called to him in that husky tone that disturbed him because it turned his insides to mush, "Alexander, it's getting cold in here. I forgot to close the door. Would you please close it before you go?"

He moved warily across the room to oblige her, but at the sight of her naked reflection in the mirror on the bathroom door, his heart began to pound violently. She was provocatively immersed up to her pouting nipples in fragrant suds. Again the war of emotions began.

Unaware that he was standing outside the door, his brown hand shaking on the knob, she leaned back lazily to soak, and he could not tear his gaze from the voluptuous sight of her body. His gaze lingered on her breasts, and he inhaled a swift, painful breath when she parted her legs and the washrag slid down them. Then, with a splash of water, she stood up and reached for a towel. His eyes were riveted to her narrow waist, the enticing swell of her hips.

"I'm freezing," she called, louder and more impatiently than before. "Alexander—"

"I'm here," he replied, his deep tone like velvet as he stepped into the bathroom, where she stood in shimmering wet splendor.

Startled doe eyes met the golden fire of his. At that moment it was impossible for him to imagine evil in her. Someone else had done what he had always believed her guilty of. He must find that person; as a husband he should protect her, not accuse her. He reached for the towel, his warm hands brushing her trembling fingers. She stood very still when he began caressing her satin skin with the soft terry.

"Alexander, I imagined you would be anxious to get down to the office," she said in a quiet voice as the towel gently massaged beneath the softness of her breasts. As always, any tenderness from him filled her with joy.

"I was," he murmured, tracing the curve of her belly before he pulled her damp body into his arms. His expression was both haunted and adoring. "But I'm not now."

"Oh—" Her one word was bold and breathless.

The towel dropped to the floor, but neither of them noticed. His palm cupped her face gently, and he kissed her tenderly.

The pressure of his mouth on hers destroyed her defenses. As always, there was a quality of arrogant mastery in his kiss that commanded her into submission. His tongue stole inside her mouth, exploring. Like a narcotic, a hot invasion of languorous sensation relaxed her rigid muscles so that his roaming hands could shape her pliant flesh to his body. When she offered not the slightest resistance, he lifted her into his arms and carried her to the bed.

The coldness was gone from his handsome face, and in its place was a hot wanting he did not bother to hide. There was another emotion as well, an emotion far more powerful and enduring than mere sensuality, but in her confusion, Liz did not note it though it evoked a subconscious pleasure in her that made her even more eagerly passionate than ever before.

As always the wonder of flesh upon flesh lifted them and shook them so that they forgot all in the blazing tide of fulfillment. In the aftermath of their lovemaking, a golden glow remained between them, and he pulled her on top of his chest, so that her hair spilled over his brown shoulders.

His fingertips caressed a strand of her hair, twirling a length of the flame wisps between his fingers. "You always smell like flowers. Jasmine and lavender." His drawl was soft and mesmerizing. "I hope you won't always prove so distracting in the mornings, or I'll never get to work."

The warm light in his eyes tinged her cheeks becomingly with a blush. She loved him; in that moment she would have given anything if he'd loved her too. Instead of telling him how she felt, her lips lowered and touched his in a brief, sweet kiss.

The phone began to ring.

"Oh, dear," Liz cried, jumping from the bed.

She had forgotten not to answer it.

His eyes followed her graceful movements, admiring the shapeliness of her body. He thought of other men, of Jock, and the desire her beauty would inevitably arouse in them. Jealousy jolted Alexander at the thought of another man possessing her, especially Jock. She was his, his alone, and he was determined to keep her no matter what the price.

"Hello," Liz whispered.

Princess Vorzenski's shrill voice exploded into the phone. "Let me speak to Mikhail."

Without a word, Liz handed Alexander the telephone.

As he listened to the princess, his expression darkened. When at last he hung up, he stared at his wife, and his eyes were as cold and hard as stones. Liz was filled with a sense of impending doom.

"Well?" she asked, unable to stand the suspense. "What did she say?"

"I'm sure you know already."

"Tell me, Alexander."

"Paul's formula was stolen out of my safe in the Dazzle offices last night." In his voice there was a deadness that she had never heard before. "I have lost the presidency of Dazzle. Maman has temporarily filled the office herself."

"And you think I took the formula, don't you, Alexander?" He stared at her in silence. "Well, don't you?"

In his eyes she saw the unspoken accusation.

"Don't push me, Liz, about what I think."

She turned from him, unable to bear that look that killed her soul, that hopelessness in his eyes that destroyed the illusion that their relationship was salvageable.

Their marriage was as dead as ashes.

He got out of bed and dressed quickly, ripping clothes from hangers, shirts from drawers. He was at the door when she called to him. "Please tell me where you're going, Alexander."

"Where do you think? To work, love. To see what, if anything, can be saved from this latest disaster. Get dressed. You're coming with me. I'm not leaving you alone and risk you running off to Jock and your father."

She turned her face to the wall so that he

could not read her face. Those had been her precise intentions. If anyone knew what had happened to the formula, her father surely must. He had been against her marriage from the first, and she'd believed he was behind the theft of the formula even before Jock had practically confirmed it as the truth. Didn't logic point to his being guilty again? Fury consumed her that her own father could be so treacherous. No matter what she'd promised Alexander in Mexico about not seeing Roger, she had to go to her father and convince him once and forever to stay out of her life. But if she went, she risked losing Alexander.

"You realize," Alexander said grimly, "that if you run away now, to Paris or anywhere else, everyone will be convinced you had some part in this. Since I have brought you back and established you as my wife, I will be condemned a fool, if not worse. I want you to stand by me, no matter what happens. You made a promise to me in Mexico about your father and Jock. I want you to tell me—now—that you intend to honor it."

"I-I—" She couldn't utter a sound. Did he really believe she would let Roger get away with this a second time? Even if it cost her her marriage, she wouldn't promise that she would stand by and do nothing while someone wrought utter destruction upon their lives.

"Liz—"

His eyes captured hers in a hard and relentless gaze that stripped away her defenses, leaving her shatteringly vulnerable. Why did Alexander make her feel that she betrayed him, when all she wanted to do was help him?

"I was a fool to make such a promise to you," she admitted at last.

"I see," he said in a low, dead voice. "And I was a fool to think you possessed even an ounce of honor where I'm concerned. I should have left you in Mexico."

"No! You don't see at all! I—"

"Save your lies." Refusing to listen, Alexander pivoted sharply and stormed down the stairs. She heard him calling for George, talking to Mrs. Benchley, behaving toward the servants as if nothing out of the ordinary had occurred when in reality the fabric of their lives had just been ripped into shreds. The house was eerily silent when he went outside. Then she heard him climbing back up the stairs, and, realizing that she hadn't even started dressing, she went to the closet and pulled out a silk shift.

Alexander strode into the room and saw that she hadn't dressed. Her slowness further infuriated him. "Hurry up, or I'll strip you and dress you myself, love."

She started toward the bathroom, but he stopped her with a rough command. "Take off your clothes in here where I can make sure you're not being slow deliberately."

Her heart was near bursting with bitter pain, but she knew it was useless to cross him when he was in this kind of mood. Without a word she slid off the robe. She was aware of his dark gaze devouring her naked body as she fumbled to undo the buttons on the front of her dress so she could step into it.

The buttons would not come loose, and she turned scarlet with shame. He came to her and took the dress from her and undid the buttons himself. Next to her, he was so tall, so male. Her senses catapulted in alarm. When he had finished with the buttons, he handed her the garment. His brown hand cupped one breast in primitive possession.

"Do you have to be so hard, Alexander?" she asked. "I can imagine what you must be feeling, but . . ."

"Can you?" His mouth curled bitterly even as his

hand upon her skin tantalized. "Maman tried to teach me something once. You've completed the lesson. She's always held that a man can have anything he wants—as long as he's willing to pay the price." His fingers caressed her warm satin skin. "Sweetheart, I wanted to watch you strip so I could remind myself of the charming body I'm paying such a damnably high price for."

Tears of humiliation stung her eyelids as she whirled away and pulled on her dress. Later they left the house without speaking, but they were each terribly aware of the other.

When Alexander and Liz reached Alexander's office, they found his mother, Paul, and their cousins, Jon and Philippe, waiting for them. The latest news was that Michelle had disappeared.

All eyes were riveted on Liz.

The princess was the first to speak. "Mikhail, why did you bring her?"

"Because Liz is as deeply involved as anyone else in this room," he replied tersely.

"But she stole the formula."

No one said anything, not even Liz.

"What is, is," the princess said at last, realizing she was forced to accept Liz's presence. "But I have a plan that just may save us from disaster. Gentlemen, why don't we sit down." The men complied, and the princess seated herself behind Alexander's desk. Liz moved to the window and looked down at the flowing traffic on Regent Street.

"I have given this matter a great deal of thought," the princess began. "No one outside the thief and those present in this room know the formula is missing, and I don't think we should release this information. The sort of publicity that would result if the theft were found out would do Dazzle no good. Furthermore, I feel we should go ahead with our launch."

"But the formula has been stolen. We risk competing with our own fragrance under a Radiance label," Philippe argued.

"We can use one of the formulas Paul discarded." At Paul's dark look, the princess said swiftly, "Oh, I know, darling, this is far from a perfect solution, but one of your discards is better than anyone else's creation. You're the best in the business. With your reputation, we can carry it off. You will be the only one to know the perfume is not up to your impeccable standards."

Paul was about to object, but Alexander cut in. "Maman's right, Paul. Her plan is audacious, but sometimes audacity—when you've got nothing else—carries the day."

"Exactly, Mikhail. And as for your marriage to Liz—"

"Maman, I've already heard your views on that score."

"No, darling, you haven't. Yesterday I was against your marriage, Mikhail, but today I'm reconciled to it as a reality. Since you've brought Liz back and established her as your wife, I now think it is very important for you to continue with your marriage. At the moment a divorce or a separation is most undesirable. Journalists would inevitably become curious, and there's no telling what they might unearth if they started digging into our affairs. I won't have anyone suspecting that the fragrance we're launching is not up to Paul's usual standards. What I suggest, Mikhail, is that you take Liz and the children to Sardinia and keep them out of sight for a while."

"While you take my place as president of the company, Maman?"

"Temporary president, while you enjoy . . . a second honeymoon. You would not have to be idle. While you're in Italy, you could iron out the distribution problems we've been having in Rome."

"I have no objections to taking Liz and the children to Sardinia," Alexander said, surprising everyone in the room, "if she'll come." He rose from his chair and joined his wife at the window. "What do you say, darling?"

She turned and met his gaze. The smoldering challenge in his eyes dared her to refuse him.

"And if I won't?" she asked in a cool tone.

His gaze narrowed, his expression hardening.

"You're either with me, or against me, Liz. Come or stay. It's your choice. But if you bolt, to Paris, to Roger and Jock . . ."

He didn't finish the threat. He didn't have to. She knew that if she did, their marriage would be over.

"So, as always your terms are the only terms," Liz said in a quiet voice. "I am expected to go along with this cowardly cover-up and leave the person who keeps making trouble for us free to go on making trouble. Really, Alexander, you amaze me."

"Did it ever occur to you, love, that my sole intention is to protect that trouble-prone individual?" He stared at her hard and knowingly, but at the same time his eyes were brilliant with the emotion he always fought to conceal.

Liz saw the flicker of tenderness shining warm and true, and it drew her like a bright beacon. Suddenly she realized that for all his deliberate harshness, Alexander was deeply in love with her, so deeply he was ready to throw his career aside to protect her. For a moment a wild joy filled her.

Alexander loved her! Her joy quickly gave over to fresh pain. He was so in love he was willing to stay with her even when he still believed her guilty of having tried to destroy him, even when he thought she held some part in this new scheme.

She reached out and touched his hand, and his fingers curled possessively over hers, gripping hers, imparting warmth and strength and determination. She held on to him with equal fierceness.

It would be so easy, she thought, to go to Sardinia with him. They would be together. She could hold on to what she had with him. The nighttime passion. The wildness and ecstasy only he could give her. The children would have their father. All of that would be hers for the rest of their lives.

It was terribly tempting to do as he asked, but she was troubled. If she obeyed him and went with him to Sardinia, yes, she would have her marriage and Alexander's love, but forever Alexander would believe her guilty of this unspeakable treachery. It was thrilling that he loved her enough to make a life with her even when he was tortured by his doubts. But could she do that to him?

Over his shoulder she saw the painting of Cornwall she had once so lovingly given him. That time when they had loved each other completely and happily came back to her.

Suddenly she realized she couldn't do as he asked. As much as she loved him, she would give him up before she would subject him to a lifetime of a less than perfect marriage. He would never be really happy with her if he couldn't trust her. No, she was going to have to try to establish her innocence, Liz thought, even if it cost her the one thing most dear to her—Alexander. In the end, wouldn't he be better off without her if he couldn't believe in her? Wouldn't it be better if he married someone else whom he could trust, even though that would mean her own heartbreak? She squeezed her eyes shut against the agonizing image of losing him.

But if she went to Paris to see her father, might she not hurt Alexander just as terribly? Alexander would not understand. It would look as if she were running away because she had betrayed him and was guilty. He would be incriminated by her actions, and he might never regain the presidency of Dazzle. The press would lacerate him; his reputation and credibility would be destroyed. He would think that she didn't love him. Inevitably the children would suffer.

Her thoughts raced in painful chaos, and she jerked her hand from Alexander's and turned her back to him.

"Liz—"

"Don't ask me now to give you an answer," she mumbled in a low, choked tone. "Because I can't. I don't know what to do."

She lied. Oh, she knew. She knew. She was going to Paris to confront Roger.

"All right," he said.

There was death in his voice. She fought against the impulse to fling herself into his arms and promise everything he wanted.

At last he said, "If you go to Paris, I hope you understand it will be the end of . . . us.

Oh, she understood.

She met his deep, dark gaze. The vision of his too-dear features wavered. She turned blindly.

She knew Alexander was lost to her forever.

Chapter Sixteen

L iz's fingers curled around the steering wheel of her
rental car as tightly as hawk's claws. The ugly suburbs
of Paris swept past in a blur of tall houses with
wrought-iron balconies and slatted shutters. Shabby
little *tabacs* and bright café-bars edged narrow streets.
A man stood on a corner selling lottery tickets.

At the thought of the way Alexander had looked
when she'd run out of the Dazzle offices, Liz's stomach
knotted as tautly as her clawed fists. His dark face had
been a portrait of mute agony.

Well, she mustn't think about Alexander now, of the
torment of losing him. She had to concentrate on Roger
and what she would say to him. What did one say to a
man as callous as Roger?

Once she had not thought her father callous. How
differently she had felt that last time when she'd
secretly flown to Paris to tell Roger of her marriage.

Shocked at first, Roger had pretended to understand.
He'd gathered Liz into his arms, kissed her, acting as if

he shared her joy. He had even gone as far as to say he hoped that this marriage could bring a reconciliation between himself and Alexander's family.

Oh, he'd fooled her completely. Liz had never suspected his ruthless intentions. They had lunched at her father's favorite restaurant, the Auberge du Vert Galant, on its summer sidewalk terrace beside the Seine. There Liz had poured out her heart, confessing the golden emotion that had overwhelmed her and made her go against her father's advice.

He had thrown back his silver head and laughed, and the sunlight that glinted on the river's surface shone in his eyes as well. He was very handsome for his age, romantically handsome.

"You speak so earnestly when you speak of him, Liz. I can almost remember what it was to be young and in love." The dark skin beneath his black eyes had crinkled. His expression was intense with the memory of that time.

"You have not forgotten what love is, Roger. You have Mimi."

"Ah, yes," he said. "Mimi." The intensity vanished. "I have Mimi to comfort me—in my old age."

Something in his voice had troubled Liz.

He patted her hand. "I'm very happy for you, my dear. Another glass of wine, Liz? This is from my own vineyard in Burgundy."

A week later it was discovered that Paul's formula had been stolen. Shortly afterward Radiance launched the pirated perfume under the name Liz, using publicity pictures that had been originally intended for another Radiance fragrance, pictures Roger had promised to destroy when he'd learned of her secret marriage.

After what Jock had said yesterday, Liz was convinced that what she'd always suspected was true, that her father had been behind the theft and launch because he wanted to break up her marriage. After all, hadn't he warned her when she first came to Paris that he considered Alexander his enemy?

When she'd left London for Mexico, she'd felt betrayed by both Jock and her father. A year later, when Jock found her in Mexico, he begged her to believe that he had had nothing to do with the theft of the formula. Jock even defended her father, saying that Roger had nearly fired him over it and that Roger had immediately withdrawn the perfume. In the end Liz had believed in Jock's innocence, if not in her father's. Dazzle had won damages in a lawsuit, even though Radiance had already taken the fragrance Liz off the market.

But why had her father done it? It had scarcely been a profitable venture. Only one reason that fit with his character came to mind.

Mimi, in one of her rare moments of candor, had told Liz once that Roger was possessive of everything he owned or loved, and Liz, remembering how forcefully he had come into her life and persuaded her she was his daughter, believed Mimi.

"He saw me, and he wanted me, and he bought me, *ma petite*," Mimi had said, tossing her golden head in that famous, sensual way of hers that made yellow silk ripple over tanned shoulders. "He owns the studios that make my pictures, the theaters where they are shown. I have nothing that is not his."

"And doesn't that bother you?"

"Very much." Mimi's smile scarcely curved her unpainted lips. Her voice was matter-of-fact.

"But why do you let him own you?"

"When you have had a life like mine, there is one thing you learn, ma petite, and that is that life, at its best, is a compromise. No one can have it all." Mimi's shadowed eyelids lowered enigmatically, and she pulled her lustrous sable jacket over her shoulders. "Yes, I have enough."

And yet Mimi had not looked satisfied.

Did Roger consider his daughter another possession he could dominate? Liz had wondered. Well, if so, Liz had decided to reject his brand of love. Unlike Mimi, she would not be owned, not after losing Alexander, not by the man who had betrayed her trust and destroyed her chance of happiness with such callous disregard for her feelings.

Still, it had been difficult in the beginning to believe her own father would betray her. He had convinced her during the three months she had spent in Paris that he genuinely loved her.

Liz hated remembering that time; it did not make the thought of seeing him easier. She shifted restlessly and rolled down the window and caught the familiar scents of Paris. The smell of wine, coffee, cats and damp air assaulted her. She switched on the radio, and the husky sensuality of French music filled the car. Oh, how she loved French music. It reminded her a little of Barbra Streisand. Almost, almost, she could forget the pain of the past and the ordeal of facing her father.

Half an hour later the car thrust its way down the confusion of the Rue Royal and then onto the great expanse of the Concorde where the Crillon was veiled with leafed-out chestnut trees.

Soon after that she reached her father's opulent flat, and Armande let her inside and showed her to her father's study. The shades were drawn, and the elegant silver room was as dark and silent as she remembered.

Liz paced before the long windows overlooking the Rue du Faubourg Saint-Honoré.

Armande returned. "Madame, I've reached your father's office. Monsieur Chartres is on the telephone."

Liz lifted the silver receiver. It was as cold as ice in her shaking fingers.

"Liz!" The deep, sensually accented baritone was warm with welcome.

For a moment, she was too shaken to answer. A

treacherous fondness filled her. The horrible realization that she still loved him no matter what he'd done struck her. That was the reason she had run from him, the fear that her love would give him a ruthless control of her. How would she ever be able to stand up to him?

He went on easily, "Did Jock tell you I wanted to see you?"

"Yes."

"And is he with you now?"

"I'm alone, Father. I-I tried to call him before I left London, but he didn't answer."

"Odd." There was the faintest trace of alarm in his low voice, but when he spoke again, it was gone. "I've been unable to reach him myself. He was to have called me this morning."

"I did not come because of Jock or because of you, Father. I came to stop you from hurting Alexander again."

After a long pause, "I see," he said.

"Jock said you admitted having stolen Paul's formula seven years ago."

"In a way I do feel I am responsible. I—"

"Father, I would rather speak to you in person. When Paul's formula was removed from Alexander's safe last night, I'm sure you wanted me to be blamed. If you could come home—"

"Paul's formula? Last night?"

The line went dead.

"Father?"

There was no dial tone. Liz called for Armande, but he had disappeared. Upstairs a door opened and closed. Liz called out again for Armande. Her words sounded hollow and wavery. She felt alone and yet not alone. Again she was aware of that ridiculous sensation of danger she'd felt earlier.

A velvet reply rippled down the stairs, the French purr that was the most famous voice in all of France.

"Liz, I am so sorry I was asleep when you arrived. I sent Armande on an errand a few minutes ago when he told me you were here. He has gone out to buy a special wine for us to celebrate your return. I will be down in a minute."

A few minutes later Mimi swept into the room. Her lips were as red as blood. Her golden hair was caught in diamond clips. Despite the sophistication of pink silk clinging to her voluptuous figure, there was still a little-girl quality in her face. It was that mixture of innocence and worldliness that gave her such a sensual aura.

As always, Mimi acted warm and welcoming, and yet Liz did not feel welcomed. Mimi embraced Liz. Mimi's perfume was rich, and Liz felt she was being suffocated.

At last Mimi released her. "For seven years your father and I have worried about you. I saw pictures of your children in the papers. They are precious. Roger and I already love them. You may remember that I was never able to have children of my own. I went to every doctor in Europe." The famous blue eyes were sad.

"I remember."

"Life does not always give us what we want," Mimi said. "But I try to be content. I have so much." Fingertips made sure the diamond clips were secure in her hair.

"Mimi, a while ago I was talking to Roger. The phone went dead before we had finished speaking."

"It happens. There is some construction in the area, I believe. It has been a nuisance lately, *chérie*. Let me check the other line for you and see if I can reach Roger."

Mimi left the room. She returned with an opened bottle of Burgundy in one hand and a glass of wine in the other. Liz remembered that Mimi's enthusiasm for wine was more than the usual French fondness of wine.

Mimi smiled. "Don't look so worried, Liz. I was able

to reach Roger, and he wants to meet us at Charmont in an hour. An emergency has detained him at the office." Charmont was Roger's château not far from Paris.

"Charmont?" Liz felt even more deeply upset. "But I had hoped to see him sooner. I—"

"He works too hard, your father. I'm afraid I suggested Charmont. Paris is so hot in the summer. I'm sorry, Liz, I did not think to consult you. This is the wine I sent Armande after. He's gone down to get the car to drive us to Charmont." Mimi poured a glass of wine and handed it to Liz. "This will give us time to visit," Mimi said, "to talk girl talk."

Liz felt impatient. The last thing she wanted was to spend unnecessary time with Mimi. She was filled with dread at the prospect of seeing her father, and yet she wanted to get the interview over as quickly as possible. Mimi was acting as if this were to be an amicable reunion.

"Drink the wine, *chérie*. It will relax you," Mimi purred, pressuring.

For an instant Liz considered telling Mimi exactly how she felt. Then she reconsidered. That would be unforgivably rude. After all, no matter how Liz felt toward Mimi, Mimi was hardly responsible for her father's actions.

Liz lifted the glass and drank deeply. It had an odd, crispy sweet taste, and yet it was not unpleasant. The glass was soon drained, and Mimi coaxed her to take another.

"But I haven't eaten. Wine always affects me—"

"What then, *chérie*, is the point of wine? You need to relax before you see Roger." She poured the wine.

So, Mimi did realize how she dreaded seeing Roger. The wine was her way of being thoughtful. Liz felt a twinge of guilt for her negative feelings toward Mimi and did not have the heart to refuse her.

A horn sounded outside. It was Armande with the car.

With Armande at the wheel of Roger's Lincoln, the suburbs of Paris swept past in a blur. Mimi talked very little to Liz on the trip from Paris, and for that Liz was grateful. Although as always Mimi had taken great pains to be both pleasant and thoughtful, Liz felt even more ill at ease with her than ever. Perhaps it was the lapse of seven years. Perhaps it was the knowledge that Mimi was her father's mistress and no doubt condoned all that Roger had done. Perhaps it was only Liz's own dread of the coming visit with Roger.

There had always been a wall of reserve about Mimi. No matter how nice Mimi acted, Liz always had the impression that Mimi kept much of herself hidden. Jock had hinted that Mimi's upbringing had been a brutal one. Mimi was an actress, and Liz found herself wondering how much of the Mimi she knew was real. Mimi tried to appear warm and friendly, but somehow Liz never felt that Mimi was wholly sincere. Perhaps it was enough that at least Mimi always did make the effort to be nice.

For a while Liz lay back against the seat. Suddenly she felt woozy, unlike herself. She should never have drunk the wine on an empty stomach. The road seemed to be a perpetual zigzag, and Liz felt less and less well. It was only her nerves, of course, the wine, and the motion of the Lincoln. For a long time she lay with her eyes closed, but the dreadful feeling did not subside.

When she managed to open her eyes again, the car was roaring through prosperous, densely farmed country. On the right, through thickets of willow, the gleam of Charmont Lake showed itself through the trees. On the left, the countryside rolled until it blended with a line of fir in the purpling haze.

Mimi's head lay upon the back of the seat too; her eyes had been closed since they'd left Paris. She looked both exhausted and preoccupied, and Liz felt a pang of guilt when she remembered that she had interrupted Mimi's nap with her unannounced visit that evening. Liz remembered Jock saying that she had been hospitalized several times.

Liz rested her feverish forehead against the cool glass of the window as the Lincoln exploded through the somnolent village of Charmont, which lay at the base of the château. The car was climbing now. Trees lined the narrow streets. At the edge of the pavement in front of the shops were tubs of flowers—the last of the tulips and freesias and scarlet ranunculus. Vivid-eyed daffodils bobbed their brilliantly yellow heads beside clumps of purple pansies and a multitude of other flowers, crowded into their pots French-fashion. Liz shut her eyes as a wave of nausea swept her.

The car plunged into a thick fir forest, and then snaked upward on the hilly road. Liz's stomach tightened, and she was suddenly afraid she was going to be ill if they didn't reach Charmont soon. Her throat felt so dry she could scarcely swallow.

Great gray beeches rose from tangles of hawthorne. The Charmont Woods. Then Charmont itself burst into view, standing proud and high as a solitary sentinel on the crest of its hill as it had for centuries, the sweep of its lonely valley and wild forest beneath it. Near the road, oak and birch were wreathed with bright holly. The pale stone of the house stood out against the dark green of the forest. Polygonal towers, crowned by slate roofs shaped like witches' hats, defended every corner of the building. The last rays of the sun made the windows of the château gleam like scarlet foil.

The car shot through the tall, powerfully fortified gate. High, corbeled, rocket-shaped towers rose on either side of the entrance arch.

The tires bit gravel and Armande parked the Lincoln in front of the enormous south door. Armande came around to open the back door and help Mimi out. Liz felt so weak and shaky she almost fell when she tried to stand up.

"Madame, are you all right?" Armande asked.

Liz held on to the car for support. The ground wavered. She was too unsteady to answer.

"Liz, you're as white as a sheet," Mimi said with concern. "I feel a little sick myself. The road to Charmont is impossible. When we get inside I'll make you some hot chocolate before dinner." Mimi took her gently by the hand.

Without a word, Armande lifted the two suitcases from the trunk and led the way toward the château. Liz found herself leaning rather heavily on Mimi's arm the whole way.

Mimi was fumbling in her purse for the keys, chattering now, as she had not in the car, but Liz could make no sense of what she was saying. The house was still, so unlike the Charmont she remembered. Suddenly Liz had the impression that something was wrong. She felt sick and strange, and yet it was more than that. Charmont was not as it had been seven years ago. The hedges were wild, the garden untamed. No flowers graced the enormous beds. Instead they were choked with weeds. Even the house itself seemed forbidding.

The sun sank in a rim of fir as Armande opened the great door and helped the women inside. He flicked on the electric lights. The furniture was draped with dust covers, making the house seem filled with silent, misshapen ghosts. Liz stepped into the high-ceilinged hall of the château. Long black shadows fell eerily across the chilled white marble floor. At one end of the vast room the staircase rose to the wide landing, which was shrouded in darkness. The air was damp and musty as if the house had been shut up for a long time. Something felt terribly wrong.

Liz fought the strange impulse to dash back outside

where the evening was golden and smelled of fresh pine and fir, but when she turned, she stumbled. Mimi's fingers were tight on her wrist, and had they not been, Liz would have fallen.

Mimi sensed her fears and said lightly, "I should have warned you, Liz. This is the month we give the servants their holiday. I'm afraid we'll have to do for ourselves tonight. I don't mind, myself. I'm surrounded by people so much of the time, I love to come to Charmont and be alone. You'll find the kitchen well stocked. I was here last weekend, and a lady from the village shopped for me this week."

"I'm not even hungry," Liz mumbled. "Why isn't Roger here?" Her voice sounded thin, like a frightened child's. For the first time she thought of seeing her father without dread.

"He is so terribly busy, *chérie*. He'll be here soon. Probably some business problem came up before he could get away. He and I come down often on the weekends."

Charmont did not look as if Roger Chartres came down on weekends.

The white shapes spun like whirling ghosts as a wave of dizziness hit Liz. "I need to lie down, Mimi," she murmured.

"Of course," Mimi replied. "I will show you to your room and then go down to the kitchen and bring you some warm chocolate milk. That will settle your stomach."

"You are so kind," Liz managed faintly. Her voice trailed off as if it were something that didn't belong to her. Vaguely Liz was aware of Mimi leading her up the stairs to the bedroom she had always used when she had come to Charmont with Roger. It seemed to her that the two of them floated weightlessly as they mounted an endless white staircase.

Once inside the bedroom, Liz sank down upon the

elaborate bed. Her gaze skimmed the Louis XVI chairs, which were draped and upholstered in flowered chintz. The room began to spin. She shut her eyes, but the sickening feeling did not subside.

She lay there for a long time wishing Mimi would hurry. In all her life she'd never felt so sick. Then she heard the quick skittering of high heels on the uncarpeted marble stairs, tappings that sounded like sharp, panicked beats. The sound was somehow familiar.

Mimi opened the door and came inside. Her eyes were downcast, hidden. She said softly, "Drink this. It will make you feel better."

Liz obeyed, and the warm chocolate was soothing, or perhaps it was Mimi's concern that made her feel better. For once she was glad to be with Mimi.

A few minutes later Mimi said, "I'm beginning to worry about you, *chérie*. You are too pale. I think I will call the village doctor. Just in case."

"No, really . . ."

"I insist."

Liz shut her eyes, thankful that Mimi was there to take care of her. She felt even dizzier and yet sleepier than before. She heard the retreat of Mimi's footsteps on the carpet and then the rapid, gunfire taps on the marble stairs. Again the sound reminded her of something.

Mimi was going to call a doctor. How sweet of her. How thoughtful. Liz opened her eyes and focused upon the golden phone on the gilt table by the window.

There was a phone in the room!

Why hadn't Mimi used the phone in this room? Why had she gone downstairs? A wild baffling panic possessed Liz. Muddled as her mind was, somehow she knew something was wrong if Mimi had gone downstairs to use a phone when there was one right there.

Liz rose and stumbled from the bed. She was so dizzy

she couldn't stand. She felt thickheaded. *Drugged*. She had to crawl across the thick flowered carpet to reach the phone. She pulled the cord and the telephone crashed onto the floor. She lifted the receiver and held it against her ear.

The phone was dead.

"Hello. Hello." She screamed into the phone, shaking it.

Of course, there was no answer.

It came to her then. Mimi had not gone downstairs to call the doctor. She had had some other reason.

Liz heard the Lincoln's engine roar in the drive downstairs. Armande was leaving! Mimi had gone downstairs to send him away. Somehow Liz had to stop him.

Slowly Liz dragged herself to the window. Her fingers fumbled with the lock, and at last she managed to unfasten it. She threw the window open and screamed out into the purple twilight.

The Lincoln shot toward the tall, fortified gate. Armande had not heard.

But someone else had.

Mimi was standing in the drive staring up at her. Her pink gown billowed in the breeze. Her hair flew wildly. Even from that great distance, for the first time Liz was struck with the burning power of Mimi's true personality. It was a force as powerful as the roll of a surging surf in a violent storm; a force as feral and vicious as a tiger's fury.

Then Mimi raced inside, and Liz collapsed onto the floor. She heard the staccato tappings of the heels downstairs, and she knew where she had heard them before. In the stairwell at Dazzle's office building. Mimi had been there that night, the night the formula had been stolen.

The words of the woman in front of Dazzle's office building came back to Liz. "I seen it happen

. . . Almost looked as if the man in the car did it on purpose . . . Didn't stay around, not him that done it."

That accident had not been an accident. Mimi had deliberately planned it as a distraction so that she could enter the Dazzle offices undetected.

It was Mimi. Not Roger. Mimi had wanted to destroy her marriage.

Suddenly Liz knew that Roger was not coming, that he had not been to Charmont in years. Mimi had brought her there because the château was the last place he would think to look for her.

Liz was alone in the vast house with Mimi, and Mimi had drugged her and brought her there to kill her.

Liz thought of Alexander. She longed for him. If only . . .

She called his name softly. He would never know how much she loved him.

Even as she screamed his name she tumbled like a madly hurtling bullet into a black and terrifying void.

Chapter Seventeen

*I*n the hospital corridor outside Jock Rocheaux's room, Inspector Walters spoke to Alexander in hushed tones.

"I'll come to the point, sir. Last night your cousin was run down by an automobile shortly before midnight. Mr. Rocheaux is not expected to live. This was no accident. The driver turned around to come back and strike him again."

The inspector's suspicious gaze was both avid and assessing.

"How horrible," Alexander murmured.

"The only thing that stopped him was that three people ran out into the street to render aid to your cousin. It was so dark, no one could give us a clear description of the car."

"Have you been able to speak to Jock, Inspector?"

"Only briefly. He wasn't able to say much before he lapsed into unconsciousness. He mentioned your wife, and then he asked me to find Mikki Vorzenski. That's

why we rang you. He said, 'Inspector, it's a matter of
life and death.' He kept repeating that phrase. 'A
matter of life and death.' His last words were, 'Find
Mikki.' Do you have any idea what he meant?''

"Not the slightest." Alexander's smooth voice did
not betray the sudden fear that gripped him. Liz was
gone. Someone had deliberately tried to kill Jock.

Attempted murder.

Suddenly Alexander realized that Liz was innocent,
and because she was, her life was in danger. She had
not left him because she was guilty but because she was
innocent. She had gone to confront the person she
believed to be guilty of the theft. That person would
not stop at murder. Jock had known, and he had come
to warn Liz. Because he had known, he lay near death.

The inspector was pursuing his own train of thought.
"I was informed you and your cousin quarreled earlier
in the evening, Prince Vorzenski."

"My cousin and I have not been close for many
years."

"I understand he maintains a close relationship with
your wife."

Alexander realized the remark was a deliberate
attempt to inflame him, and it did. "What exactly do
you mean, Inspector?"

"I understand as well that there is some possibility,
remote at the moment, that you were involved in the
explosion of your company's lab in Switzerland."

In a voice of steel Alexander replied, "Inspector, I
was not involved with what happened to Jock last night
nor with the explosion in Switzerland."

"Nevertheless, Prince Vorzenski, you must realize
that you are a prime suspect. I don't want you to leave
London. The charges that may be brought against you
are very serious."

The two men regarded one another grimly. Inside,
Alexander went wild. Liz was in danger because he had

bullheadedly distrusted her. By doing so he had forced her to run to France, straight to the person who wanted to destroy her.

And he could not leave England.

Liz awoke to the soft blur of sound in the room and the cloying fragrance of Mimi's perfume. In her confusion Liz mumbled, "I don't know if I can wait for Father. I'm so sleepy."

"You will never see your father again." These words rang, vibrating like a gong.

Liz remembered everything. For an instant she managed to focus on Mimi, whose golden face was naked with hatred.

"I put something in your wine and in your chocolate, Liz, so that your death will look like suicide. An overdose of sleeping pills. It will be easy to say that you were distraught because of your failed marriage."

Mimi's words swam in a fog of sound. It was difficult for Liz to make her own lips move because they felt numb and stiff.

"But why, Mimi? What have I ever done to you?"

"Nothing."

"You must be crazy."

"Don't say that!" The purr became a shrill, tormented burst. "I have a reason." The purr was back and filled with bitter sadness. "You see, my sister died of an overdose . . . many years ago. A tragic accident, the authorities said, but I always believed it was suicide."

"W-what do I have to do with your sister?"

"Rochelle was my little sister, my innocent sister that I cared for like a baby, that I protected even when we were so poor in Marseilles. We were orphans. Everything I did, I did for her. For her I climbed from the gutter to stardom. No one knew we were sisters. Then in Deauville, because two playboys, Jock Rocheaux and Mikki Vorzenski, amused themselves and made a game of my sister's love, she died. She was so idealistic. After my wedding, she took pills because she was too excited to sleep. Or so they said. When she died, I wanted to die, but, of course, I went on living. Only my heart had died. It is not bad, Liz, to die. It is the living who are really dead that suffer. My last words were said to her in anger. You see, she did not approve of my marrying a count, simply because he was a count."

"Rochelle's death must have been no more than an unfortunate accident," Liz murmured. "It is wrong to blame—"

"Her death choked me with hatred. I had to have revenge. So I slept with Sasha Vorzenski, and then the night before one of his races, I told him that I was sleeping with his cousin Jock as well. Sasha was so jealous that he tried to kill Jock on the racetrack the next day, but he died himself."

"Mimi, how could you . . . so coldly . . ."

"Sasha's death did not matter to me. After Rochelle, nothing like that could ever matter to me. All that mattered was that Mikki Vorzenski suffered as I suffered."

"There is no profit in revenge. Mimi, you must . . ."

Mimi was not listening. Her eyes were glazed. "I became Roger's mistress to get close to Jock. I persuaded Michelle, my niece whom I supported, to go to work for Dazzle. Michelle rose in the company quickly, and we waited for an opportunity. Then you came to Paris. You were so young and beautiful, and, of course, Roger wanted you for Jock. I did not want to hurt you. I was by that time fond of Roger, but when Jock fell in love with you, I had no choice. Through you I could make Jock suffer. I took you down to Deauville so you could meet Mikki Vorzenski. It was fitting that you should fall in love in Deauville, don't you think?

"Your father told me of your secret marriage, you

know. He thought he could trust me. I went to Michelle, and she said there was to be a Dazzle launch soon. So I had her steal the formula. She was sleeping with one of the chemists. It was really quite easy for her. I, too, had chemists who were loyal to me. Radiance was on the verge of a launch, so I was able to substitute the stolen formula at the last minute, and then I discovered that you had run away to Mexico. Jock was nearly ruined because he used your publicity pictures. You see, I had torn up Roger's orders not to use them. Mikki Vorzenski nearly lost his presidency. The only problem was that Roger found out what I had done. He took the perfume off the market. He was furious, but he still wanted me enough to forgive me. Men can be so stupid.

"Later I almost left Roger, but I was afraid that if I did, you and Mikki Vorzenski might somehow find each other again. So I let Jock find you. I tipped Mikki Vorzenski's detective agency so you could be found. I impersonated Michelle and planted the bomb in Dazzle's lab six weeks ago. You can imagine the rest. Michelle and I took the formula last night, and then I helped her run away. Jock is dying in a London hospital right now. Soon it will be discovered that Mikki Vorzenski's car ran Jock down. Mikki will lose you. He will be accused of murder. His career will be ruined."

The words were a jumble in Liz's weary brain. One thought remained with her. Alexander would be destroyed. She had to find a way to save Alexander. She had to stay awake. Her eyelids felt as heavy as lead weights, but she forced them open.

Sleep was death.

"W-what about my children? If I die, and you destroy Alexander, they will be orphans—like you and Rochelle were."

Mimi's resolve weakened. "It is always the children who suffer." She was clearly upset at this thought.

"You must help me—to save them," Liz said.

"I-I don't care about them. Don't you see. I *can't* care!" Mimi screamed wildly. Then she fled the room, turning a key in the lock, imprisoning Liz. High heels clattered on the stairs as Mimi flew down them.

For a moment, Liz thought Mimi might change her mind, but Mimi had vanquished the last remnants of her conscience. Her grief and hatred had warped her, and she'd left Liz to die.

A deep, inviting blackness seemed to swirl around Liz. It was so tempting to close her eyes, to go to sleep, but if she did not fight, she could not help Alexander. She thought of her children, and she knew she had to force herself to struggle.

Groggily she dragged herself to the window and pulled herself up so that she could see out. The night was dark and moonless. The cool air revived her as she leaned out. In the distance she saw white, darting lights on the Charmont road. Then they disappeared, blinked, and then disappeared again. Was someone coming up to the château?

Beneath the window was a ledge that was at least twelve inches wide. The windows of the bedroom next to her had been thrown open earlier, doubtless by Mimi, who must have taken that bedroom for her own use. If Liz could walk along that ledge the ten feet to the next window and crawl inside, perhaps she could get downstairs.

Liz stared down at the gravel drive fifty feet beneath. If she fell, she would die. But if she stayed . . .

The car lights twinkled on the road. The car was coming to the château. Liz pulled herself up onto the windowsill and swung her feet outside, sliding her body out the window until her toes touched the ledge. Shivering with fear, she told herself not to look down.

She could scarcely stand, but somehow she managed to lean back against the stone wall of the château, her arms spread wide to brace herself, her fingernails digging into the stone. Then she began to inch her way along the ribbonlike ledge to the other window.

The car was in the drive, and then it disappeared from view as it swerved toward the north entrance. A terrible blackness swamped Liz, and for a moment she thought she was going to pass out. Her knees became jelly. Her foot slid over the edge. Then, just in time, fear jerked her back to consciousness. She forced herself to keep moving toward the window. If she were going to faint, better that she fainted inside instead of out here where to do so was certain death. At last her hand curled over the windowsill. For a long moment she just gripped it, too weak to move. It took all her strength to pull herself inside, and when she did, she collapsed headlong onto the floor. A table lamp smashed beside her, and her last thought before she fainted was that Mimi had heard and would return to kill her.

Fighting her way back to consciousness, Liz sat up. The room was a blur. The blood in her head seemed to be a pounding force. Gathering her remaining strength, she half-crawled, half-staggered across the thick carpet toward the door. At last she reached it, and when she twisted the doorknob, it opened.

Deep baritone voices thundered from below. Liz crawled to the edge of the landing and pulled herself up.

Leaning against the balustrade, Liz lurched toward that welcome sound of voices. When she reached the top of the stairs, she stared down the dizzying spiral and felt faint. She could never make it down those stairs. She clung to the banister.

Alexander and Roger strode into the hall. Mimi was right behind them, trying to stop them.

Liz called out to them, but it was the terrible, soundless scream of nightmares. She clutched the newel-post so tightly that the pointed ears of the carved fox dug into her palm with sudden, rejuvenating pain. "Alexan—" Again no sound came.

Alexander and Roger were walking outside, out of the south entrance.

Liz heard Mimi say quite clearly, "No, I have not heard from Liz. I came down to Charmont to rest. You know how exhausted I've been, Roger. The film—"

"But to Charmont?"

The door banged as it was opened. They were leaving.

In her panic, Liz let go of the newel post and lost her balance. She screamed. The frail sound cut the air like the thinnest blade.

Alexander's voice rang out. "What was that?" He dashed toward the stairs and glanced up, his eyes filling with terror. He raced swiftly up the stairs, taking them two at a time, as Liz fell.

A violent stab of pain jolted her when she landed with a thud on a thick slab of marble. Too weak to catch herself, she rolled over and over until her soft body reached Alexander, who had climbed halfway up the stairs.

He wrapped her unconscious body in his arms and bent his black head very close to her face. He searched for her pulse, and when at last he felt the weak throb, he began to weep. It was the first time in his adult life he had ever cried.

He lifted her into his arms, his tears falling upon her face that was as cold and still as death.

But she was alive. There was a chance that he had not been too late. For the moment, that had to be enough.

Chapter Eighteen

The sound of music—Barbra Streisand—filled the sun splashed villa that hung from the sculptured edge of a cliff high above Sardinia's Porto Rotondo. Across a silver, mirrorlike sea, Porto Cervo was clearly visible.

A thousand bejeweled guests were crammed inside the villa or clustered upon the wide decks around the aqua expanse of the glistening pool. Scarlet and gold hot-air balloons hovered above the mansion. From the balloons, beautiful maidens cast perfumed silk petals down onto the villa so that the sky seemed filled with golden rain. Samantha and Alex were splashing in the pool. Alexander's Swan was anchored in the quiet harbor beneath.

From her balcony, a pale, thin Liz watched the milling crowd—executives from the highest echelons of both Dazzle and Radiance. Her red hair was braided with golden ribbons, and she wore a white flowing gown that made her look like a Roman princess.

Never had so many people been crushed into such a

small space, and yet never had Liz felt so alone. Liz smiled as she watched Jock limp across the deck and join her father, who was standing beside the pool watching Samantha and Alex. Somewhere in the press of people was Jock's new wife, Sarah, the lovely English nurse he'd fallen in love with when he was recuperating.

So much had happened in the month since Alexander had driven to Charmont with Roger and saved her from certain death. Mimi had been institutionalized in Switzerland. Michelle was behind bars. Roger had confided that Mimi had been repeatedly hospitalized for psychiatric reasons over the past few years, but that he had not realized how dangerous she was. He said that in reality Mimi had blamed herself for Rochelle's death, but, unable to face her own guilt, she'd tried to convince herself Jock and Alexander were to blame.

The night Mimi drugged Liz, Roger and Alexander had forced Armande to tell them that Mimi had taken Liz to Charmont, which had been closed for over a year because Roger was planning to renovate it. The formula that had been stolen the night before Mimi tried to kill Liz had been a fake substituted by Alexander as a precautionary measure.

Liz had recovered after two nights in a Paris hospital. Roger told her that Alexander had hovered at her bedside until she was out of danger, but that when she had regained consciousness, he'd left Paris and returned to London.

"He loves you," Roger had confided at her bedside.

"Perhaps—in a way. But too much has happened between us. I suppose it is for the best that he has gone."

Brave words. The truth was that Alexander's leaving her had ripped her heart to pieces.

A letter from Alexander came to her in Paris. He offered her his villa in Sardinia to recover. When she accepted, in the hope of seeing him, he sent Ana Lou and the children to join her.

But he had not come himself.

Nor had he written again. The only letter that came from him was one he forwarded from Manuel, who wanted to buy the doll factory. She wrote Alexander and told him that she agreed to sell. She received no further communication.

Within a week, Liz had decided what she would do. She called Roger in Paris and invited him to Sardinia.

The night Roger arrived, Liz picked him up at the airport in Olbia and took him to the Piazza San Marco. She ordered him a Bellini.

Roger lifted the frothy pale peach elixir of juice, sparkling white wine and ice to his lips. Across the café table he asked, "Why did you ask me to come?"

"I need your help. Because of me, Alexander has lost the presidency of Dazzle. I know that everything regarding the explosion has been resolved, that all charges against him have been dropped. But the news stories in the papers were so lurid, his career may never recover."

"Men like Mikki Vorzenski have a way of landing on their feet. Give him time, my child."

"But, don't you see, he's not fighting for himself. His mother will never give him a chance. And it's my fault."

"What do you want me to do?"

"Could you . . . Could we buy Dazzle?"

"And they call Mikki Vorzenski a pirate." Roger began to laugh, but his eyes were filled with love. "Order me another of these . . . these . . ."

"Bellinis."

"Alexander owns a great deal of stock in Dazzle, Father. So does Paul. Perhaps you could approach them?"

"Perhaps . . ." Roger folded her hand in his. "For

you I will buy Dazzle. It will not be easy, but I will find a way."

"Then Alexander can be president of Dazzle again."

"You do realize you might be making a very grave mistake. Some men do not like to be bought by a woman."

The memory faded and the present came back with violent force, but Roger's words lingered.

Some men do not like to be bought by a woman.

The aqua pool glimmered; the sensual music made Liz shiver. Roger looked up from the deck and waved to her to join them.

This party was in celebration of the upcoming merger of two of the greatest names in the perfume world—Dazzle and Radiance. The financial papers had made much of it. Jock and Roger had been interviewed. Paul had spoken to the press. Only Alexander had declined to comment.

Suddenly a hush swept the party, and Liz saw a very tall black-headed man leading a silver-haired woman on his arm. They were Alexander and the princess. Roger extended his hand and Paulette took it. After a long while she knelt and leaned over the pool. She didn't seem to mind that the children splashed her when they swam near. Even from the great distance, Liz could see that the princess's smile was radiant.

Liz remembered something Alexander had told her once about his mother, that his mother was always on the side of the winner.

Liz was the winner. The princess had come to her.

As if drawn to a magnet, Liz's gaze melded with Alexander's. For a long moment he stared up at her. He was as still as a statue, and then he was running.

And so was she.

The staircase curled down the cliff's edge. High-heeled sandals scampered down red tile stairs. Liz flew into his arms. She was breathless, but not from running. He crushed her against his hard chest. He was kissing her, whirling her in his arms. Tears were falling, but they were tears of happiness.

After a long time he set her down and held her tightly against the white wall. Beneath them the cliff plunged a thousand feet to a sparkling sea.

"I love you," he said. "I don't know if you can ever forgive me for being so stupidly blind to the truth."

"I thought you were mad because I bought Dazzle."

"Mad?" He threw back his black head and laughed. "Mad? I thought it was one hell of a way to tell a guy you love him. It was insanely reckless, of course."

"I do love you, you know."

"I don't deserve you," he said. "I tried to be gallant and stay away, but, Liz, I can't live without you."

"Nor can I."

"So I'm to be president of your company?" he murmured.

"Our company."

"I bought you a gift," he said.

Her eyes flashed with excitement. "What?"

"Of course, it's not nearly so grand as the presidency of Dazzle and Radiance."

"I'm dying of curiosity."

"I went down to Cornwall and bought that crumbling antiquity you're so insane about."

"Killigen Hall?" She shrieked with joy when he nodded.

"Ghosts and all."

"How did you manage it?"

"By paying three times what it was worth."

"Whatever you paid, I'll make it worth it." Her voice was low and deliberately suggestive.

He lowered his mouth to hers. After a long time he said, "Do you remember that grotto where you taught me that an innocent can know more about love than a rake?"

She began to laugh as he lifted her into his arms. "Where are you taking me?"

"Somewhere private where you can start earning your keep."

"Why don't we go up to our bedroom and save the grotto for later—when our guests have gone?"

The husky voice of Barbra Streisand was a rush of sound. Slowly, hand in hand, they began to walk up the stairs to the sun-drenched terrace outside the master bedroom.

They kissed again, surrendering at last to the brilliant and fulfilling dazzle of their everlasting love.

READERS' COMMENTS ON SILHOUETTE SPECIAL EDITIONS:

"I just finished reading the first six Silhouette Special Edition Books and I had to take the opportunity to write you and tell you how much I enjoyed them. I enjoyed all the authors in this series. Best wishes on your Silhouette Special Editions line and many thanks."

—B.H.*, Jackson, OH

"The Special Editions are really special and I enjoyed them very much! I am looking forward to next month's books."

—R.M.W.*, Melbourne, FL

"I've just finished reading four of your first six Special Editions and I enjoyed them very much. I like the more sensual detail and longer stories. I will look forward each month to your new Special Editions."

—L.S.*, Visalia, CA

"Silhouette Special Editions are — 1.) Superb! 2.) Great! 3.) Delicious! 4.) Fantastic! . . . Did I leave anything out? These are books that an adult woman can read . . . I love them!"

—H.C.*, Monterey Park, CA

*names available on request

Silhouette Special Edition. Romances
for the woman who expects a little
more out of love.

If you enjoyed this book, and you're ready for more great romance

...get 4 romance novels FREE when you become a Silhouette Special Edition home subscriber.

Act now and we'll send you four exciting Silhouette Special Edition romance novels. They're our gift to introduce you to our convenient home subscription service. Every month, we'll send you six new passion-filled Special Edition books. Look them over for 15 days. If you keep them, pay just $11.70 for all six. Or return them at no charge.

We'll mail your books to you two full months *before they are available anywhere else.* Plus, with every shipment, you'll receive the Silhouette Books Newsletter absolutely free. *And with Silhouette Special Edition there are never any shipping or handling charges.*

Mail the coupon today to get your four free books—and more romance than you ever bargained for.

Silhouette Special Edition is a service mark and a registered trademark.